These Vengeful Souls

TARUN SHANKER
KELLY ZEKAS

Swoon
READS

SWOON READS | NEW YORK

A Swoon Reads Book

An imprint of Feiwel and Friends and Macmillan Publishing Group, LLC

These Vengeful Souls. Copyright © 2018 by Tarun Shanker and Kelly Zekas.
All rights reserved. Printed in the United States of America. For information,
address Swoon Reads, 175 Fifth Avenue, New York, N.Y. 10010.

Our books may be purchased in bulk for promotional, educational, or business
use. Please contact your local bookseller or the Macmillan Corporate
and Premium Sales Department at (800) 221-7945 ext. 5442 or
by e-mail at MacmillanSpecialMarkets@macmillan.com.

Library of Congress Cataloging-in-Publication Data is available.
ISBN 978-1-250-18306-4 (trade paperback) / ISBN 978-1-250-18305-7 (ebook)

Book design by Liz Dresner

First edition, 2018

10 9 8 7 6 5 4 3 2 1

swoonreads.com

For restless souls

Prologue

T HE WORST MOMENT of my life was not the one in which one hundred and twenty-two people died due to my selfishness and a monster's rage.

It was not the moment I nearly lost Sebastian on the bridge, either.

It was this moment.

It was this moment, hours later, when the enormity of what had happened finally sank in. This moment, when I could no longer convince myself it was a dream. This moment, when the moon and the stars were shrouded by the smog, leaving a darkness with only one thing to say: There was nothing left.

Sebastian and I sat in a frigid church, the wind howling against the stone. He lay in my lap, staring straight ahead. He did not cry. He did not curse the heavens. He did not pray. He just stared and stared at the wooden pew in front of us, his eyes empty.

I ran my fingers soothingly through his black hair. I rocked him back and forth, hoping it might put him to sleep and give him a moment free of misery. I whispered the words I'd been repeating for hours.

"It will be all right, Sebastian. It will be all right."

But they rang hollow and I no longer believed them myself.

I was frozen with despair for my friends—the ones I had seen die and the ones I hadn't.

The fate of anyone besides Sebastian and myself, I did not know. I could repeat words of comfort to Sebastian, but I could not even convince myself that it would ever be all right again.

Mr. Kent, Miss Chen, Emily, and Laura had been shot out into the sky with more power than they could control. Rose and Catherine had been left out on the street with no power to defend themselves. I only clung to the thought of finding them because I couldn't fathom the alternative—that we might be completely alone.

And it was all the fault of Captain Goode.

I crumpled the skirts of my dress, the fabric stiff with his blood. I couldn't get Captain Goode's message out of my head. The message I had seen in the dim light as we'd passed by 43 Belgrave Square. The message he had written in blood on the front of my home, just to tell me he had survived.

We will find you.

He still wasn't satisfied. Even after he'd made me choose between my sister and everyone else. After he'd taken them all from me. After he'd taken every place I'd ever considered a home. My parents. The Lodges. The Kents. He'd left me with nowhere else to go, no idea what I was fighting for, and nothing more I could do.

A draft whistled into the church, flickering the low candles, bouncing their light off the statues and sculptures. Twisted shadows were painted across the wall, figures in agony.

There was one thing I could do. I could cut Captain Goode open from head to toe, listening to him beg for mercy, for me to spare him. Eventually I would give in and heal his wounds, all so I could serve him arsenic in his food, which was a second thing to do. It would tear apart his insides, but I'd keep him healthy enough so he could scream at me to end his life. But then I could find a collector of medieval torture devices and offer to test whether their rack was in working order. Three things. Three things to do.

My mind swam with visions of blood for minutes or hours, so long I began to doubt what was real and what I was seeing through a sleepless stupor. But the vengeful fantasies got me through the long night. By the time dawn came, I had a list of thirty-six things I could to do to make Captain Goode pay.

And one thing I could do to find my friends.

A door squeaked open, sending my heart racing for a moment. A quiet young man slipped in to extinguish the candles. The morning light had started to leak in through the dusty windows. I looked down to see Sebastian's breathing had turned easy and slow. His eyes were finally closed. But even now, he did not seem fully asleep, his eyes moving rapidly behind the lids. I reached out to gently touch the crease between his brows, the one that never seemed to go away. How much deeper had it been made tonight? Was there anything I could do to help him rest easier, to find a measure of peace?

That fierce sensation of our clashing powers traveled up my fingertips. I sighed, hoping to draw a little comfort or strength, to make myself move. I'd promised him that I would be with him. I'd told him that we would help people. None of that was going to happen if we stayed here.

"Sebastian," I whispered.

Immediately, he sat up. His hand clenched around my knee, his muscles bunched, and his eyes flew open, whites showing as he looked around wildly.

"It's all right; it's all right." I tried to soothe him, but my voice cracked repeatedly after our cold, silent night and lack of sleep. "It's just me."

Slowly, his eyes found their way back to me, his hand unclenching slightly. His chest heaved rapidly beneath the grubby and torn white shirt.

I swallowed hard and tried to sound confident. "We should go. I have an idea."

He looked to the door, then back at me, and I felt sure he was pleading for something, but he said nothing.

He had not spoken since the bridge.

I wanted so badly to find the words that would make him understand how it had not been his fault. But I had only the coldest of comforts to offer him. What could I possibly say? At least the two of us had survived? It *wasn't* his enhanced power that had killed so many?

Tell him it was actually my own selfish fault?

I took a deep breath and stood only to immediately lurch forward as my numb legs failed to support me. But Sebastian was there, from sitting to standing before I could even register what had happened. His arms went around me, pulling me up against his chest. I clung to him, his breath in my ear all I heard for a moment, and even that sounded full of misery.

There it was again: the despair that wanted to sink me. I stepped back, letting my hand fall into Sebastian's. His eyes were hooded now and downcast as I pulled him from the pew.

"We have business with a newspaper." He did not acknowledge me in any way, just let himself be led down the aisle.

Our steps echoed a little in the small space as we headed to the back of the church. Doom was building inside me as we reached the door, panic filling my head, shrieking its protest. I had no idea if this would work. I had no idea if I was going to make everything worse, yet again, but I had to try. I had to claw back into the world, dig in no matter if my nails cracked and bled, hold on with everything I had. I owed it to Sebastian, to Rose, to my parents, and to everyone else we lost last night.

I gave the altar one final glance, then we were outside in the bright light of morning.

Chapter One

"MY MA'S LANDLORD was there! She swears it were a man with glowing red eyes that burnt them alive!"

The city was still full of talk of the ball three days later.

We had already heard two arguments the day prior about who could have committed such crimes. The French were suggested, but, more disturbingly, so were unnatural people with unnatural gifts. The Queen was even planning to make a rare public appearance to quell the panic. Which, of course, only made the rumors grow more outlandish.

"And the only part he didn't burn were his victims' eyes. He left 'em behind as a warning. A ballroom full of ashes and eyes!"

I resisted the urge to reach out and smack the loudly arrogant fool trying to convince his companions. I did not know if it was my paranoia or if London really was bubbling over with suspicion and fear of something more than human responsible for the crime. But either way, I knew I'd feel safer if we found our friends soon.

The air was still and almost warm, but Sebastian and I huddled together as we walked toward Hyde Park Corner, faces down, hoping to draw little attention. The streets were filled with the usual morning crowds—the ton in carriages on their way to Rotten Row, bakers finishing the last of their morning sales, young men on their way to apprentice and clerkships. Nothing inherently suspicious, but I remained full of dread. I glanced up every few feet and everywhere I looked, I saw a potential threat, a potential ally of Captain Goode's waiting for us, waiting to finish the job started at the ball.

We were almost at the park when Sebastian stopped midstep, jerking me back. I turned to see what had finally arrested his attention after these three days. The answer was pastries.

In the dusty window of a pastry shop, a police notice was posted for a tall, dark-haired, high-cheekboned young man last seen fleeing from the scene of the Belgrave Ball three nights earlier.

A sketch of Sebastian's face filled the page, a caricature made of his deep-set eyes and thin lips. He looked vicious, monstrous. But he was still recognizable. A lump filled my throat, and I swallowed it down like a stone. In all my worries about Captain Goode and in the rumors flying across the city, I hadn't thought that the police would be looking for Sebastian. I surveyed the street. One, two, three, four, five of the notices decorated building walls and lampposts, and those were just what I could see from where I stood. Which likely meant hundreds if not thousands were plastered across the city.

"Why, it's . . . it's ridiculous," I said shortly, looking between Sebastian and the warrant that looked too much like him. Why didn't he have a scarf he could pull up over his face? A hat to pull down? The man didn't even have a blasted hat to wear!

I turned him to me and pulled the collar of his coat up around his ears, wishing for the hundredth time that he was less tall and striking. He did not respond, did not look nervous, just utterly defeated.

"We will find our friends." I stared at him, willing him to believe it. "We will find our friends, find Captain Goode, and make him confess."

He still said nothing. I continued walking, gathering his arm in mine and pulling him down slightly so he was hunched over, hopefully disguising him somewhat.

"The plan is still the same," I said, wondering why I was even bothering. Sebastian did not notice, let alone care, what I was saying.

My eyes darted around till I felt almost sick. My heart was beating uncomfortably by the time we reached the park entrance. Any person could stop and notice Sebastian, could cause a scene and ruin everything.

As soon as was possible, we turned off to smaller paths, winding quickly toward the south. "Good morning," a male voice said. A well-dressed stranger approached us on the path, tipping his tall hat. Was his scarf tied a little too tightly? Did his eyes linger too long?

"I— Good morning," I muttered back, tightening my hold on Sebastian's arm. I tensed as the man passed us by, my lips painfully caught between my teeth until I realized he wasn't here for us.

"They will come today," I said, eyeing the sword of the Achilles statue ahead. "Catherine and Mr. Kent will see the Agony Column and know what it means."

Sebastian's arm moved slightly then, and I realized I was still gripping it far too tightly. I began to slip my arm from his to stretch my stiff fingers, but he reached out and clutched my hand. Even with our powers returned to their normal levels, he refused to put any distance between us. I turned to catch his eyes on mine, as bleak and broken as a dead tree in winter. His tongue darted out and wiped the smallest drop of blood from his chapped lips.

I squeezed again, leaving my aching fingers in his. His breath warmed my skin slightly, his head so near my shoulder. How tired he must be. How tired we both were.

The statue of Lord Byron loomed ahead, fittingly, in such a remote corner of the park. Surrounded by trees, Byron sat high above us, chin held arrogantly in his hand, passing judgment on those of us who dared to continue living after he and his brilliance had passed on.

Cautiously, we approached. Sebastian's eyes did not seem to see anything, but mine were straining to look for signs of danger and signs of hope. The only figure I could make out was an older man smoking on a bench some distance away. There was a carriage on the road just outside of the park but not another soul in sight. Damn and double damn. As grateful as I might be that no one was here to spot Sebastian and accuse him of the murders, it was yet another blow that our friends were not here to meet us. I needed to see my sister, needed it more than I needed to breathe.

A slight breeze provoked a chill, and as I pulled my cloak tighter, I chanced a quick glance behind me and felt my hopes fall even further. Two men were on the path behind us, one with a tall hat. The man who had greeted us not five minutes ago.

"We're being followed," I told Sebastian, tightening my grip. I veered us north on a path away from the Byron statue.

He said nothing.

"We have to go," I said, filling in his side of the conversation. We had to get them off our trail before returning. We couldn't lead them to our only meeting place. I prayed we hadn't already given away the secret with that brief pause.

Steering Sebastian down another path, I continued to sneak looks behind us. Our pursuers had increased their pace. Wonderful.

Why, oh why, had I chosen a statue in *Hyde Park* of all places! The entire point of Hyde Park was to see and be seen. And now it was going to get Sebastian arrested.

And suddenly, our luck got even worse. For entering the park from the opposite direction of our two pursuers was a pair of policemen, their proud, bright uniforms gleaming in the morning sun.

As they quickly closed in, I could make out a sheaf of police notices held in one man's hand.

"Oh blast. Oh blast," I muttered, trying to calculate my options. Could we duck off the path and run? But the murmurs behind me were equally suspicious and growing louder. I chanced another look behind—the man in the hat was indeed pointing at Sebastian. And now we were coming up on the policemen. The only saving grace was that they were not paying us any attention whatsoever. If Sebastian wasn't going to help (and he wasn't), it was up to me to decide. And I decided to brazen it out.

Just before we crossed paths with the police, I reached for something absurd to say and pulled out the catty purr of the worst debutantes I had encountered during my Season.

"It's simply *terrible*, John! She copied my hat *entirely*! I had not even worn it yet! Can you imagine such a horrid creature to treat me so? And I considered her my greatest friend! You *know* how I feel about my haberdashery!"

Sebastian did not pay my change in character any mind, but most important, neither did the police as they continued past us.

Safe, for now. I continued my nonsense for another second in case they turned their ears to us, but I also moved us forward at a quicker pace, increasing the distance between us.

"You! Wait!" The shout came from behind us at just the right moment for the police to have crossed by the suspicious men following us. Blast and damn *and* bloody damn.

We kept moving, exiting the park where the police entered, crossing the street to a narrower, empty one. I chattered about something earnestly at Sebastian, hoping maybe the men were yelling for someone else out there. But their boots clicked determinedly closer and closer, echoing off the brick buildings around us. Should we run? Or pretend to know nothing? Play mute? No, they had already heard me speak.

"Oy!" A hand reached out and turned Sebastian around, swinging me with him.

"Well, I never!" I twittered, fluttering my hand nervously. "What on earth is the meaning of . . ."

But they weren't paying attention to my babble. Their eyes were only on Sebastian. One of them was pulling a club out cautiously.

"You're the one, aren't you?" he spoke up, taking a brave step toward us. "Killed a lot of people, we hear."

"Just come quiet," the other said. "Don't want your lady to g—"

I didn't wait for him to finish. I seized Sebastian's hand, yanked him in the other direction, and felt myself anchored. One of them had grabbed Sebastian, and the other one was striking from behind with his club.

Sebastian winced and struggled against their hold, but he refused to fight back, to hurt anyone else. I held on to his hand as long as I could, our fingers turning white with strain, but one of the policemen struck his arm, and Sebastian lost hold. They pulled him away and shackled his hands behind his back. He looked helplessly at me, confusion and panic flitting across his features, the first emotions I'd seen from him in days. His power would overwhelm these men, and he knew it.

"Stop it! He's terribly dangerous!" I shouted.

Sebastian was moaning, wriggling hard to free himself as they dragged him away and the distance between us widened. My mind scrambled to think of what to do. Unfortunately, violence was at the forefront of my thoughts. I flung myself at one of the policemen, slapping him solidly across the face. My palm went numb for a second, then prickles of pain bloomed across it.

"We're both terribly dangerous. Arrest me, too," I yelled in the shocked silence.

The policeman pushed me away, and I immediately latched on to Sebastian. The man looked at his companion, a sneer on his face as they both began to laugh. "She says she's dangerous!"

"The little lady!"

Which was ridiculous. I wasn't little at all.

And less and less a lady.

I threw myself at them again, this time with dagger fan in hand. The blade sliced deep into an arm, and the smaller man recoiled back in surprise. "She stabbed me!"

"It . . . it was a stab to help you!" I argued back.

Ignoring my poor reasoning, the other policeman pulled out his club to strike me, but Sebastian slammed his shoulder into the man's gut, throwing them both off balance.

My hand found Sebastian's jacket, and I pulled him to me. "Run."

And run we did, a whole five steps.

"Stop there!" A huge policeman stepped out from an alleyway, triumphantly blocking our path. He held up a policeman's club, but it was his sheer bulk and his eager crouch that bothered me more. Sebastian and I were both dazed and weary from the fight, little sleep, and less food, while the policeman looked ready to pounce. I doubted we could slip by him. I doubted even more that Sebastian wanted to risk hurting him.

"Harrison!" The other two officers were back on their feet, trapping us from the other side.

"See, I told you it works. Wait off to the side and then catch them off guard!" Harrison smiled proudly at the other two. "They never suspect a third."

A gun cocked loudly behind the big policeman. "By God, you're right; they never do."

A man appeared behind Harrison and pressed the muzzle into his head. He wore the most hideous hat I'd ever seen, a bushy mustache, and pince-nez. He didn't look familiar, but that voice, equal parts silky and cutting, I'd recognize anywhere.

"Mr. . . . Kent," I managed to gasp out.

"Mr. Lent," he corrected with a pointed look. He pulled the policeman back into the alleyway. "Now, all of you come in here and join your friend."

Once we followed him in, he nudged his hostage forward with his gun. Harrison slipped past us and stood in front of his partners. They whispered something to one another.

"I didn't hear that," Mr. Kent said. "What did you say?"

"I said we could charge you at once because you can't shoot all three of us," Harrison admitted.

"Oh Lord, why'd you tell him?" the mustached officer groaned.

"I don't know."

"Officers, let me tell you what you will do. One of you is going to come over here and gently uncuff this man, then you'll let us be on our way, while you return to your station and tell your superior that a Captain Simon Goode is truly responsible for the Belgrave Ball."

"I liked my suggestion better," Harrison replied.

"But my suggestion doesn't involve the three of you having your darkest secrets revealed to the public," Mr. Kent said, waggling his eyebrows. They didn't look convinced. Mr. Kent gestured to the stout officer. "You, what is your darkest secret?"

"My father couldn't afford to keep his bakery because he owed too much money, so I told him to purchase insurance for the shop, and then one night I got a barrel of kerosene by robbing a local factory owner who was—"

"You committed arson and fraud, yes?" Mr. Kent interrupted.

"Yes."

"All right, that's plenty, thank you. Now come over here slowly and remove this man's handcuffs." Mr. Kent kept his gun on the officer as he meekly stepped forward and unlocked Sebastian's restraints. Mr. Kent looked to the mustached officer. "And what is the abridged version of your darkest secret?"

"I have been unfaithful to my wife," he said, looking shocked and ashamed.

"Fitz!" Harrison exclaimed. "How could you do that to Mary?"

"I . . . It was a foolish mistake," Fitz said remorsefully.

"It certainly was," Mr. Kent said. "I'll do my best to make sure poor Mary doesn't find out. Now you, tall one, what is your darkest secret?"

"I once lied to a man and said his hat looked very good when in fact it did not."

"Oh Lord, you're one of those," Mr. Kent said, rolling his eyes. "Fine, what question would be the most damaging one to ask you?"

"Which of my friends I like more," the officer answered, his eyes nervously flitting to the other two officers.

Mr. Kent let out a faint snort. "Good. Handcuff yourselves to one another and start walking toward the northwest corner of the park, and I won't tear apart your friendship. Though, dammit, now I can't help but be a little curious. I like that Fitz's mustache but—"

"Mr. *Lent*," I said, backing away to our escape.

"Fine, fine," Mr. Kent said. He eyed the policemen threateningly. "But remember: Do what I said. Or Lent . . . will give *you* up."

He allowed a moment for the threat to sink in, then slipped the gun into his coat and turned on his heel to lead the way out.

"Thank you, Mr. Kent," I said.

"I've been saving that one for you two," he replied.

"Truly," I said. I wanted to tell him my thank-you was not for the horrible quip but for the rescue and for . . . well, being alive. I didn't quite know how to say that.

He seemed to figure it out anyway and gave me a sad sort of smile. The bravado fell from his face, and I could see the grief and

exhaustion the last few days had wrought on him. "Of course."
He eyed us both for a long moment, lingering on Sebastian, then
cutting to me. I nodded at his unasked questions: Yes, Sebastian
was in a very bad way. No, I did not know how to snap him out of
this.

Except by murdering Captain Goode in thirty-six ways.

"Come." Mr. Kent clapped his hands together bracingly. He
led us out of the alley to an idling carriage and opened the door
for us.

I shook my head. "No, we still have to wait for—"

Rose.

Chapter Two

F OR A SECOND all I could make out were the essentials. Tired but clear blue eyes. A constellation of small freckles on the right cheek. A faint crease between the eyes. All the tiny little things that made up Rose.

We stared at each other for a long moment, and mixed with pure relief was a hot flush of guilt. I closed my eyes and threw my arms around my sister, but I still saw everyone who had died so I could have her here with me. She returned the hug, but it somehow seemed a little less full, as though an essential bulk of her was missing, gone when we watched our parents die.

I squeezed harder. "Thank heavens you're all right," I said, half-considering holding on forever. "You're safe."

"And you," her muffled voice came back. I released her and checked again to be entirely sure she wasn't a figment of my rather active imagination. No, it was certainly her. She gave me a weak smile and quickly darted her eyes away, shifting the attention to Catherine.

"Catherine did it all. She kept us safe and found the newspaper listing."

I scrambled into the carriage, pulling Sebastian after me and unleashing my hug upon Catherine next, crushing her spectacles into my neck. "Thank you for being your brilliant self."

"I'm just glad we saw the Agony Column listing," she replied, but she was looking at Sebastian, who settled next to me, stiffly pushing himself into the corner as far away from the other carriage occupants as humanly possible.

All of them were eyeing him, actually. Mr. Kent gestured at Catherine to shove over so it was the three of them on one side, Sebastian and me on the other. I made a show of grabbing his hand firmly and forcing them to meet my eyes. If I couldn't even convince my *friends* of Sebastian's innocence, we would have no chance against the rest of the world.

In the tense silence, Mr. Kent reached up and tapped the carriage ceiling. We began to roll forward, and that's when I noticed it wasn't as full as it should have been.

"Where is Laura? Emily? Miss Chen?" I asked. "Are they—"

"They are safe," Mr. Kent assured me. "I sent them ahead in a separate carriage in case something went wrong here."

"Sent them ahead where?" I asked. "Do you . . . already have a plan for Captain Goode?"

Everyone in the carriage half looked at me with a sort of awkwardness, like there was something they didn't want to tell me.

Finally, Mr. Kent cleared his throat. "I sent them to the train station, Miss Wyndham. Our plan for Captain Goode is getting ourselves out of London and as far away as possible."

I stared at them, half expecting it to be a very strange joke. "But . . . we have to stop him."

Rose's mouth puckered, and Catherine sighed.

"We don't know that he will do anything else," Mr. Kent said.

"Of course we do—"

"The only thing we do know," Rose said, her voice quivering a little, "is that he plans to find us."

My angry response died in my throat. His message on our home.

"You saw it?" I asked.

Rose and Catherine nodded at the same time, little jerks of their heads that made it clear they wished they had seen nothing.

"The only smart option is to join Catherine's aunt in Liverpool." Mr. Kent looked so tired. But to run? Let Captain Goode live without paying for what he had done?

"We are not running away from this murderous, evil . . . murderer!"

"I did not suggest running. I told you, we are taking a train." Mr. Kent's poor attempt at a jest landed heavily, ignored by everyone.

"Evelyn, it isn't safe for us here." Rose's voice was thin with worry.

"What would you want us to do if we stayed?" Catherine's practical firmness felt somehow frustrating now.

"We are going to kill him," I said evenly. Just the thought of watching Captain Goode choke for air, begging for mercy and receiving none, eased some of the pain that threatened to bubble over into hysteria.

The carriage's occupants all frowned at my proclamation. Except Sebastian, who was staring out the window, not following along at all.

"Lovely idea, but how are we going to do that?" Mr. Kent said.

"Bare hands," I offered blithely. That was my favorite on the list.

"We don't even know where he is," Catherine pointed out in that annoyingly correct way.

"We'll follow the trail of bodies. There are only going to be more." I turned to Rose, looking at her beseechingly. How were they all so calm? So ready to run with our tails tucked?

"We don't know that. And what about . . . him?" Rose did not—it seemed *would* not—look at Sebastian, but her meaning was clear.

"He can borrow Mr. Kent's disguise." Really, why was everyone so focused on these trivial little things?

"Evelyn, there are notices all over the city." Catherine's voice was beginning to grate.

"So we will kill Captain Goode today and make sure the whole country knows it was *he* who killed our friends and family. Not Sebastian." I glared at them to make the point clearer.

"We all know it was not Mr. Braddock's fault." Surprisingly, that came from Mr. Kent, who was looking at Sebastian almost gently.

Catherine nodded in agreement. "And we want to do everything to help."

"Exactly. And that means making Captain Goode pay. He is entirely responsible," I continued evenly, ignoring the voice that told me this wasn't *quite* truthful.

No one seemed to guess, though.

Except Rose, who knew the truth about that night. She looked down at her lap, avoiding my eyes. She knew what I had chosen. Whom I had chosen.

London was flying by outside the windows, and I didn't have long to persuade my friends to stay and fight.

"What do you propose as the alternative? We simply leave and never come back?" Perhaps I could persuade them not to leave, rather than to stay.

"My aunt can take us in until we decide what to do further," Catherine said. "And if necessary—"

"We cross the Atlantic and hide forever in America?" I scoffed.

"No. We take a little bit of time to be rational," Catherine answered, her eyes narrowing slightly as I challenged her admittedly sound plan.

"We have to find a way to clear Sebastian's name," I tried again.

"And we will. From a safe distance. In Liverpool," Mr. Kent rebuffed me. Rose's lips were drawn tight, and Catherine was still faintly glaring. I gestured at Sebastian.

"How can you think to let Captain Goode blame Sebastian for this? If we don't tell the world that a murderer *used* him entirely against his will, he will not get to have a normal life!"

"No one is saying we leave forever!" Rose cried, looking at me pleadingly. And I so badly wanted to listen to her. Whether it was my sister's power at work or just her deep unhappiness, I softened some.

"I want to go." Sebastian's voice barely made it across the carriage.

I snapped my head to him in surprise. His first words in three days. He still wasn't looking at me or anyone else.

"You want to leave?" Rose sounded as surprised as I felt.

Sebastian nodded, his hair falling in front of his eyes.

Mr. Kent stamped his cane a little, and Catherine's hands clapped together briskly.

"Good. Settled just in time. For we are here."

I searched for words as everyone piled out at Victoria Station, the bustling center that could take us anywhere. The last time I was here, I'd come from Bramhurst searching for Rose. Now, I had her back by my side at the cost of so many other people I loved.

This felt so wrong, so terribly wrong to be leaving, but no one else seemed to agree. That Sebastian and Rose both wanted this . . . I swallowed my dread back. Maybe they just needed a day or two. Maybe I just needed to find the right argument.

Mr. Kent paid our driver and gestured down the street. "The others should be just this way."

He hurried a little ways from the station, down a smaller adjacent street. A carriage waited there, curtains drawn. Mr. Kent gave it three rhythmic knocks and the door clicked open. Only when he saw the carriage occupants did his shoulders relax a little.

Miss Chen was the first to step out. She looked paler than usual, but still calm. I would never guess just by looking at her that she had been through all the horrors of the past three days.

"Miss Wyndham." She nodded a little at me, her arm held stiffly in front of her. "If you wouldn't mind, I very much need you to heal my arm."

I looked more closely. It was indeed held at a very strange angle, and I quickly took her hand, shaking my head. "I'm sorry I didn't find you sooner."

She grimaced lightly. "I've been in worse pain. Not much worse, but some."

I let my power do its work before realizing it couldn't.

I turned to Sebastian, searching for the gentlest words. "Sebastian, I need to heal Miss Chen. Her arm is quite broken."

From the way Sebastian's jaw tightened, it felt like I had told him I never wanted to see him again.

"Do you think you could move away, just to the edge of our range? There's no one behind you." Catherine and Rose were helping the others down from the carriage.

He looked to be sure I was right and took a deep breath before stepping back from us, counting the ten feet to make sure he stayed as close as possible.

Miss Chen's eyes caught mine for a quick moment, and finally

I saw the pain she was carrying with her. Even though she hadn't lost a parent or someone she loved that night, she still saw that madness fly around the ballroom—and had been a part of it, too. Captain Goode cut through her carefully held control and forced her to hurt people. That would be devastating, even for the strongest of us.

"I'm sorry for . . . well, your losses. Both of yours." She looked at the ground a little, clearly uncomfortable with expressing much. Or perhaps she simply was worried I might fall to pieces if she looked at me too long.

"Thank you." I felt odd accepting her condolences, but I gave her now-healed arm a light squeeze.

"Evelyn." A mournful little voice came from behind Miss Chen. Laura was being held protectively underneath Emily's arm. Her hair was lank and plastered to her cheeks. There was no light of fervor in her eyes as there should have been. She didn't look to be scheming or full of impossible plans. A deep twinge pulled at my heart. The poor girl. Her parents were gone, too.

And I had let Captain Goode do it.

"Oh, Laura, I'm so glad to see you." I wrapped her in a hug, holding her thin body to me. "I'm so, so sorry." She seemed to muffle a sob, and I held on longer, eyeing Emily over her shoulder. Rose fussed at a bruise on Emily's arm.

"Emily, you are injured?" She shook her head but didn't take her worried eyes off Laura. I took some comfort in knowing that Laura had not only her fierce older brother as a protector but her new friend as well. Rose shook her head a little at me, indicating that Emily was fine.

"Here." Mr. Kent tossed his hat to Sebastian, distracting him with the task of transferring his disguise. I walked back and took his hand, hoping it made him feel a little more comfortable.

"Pull the hat down over your ears. Take the pince-nez, too. The mustache sticks on. Should last long enough to get on the train." Mr. Kent didn't quite catch Sebastian's eye as he said it. But Sebastian raised no argument, not even to the hideous mustache. He just gingerly pressed it above his lip. It almost looked real.

Catherine and Rose helped Laura and Emily into their coats as Mr. Kent paid the driver. The carriage clattered away, and we stood for a moment in a malformed circle, the silence between us anything but comfortable. My stomach sank again.

Wrong, wrong—leaving like this is wrong.

"It seems we're all ready then," Mr. Kent said with a decisive strike of his cane.

I tried one last time. "Are you sure we shouldn't stay and quickly kill Captain—"

"No, off we go." Mr. Kent cut me off and headed toward the station, the others following.

"This is truly what you wish to do?" I asked Sebastian as we lingered behind.

"Yes."

I tried to be cheered by the fact that he had now said at least five words. Maybe leaving would help him see that he did not need to blame himself.

"You don't need to punish yourself," I said carefully. He grimaced a little harder. "It was Captain Goode's fault." I silently wondered if that would end up being my most oft-repeated phrase. Maybe it would even be engraved on my tombstone.

He ignored me. I sighed and I gripped his hand as we entered the busy station. Two policemen in dark uniforms stood near the door. I turned Sebastian slightly to the right. He ducked his head and leaned closer to me. We wove cautiously through the crowds, Mr. Kent leading the way.

"The train leaves in a few minutes; we shall have to move

swiftly." Catherine turned to us, consulting a watch tucked into her jacket.

"To track three." Mr. Kent veered left and we followed.

"Do we not need tickets?" I tried to keep pace with him.

"I bought them early this morning," he said, a little smug, which was greatly annoying.

"With what money?"

"You don't have emergency funds stashed away in case you accidentally anger the entire city?"

"No, I try to stay on the good side of entire cities."

"Well, now you know how hard that is."

Every step forward we took felt heavier. We were leaving Captain Goode here to do God-knows-what with God-knows-whom. I could not conscience it. The need to destroy him was itching me like uncomfortable woolen underthings.

But I didn't have an argument to persuade the others. Hundreds died because they had the unfortunate luck of being caught between Captain Goode's rage and us. Because of the selfish decision I had made. And if I had it my way now, it would hurt Rose, Sebastian, and everyone else who wanted to leave.

The great black train belched smoke as we came to the tracks. Shouts and mechanical noises clamored and competed for attention between the shrieking bursts of steam, calls from porters, and loud conversations between companions.

I looked around as surreptitiously as possible, my heart beginning to pound. This was it. We were leaving.

The train gave another loud scream, sounding somehow more final than the others.

Sebastian pulled me up behind him, my shoes slipping a little on the black steps, my nerves buzzing. For just a moment, the grief on his face cleared a bit, and he frowned at me in consternation. "Are you all right?"

That little sign of awareness, his concern for me briefly out-weighing his pain, made my heart skip slightly. Of course I was not all right. Neither was he. But we were here.

Together.

"Yes."

Rose and Catherine led us past the first- and second-class carriages. Sunlight split through the windows, illuminating the little picnics that were being unearthed from hampers, the children jumping around in their cramped compartments. It was a strange place to be given our somber mood.

We found our compartment near the front of the train and everyone climbed inside, shaking out of coats and settling skirts around ankles. The screech and rumble announced our departure. We had made it, but only barely. An awkward silence lingered between all of us.

I settled against the window and peered outside. I watched as the station drifted by and the train's chugging grew more rapid against my best wishes. I watched as an unlucky couple emerged from the opposite end of the platform and hurried through the crowd to catch the leaving train. I watched as they ran so fast their hats flew off and they managed to leap onto the car in front of ours just before we left the station. The woman paused on the step, looking straight at me through the glass. A shiver tore through me, and the train felt colder all of a sudden. The woman, wrapped in a big blue coat, had a bit of a glow about her. A literal glow that I had seen before.

When she was encasing my feet in blocks of ice, deep below-ground in the Society of Aberrations prison.

Chapter Three

―――――

I FROZE BEFORE realizing that's exactly what she would want me to do.

"Mr. Kent," I strained a whisper through my teeth. "We're being followed. Please get us to a first-class compartment right now."

His eyebrows went up. "And how—"

"Full blackmail privileges," I replied. "Go."

Like a cat, he slid out of his seat and opened our compartment door, pulling Laura and Emily behind him. Miss Chen, Catherine, and Rose followed him, shooting me looks of concern and confusion.

Sebastian stood up, but waited in the narrow corridor, eyeing me as though he expected me to run off somewhere without him.

I pushed him forward, sending him a faint buzz from my fingertips. "I'm right behind you."

I kept my head down and my face hidden, hoping our escape went unnoticed. The train car rumbled below my feet as it picked up speed, and I seized the wooden wall paneling for balance. Perplexed heads glanced up at us through the ajar doors of other compartments until we reached the end of the carriage and stepped outside onto the small shelf of metal separating the cars.

The cold, bracing wind and burning fumes hit me at once. Slivers of rooftops passed by in procession to my right. Sebastian took my hand, and I hopped over the gap between the passenger cars as the wheels clattered in warning over the tracks.

We made our way into the second-class carriage, where upholstery and ornate trimming replaced the plain wood of third class. We passed a silent railway guard, who was staring rather slack-jawed at Mr. Kent, and then we were in the dining car, where a few passengers were already comfortably seated and sipping tea. I watched an unobserved cup slowly float away into Emily's hands and then get offered to Laura. Not even a ghost of a smile hit Laura's lips.

Finally, we made it through to a first-class carriage. My heart thrummed along with our steps, and I resisted the overwhelming urge to see if the woman was following us. There was another railway guard at the end, but fortunately, he seemed to be distracted by two other passengers. Unfortunately, one of the passengers was holding a poster that looked horribly familiar, while the other peeked into one of the three private compartments.

Mr. Kent spun around, pushing us back the way we came. "You know, I feel much more comfortable in second class all of a sudden. I don't know what was I thinking—me in first class."

I turned to open the rear carriage door again when I found it already opening. A chill ran down my spine, and I couldn't tell if it was dread or her—I was now face-to-face with the ice guard.

"Emily!" I yelled wildly while I could still draw in breath instead of ice.

The door slammed in the woman's blue-pallored face. It rattled in protest as she tried to open it, but Emily's power held it firm. I spun back around to find our group looking very lost.

"Maybe those police notices are for someone else," Mr. Kent said, forcing a smile. He spun around with a decisive clap of his hands to see the two passengers and the railway guard gaping at us.

The bulkier of the two passengers stepped forward, taking up nearly the entire narrow corridor. He stared hard at Sebastian, poster in hand. "This you, then?" His voice was a grating scratch.

"Right," Mr. Kent said, pulling out his pistol. "Not another step."

The bulky man took several. He ambled toward us, a clacking, metallic sound chiming with his every step, as if he were wearing a suit of armor.

I opened the third compartment and shoved Catherine, Rose, and Laura inside, ignoring the gasps from the two elderly occupants. "Stay here."

"We don't want to start a panic," Mr. Kent said, aiming straight at the man. "Why don't we continue this another time?"

The man pulled his hat off and, in his grasp, it slowly transformed from a dull black to a shiny silver, from fabric to metal. "Because Captain Goode wants his revenge now."

"Maybe . . . we should set that aside for a moment," Mr. Kent said. "You see, we recently battled this lady who can control metal, and you would get along—oh, wait, she probably died at the ball, didn't she?"

"Yes," our group responded in unison.

Mr. Kent sighed. "Ah well, it would have been adorable."

He re-leveled his gun and quickly fired at the man, who covered his face with the former hat and now shield. The bullets barely seemed to have an effect, clanking off his arms, his chest, his knees as he got closer. Shouts and screams came from the closed compartments on our left.

"Blast it," Miss Chen muttered, peering over Mr. Kent's shoulder to get a better view.

The man's metal hat cracked into pieces upon her gaze, revealing an expression of faint surprise. But before Mr. Kent could aim at the man's head, his previously quiet companion slipped in front, raised his hands, and flooded the entire carriage with smoke.

I could hear Mr. Kent groaning, and my eyes watered as I blinked away the strange smog, finally catching sight of him, trying to aim his gun through the thick, black shroud. Glass and wood shattered around us as Miss Chen tried to clear the smoke out the windows, but it did not dissipate in the least. It stubbornly clung to us, as though it were made of a stickier substance, working its way into our lungs, filling the carriage with hacking coughs. I remembered the fire in Dr. Beck's laboratory, nearly choking to death even when I had my powers. With Sebastian canceling them out here, everyone in this carriage would have a minute at most.

It seemed Mr. Kent had the same thought. "Mr. Braddock! Your assistance, please!" he shouted around a cough. His hands popped out of the smoke, wrenched Sebastian away from me, and threw him at the source.

All right. Perhaps not *exactly* the same thought.

But sure enough, the smoke started to clear. I squeezed past the others to Sebastian, who was scrambling up from the ground, climbing desperately off the smoker he had wrestled into unconsciousness. I pulled him back next to Emily, who was still managing to keep the rear carriage door tightly shut. The last bit of smoke disappeared, leaving the terrified railway guard fumbling with the half-broken carriage door at the front and the metal man vulnerable, his clothes ripping and the armor underneath cracking and

falling in thick shreds of metal. Mr. Kent cocked and aimed his pistol as the carriage door opened behind his target and the railway guard was shoved to the floor.

The ice guard. She must have climbed across the top.

Before Mr. Kent could fire, she spat out an ice shard, piercing his hand. He dropped the gun and followed it to the floor, lunging with his left hand. The metal man grabbed Mr. Kent's hand first in a steel grip, and Mr. Kent screamed like I'd never heard before. His hand seemed to harden, metal taking over his arm inch by inch, climbing terrifyingly fast toward the rest of his body. I leaped forward to do something, but Emily pulled the metal man away with her telekinesis.

"Stop it!" she cried, slamming him into the ice guard. When he tried to reach out for something to anchor himself, she flung him to our end, forcing us to duck to avoid his body, and threw him against the corridor walls, punctuating her every word with another vicious slam.

"Stop! Hurting! Us!"

Miss Chen supplied the punctuation on the last word as she blew the side of the carriage apart in an eruption of wood and metal. The man was hurled out of the train and down into the London streets.

Before we even had a moment to catch our breath, a scream brought our attention back to the front. The ice guard pulled a young woman out of the first compartment and held her captive with an ice shard by her neck. She stared at us, daring us to move.

"Please . . ." the woman stammered.

"Are you really going to hurt her?" Mr. Kent asked.

"No," the ice guard replied, but she was smiling. "No need."

The rear carriage door slammed behind me. Oh no.

We were afforded the briefest glimpse of our new enemy, gray-haired, sinewy, his right eye covered by a white kerchief wrapped around his head. He lifted the fabric, setting his eye upon us, and I was struck with an excruciating pain. Everyone around me cried out in agony as it brought us writhing to the ground. It was like every bit of pain I'd ever experienced combined and yet unlike anything I'd ever felt before. It was every burn, every cut, every break, every ache, striking a match against every nerve. It was every body on the ground at the Belgrave Ball, every life I couldn't save, every shred of guilt, horror, devastation burning like a tattoo on my brain. It was torture in every possible form, random and relentless.

"Captain Goode wanted you to know he picked this pain personally," the torturer said above me.

My breath left me. I choked and coughed and gasped for air, but there was never enough. The tight passage seemed to close in even tighter. It was like being smothered, suffocated, drowned, and then given just enough air to experience it again.

"Who first, Miss Quinn?" Through the blur of panic, I could only make out the torturer's boots approaching.

"The healer," the ice guard said. "I get the one with the big mouth."

I felt my head lifted up and my neck bared, somewhere distant between all the pain. Tears streamed down my face and my body twitched uncontrollably. I wondered if this would, at least, put an end to my torture.

And then I heard Rose's voice. "Evelyn!"

Startled, our torturer looked up at my sister emerging from her compartment. She cried out in pain from his attack and collapsed to the ground next to me.

"Oh no, no, I'm sorry."

Did I say that?

No, the torturer had. All of a sudden I could think clearly again. The pain had stopped.

I seized the moment of hesitation, taking advantage of his guilt from hurting Rose. I charged straight at him. The pain hit me again, but I had the momentum. I tackled him, low and hard, straight out the hole in the side of the train.

We fell for a brief, breathless second and then more pain struck me, every imaginable type from the torturer along with an extra dash of bruising and cutting as we slammed and bounced and rolled across a brick roof just below the train tracks. The edge was so close, perhaps this really was death—perhaps I would not heal from this fall.

And then a great tethering sensation yanked me back upward, my stomach flipping, the streets and the torturer falling away from me in a dizzying rush, and I was pulled into the train, landing on the floor beside Emily.

I gulped down a heavy breath. "Thank you," I managed to groan to her as Sebastian helped me up.

With Laura's help, Emily climbed to her feet by the hole and gave me a shaky nod, still wincing over the pain she just experienced. In fact, everyone seemed to be rather slow and shaken, save for Mr. Kent.

He had his still-metal hand over Miss Quinn's mouth and was bombarding her with questions.

"So this metal won't go away on its own?" he asked.

"Nmph" was her muffled reply.

"Can Captain Goode remove it?"

"Nmph," she said again, shaking her head.

"Is there another man or woman with this poorly thought-out power who can reverse it?"

"Nmph."

"My hand will be metal forever?"

"Mmph."

"Oh, for God's sake," Mr. Kent said. He turned to the rest of us. "Is everyone all right?"

"No" was the unanimous response.

"Well, you all responded, so I will say that's a victory. Miss Wyndham, do you heal . . . metallic afflictions?"

"I don't know. I promise to try later," I said, hobbling over to them, ignoring the dull pain in my limbs. "Is anyone else hurt?"

Everyone shook their heads. Despite the horrible pain, there had been no real injuries. The two witnesses, however, were petrified. The railway guard kept one eye on us and one eye on the carriage door he shakily managed to open. He leaped over the rail into the next carriage, shouting for help. The ice guard's hostage, meanwhile, had crawled back into her compartment and was huddled against her terrified mother.

"Stay in there. It's still dangerous out here," I told them, shutting the compartment door.

"We should find a way off," Catherine said. "We're lucky no one else saw us."

"We will," I said. "But first, Mr. Kent, ask her where the tracker is."

Mr. Kent removed his hand and aimed her in the direction of a broken window, away from us. "What tracker?"

"The one from the Society," I answered.

"The man who led us to you," Miss Quinn helpfully corroborated.

"Ah, thank you, yes, where is that specific tracker?" he asked.

"Second-class compartment," she answered, huffing out mist and squirming against Mr. Kent's hold.

"Good," I said. "Put her on the next carriage quickly, and Miss Chen, can you sever the line?"

Miss Chen helped Mr. Kent move the ice guard to the other end. "She could still damage our carriage from there."

"I'll ask her a question with a very long answer," Mr. Kent said.

With Emily's help, they lifted Miss Quinn over the gap and threw her back into the next car. Miss Chen eyed the connectors for a moment until they snapped and exploded apart.

"In order, what are my most attractive features and qualities?" Mr. Kent shouted over to Miss Quinn.

With fury in her gaze, she answered. "Cleverness. Your eyes. The sharpness of your jaw. Your confidence."

Her voice faded as our half of the train pulled away with a burst of speed.

Mr. Kent tut-tutted to himself. "Perhaps that was too harsh. She's going to spend the rest of her life answering that."

"Would have been a mercy to throw her off," Miss Chen muttered.

Rose clutched my arm as I turned around. "Ev, what are we doing?"

"I don't know," I said, pulling her along with me. "But they are going to keep finding us if we don't attend to this tracker."

I led the way back into the second-class carriage, where another railway guard stopped us, demanding to know what happened.

"There . . . was a row and a . . . a man with a gun," I stammered. "Please help us. I just want to get my sister somewhere safe."

My half-truth along with a look from my sister was enough. He squeezed by us and ordered us to take shelter with the other curious passengers peering out from their compartments. He left the carriage to investigate the next one.

The moment he was gone, Mr. Kent gave up all pretenses of

subtlety and began repeatedly shouting his question, "Tracker! Where are you?"

We got no response in the first carriage, but when we crossed over into the next one, a muffled voice answered. "In this compartment—oh goodness me!"

We found a nervous young man in his twenties, his face round and skin a deep umber, with a fidgety energy about him. He was standing by the other door to his compartment. It was open, leading to a long drop onto the London streets that he did not look too excited about experiencing.

"Mr. Adeoti," Miss Chen said, looking at him warily.

Recognition crossed the tracker's face, and he held his hands up in defense. "Miss Chen, I'm sorry, these were Captain Goode's orders. Please don't—"

"Do you know him?" Mr. Kent asked Miss Chen.

"Yes. From Society missions," she answered. "He was the one who found people before Miss Grey."

"Did Goode take control of the Society of Aberrations?" I asked. Mr. Kent repeated my question.

"Yes," Mr. Adeoti answered, his large eyes darting between us all as though he was trying to figure out who among us would be killing him.

"And what is he planning?"

"He—he said he is going to protect everyone with powers."

I hesitated, the answer throwing off my line of questioning. It wasn't just revenge he wanted, then.

"And uh . . . what did he say about the rest of the public?" Mr. Kent asked.

"He said they're going to be enlightened tomorrow."

The train lurched violently and a loud squeal filled the air as the brakes were put on. The conductor must have noticed first class had been left behind. The carriage rumbled and shuddered to a stop, and the compartment fell silent. I was sure we were all picturing the same thing in what Captain Goode considered "enlightened."

Mr. Kent looked at our group and then out the window at the surrounding rooftops. We had not even gotten out of central London.

He sighed. "Well, I take it this is our stop, then."

Chapter Four

———————

"THIS BETTER NOT be a den of thieves," I said.

"It's not," Mr. Kent said as he knocked on the front door to a crumbling house that fit in with the other buildings around us. The street was dotted with squat houses in yellow brick, and a skinny railway curved over the rooftops, bringing people in and out of London. Lambeth wasn't exactly the most fashionable area, but after the exhausting fight and our hasty escape from the train, I was willing to settle for anything. As long as it was as discreet as Mr. Kent claimed.

"And not a brothel, either," I said.

"It's even better than that," Mr. Kent replied with a wink.

Oh Lord.

But then the door opened to an unexpected but familiar face.

Tuffins allowed himself one astonished blink before greeting us. "Mr. Kent, Miss Wyndham, Mr. Braddock. My . . . most sincere condolences."

"Thank you, Tuffins. I am sorry for all the unexpected events," Mr. Kent said. "Including this intrusion. But, well, I recalled your mother runs a boarding house, and we were wondering whether you have any vacancies for, hmm . . . nine of us."

Tuffins looked out over our shoulders to the two waiting carriages on the street.

"Miss Kent is with us," I added. "She is safe."

He maintained his full butlery composure, but I could see the slightest hints of relief flooding his body. His hands relaxed their hold on the door. He let out a long-held breath. His jaw unclenched. It was the happiest I'd ever seen him. "I will inform my mother and return to fetch your belongings."

"Oh, no need, we have none," Mr. Kent replied, waving the notion aside with his metallic hand. "But if you could set up a room appropriate for a guest we'd really rather not escape? Something secure. Perhaps odd and threatening?"

"Yes, of course." The fact that Tuffins didn't even bat an eye was the final reassurance I needed that this was the right place.

We went back to the carriages to get the rest of our group. While Mr. Kent and Miss Chen escorted Mr. Adeoti to his room, I paid our drivers with the last coin I had left. I didn't know how far Mr. Kent's funds would stretch, but I tried to take my cue from Tuffins and remain calm as we climbed the stairs and entered the boarding house.

The inside of the house was completely at odds with the tired, worn exterior. Rugs that didn't quite fit together spread across the wooden floors. The walls were covered with a strange assortment of images. Landscape prints sat next to advertisement bills, which sat next to detailed sketches of insects. There was no discernible pattern—just an overwhelming enthusiasm for everything.

We made our way across a narrow hallway, past the main staircase, and into a cramped dining room decorated in more mismatched choices, from the styles of all the chairs to the trinkets lining the fireplace mantel. A moment later, Tuffins came downstairs with Mr. Kent, Miss Chen, and a stout older woman who was dressed exactly like the rest of the house: hair in an older style, green glass earrings shining brilliantly, her dress all manner of patterns, and sturdy boots on her feet. Tuffins cleared his throat and gestured to the woman beside him but found himself quite interrupted by a vicious hug.

"T-Tuffins, you-you're here. You're alive." Laura clung to him as if he'd disappear if she let go.

If Tuffins was at all put out, he didn't show it in the least. "I am most thankful to see the same is true of you, Miss Kent."

Behind him, the older woman looked around the room with a wide, slightly flustered smile, overwhelmed by all her guests and trying to decide how to welcome us.

Tuffins helped her with the decision. "Miss Kent, may I introduce you to my mother, Mrs. Eleanor Tuffins?"

Laura looked up, her eyes red and astonished, as if she'd never considered Tuffins could have a mother. She unlatched herself and made a deep curtsy.

But Mrs. Tuffins would have none of that. She waved away the curtsy with warmth. "Oh, Miss Kent, I've heard so much about you." She pulled Laura into a hug, briskly rubbing her back and tucking back her hair. She looked at each of us with so much concern and true feeling my lip began to tremble despite itself. "I'm so sorry to hear what's happened to you, my poor dears. But you are welcome here as long as you need. All of you."

Tuffins proceeded to make the introductions, and Mr. Kent helped fill in the gaps, after which Mrs. Tuffins was eager to get us settled.

"Goodness, it's been so long since I've had guests," she said, her face red and shining. "I haven't shown anyone around in months."

"Most of the lodgers left last year when two of the factories nearby closed," Tuffins explained to us.

"And *someone* insisted I sell this and find a small home for myself. But if I had," she said, shooting her son a fond look, "I wouldn't have had room here for all of you."

"It was shamefully shortsighted of me," Tuffins put in.

Mrs. Tuffins gestured around the room. "Well, my dears, we will have all our meals in here. Our breakfast is at seven, lunch at noon, and dinner at six, though of course we can alter that if it does not suit?" She made it sound like the most important possible question, and we quickly assured her the times were amenable. The brilliant smile was back on her face immediately.

"I imagine you all must be very hungry. I'll have the cook prepare some tea and cakes now." She squeezed Laura's shoulders and gently led us down a hallway toward the back of the house. She opened a door at the end of it leading to a small, well-kept garden. "The garden, as you can see, is quite modest, though we do get lovely ro—Oh! And this is Soot. He's the head of the household."

A very fat and very friendly black cat slipped in, nuzzling against our legs as he made his way through our group. Laura managed to pet him once before he continued on his way, leading our tour back inside to a small, colorful side room.

"Now, you are welcome to use this parlor whenever you wish," Mrs. Tuffins said. "We have all sorts of books, a writing desk for letters or studies, and there's an old pianoforte in the corner for those of you that are musical. I've sure some of you sing beautifully." She chucked Laura under the chin a little.

"Well, I don't like to boast. . . . ," Mr. Kent said.

Laura made a little choking sound, and I was quite convinced she was about to laugh until she burst into tears instead.

"I didn't think it was that bad of a joke," Mr. Kent muttered as he fumbled through his pockets for a handkerchief.

"Oh my poor dears, this isn't at all what you need now, is it?" Mrs. Tuffins shook her head regretfully. "Let me show you your rooms, so you can get some rest. Sleep always makes things a little better."

"We are so thankful that you have room for us." Rose took Mrs. Tuffins's arm and smiled gratefully. The older woman dimpled and reddened as she patted Rose's hand. We followed Mrs. Tuffins, winding out of the other parlor exit and up the main staircase.

Laura sniffled into her handkerchief as her brother guided her up behind us. "She's . . . just . . . so . . . nice," she whispered in between sobs.

It was impossible to argue with that, and I could feel my own eyes pricking a little. Every warm and welcoming part of Mrs. Tuffins and her house that was more a home was a reminder of everything we'd lost. Of places to which we could never return. Of people we took for granted.

"We have four rooms on this floor and two rooms above," Mrs. Tuffins said as we reached the first-floor hallway. "Some of you may have to share. I hope you won't mind terribly."

A scrabbling sound came from behind us. Emily was telekinetically dragging a small piece of scrap fabric across the floor while Soot diligently stalked it. Laura had stopped crying, watching the cat wait to pounce on its prey. The girls and cat wandered into the first bedroom, and Mr. Kent closed the door halfway, to keep the powers out of sight.

"Not a problem at all, Mrs. Tuffins. I would be happy to share with Miss Wyn—"

"I can share with Miss Chen," I cut in, seeing Mrs. Tuffins's eyes go wide at Mr. Kent's joke. I glared at him but smiled at Miss Chen. After all, I was the only one she knew even a little. "Rose, you can share with Catherine—"

"Evelyn, is it all right if I share with you, actually?" Rose asked, looking tense in a way I couldn't quite read. "I feel I've bothered Miss Harding enough the past week."

"I—yes, of course," I said, glancing at Catherine and Miss Chen. "Do you two mind sharing?"

Catherine looked a bit confused but covered it with a smile. "Of course not."

"I rarely break the ceiling when I wake up these days," Miss Chen reassured Catherine. She glanced back to me. "But what about . . . uh . . . ." She gestured at Sebastian, and everyone's eyes followed.

Right. Hmm.

Mrs. Tuffins looked rather concerned, and Mr. Kent hastened to assure her. "It's just . . . Mr. Braddock snores. Terribly," Mr. Kent explained, looking at me for assistance but then continuing on, making everything worse. "I think the only thing for it, Miss Wyndham, is for me to bunk up with you, while Mr. Braddock sleeps alone."

That was too much, even for the kindly Mrs. Tuffins. She looked properly scandalized. Everyone tried to jump in, offering worse and worse excuses. I groaned, the hallway suddenly feeling rather crowded. In everyone's haste to reassure the poor woman, Sebastian slipped back toward the stairs.

He managed to get nearly all the way downstairs before I caught him by the wrist.

"Sebastian. Please," I said.

He looked smaller than me, standing three stairs down, held back only by my grasp on him. He was already shaking his head, preemptively disagreeing with whatever I had to say.

I said it anyway. "It will be all right. You and I can stay near each other—perhaps even—"

His voice came softly. "They are going to get hurt."

"More people are going to get hurt if we leave," I said, squeezing his hand, trying to make him feel the power between us. "I promise. I'll be near."

"You were near when I killed that man on the train."

"You did not kill him."

He shook his head. "You don't know that."

"I do. We weren't standing there for a full thirty seconds listening to you kill a man. That would have been . . . well, it wasn't."

"How long was it?"

"I—Twenty . . . one seconds. I've started counting whenever I see you make contact with someone," I said, slightly omitting the fact that I had only now started. "You only knocked the man out, which in turn, saved all seven of us. So you can subtract that from the number you are undoubtedly keeping in your head."

He pursed his lips and said nothing but looked a little redder.

Of course he was really keeping a number. "What is it?"

"One hundred and thirty-two."

I frowned at him. "The newspaper said one hundred twenty-two."

He sighed and scrubbed at his face. "Victims from before."

"Then you should include people you've *saved* from before," I said. "You could cut it in half for all the people you saved from Dr. Beck."

"That was only eight people," Sebastian said stubbornly.

"Eight? That's absurd. You can't just—" I stopped. And sighed. What was I doing arguing with him about this? This was the last thing he needed.

"Well, one hundred twenty-four before today, then," I said encouragingly. "And after this morning on the train, it's one hundred seventeen."

"One hundred and nineteen. I can't count you and Mr. Kent again."

"Oh, for goodness' sakes, these rules are terrible!" I said. "If you're counting that way, then by saving me, you also indirectly saved everyone *I've* saved—I'd estimate that to be about sixty."

"You can't do that," Sebastian said, looking as frustrated as I felt, and it suddenly, loudly occurred to me . . . this *was* what he needed. Arguing meant he cared about something. Yes, that thing he cared about was the number of people he'd killed, which he was using to continually torment himself. But that was still better than the vacant gaze. A count meant there was still hope.

"Too late, I already did," I said as tartly as possible. "The total is fifty-nine now. Sorry."

"Ev—the ball . . . it's my responsibility." He was almost pleading with me now, as though he wanted me to agree that this was all his fault.

Too bad.

"It's just as much mine," I said. More so even. I was the one who chose Rose over everyone else. "And I'm always going to be near, whispering the *right* number in your ear until you can't remember the wrong one. Now come with me."

I tugged him back upstairs, pulling ineffectively at him until he finally relented and followed, a warm, heavy presence I could feel at my back. I shook my head a little, feeling even guiltier.

I managed to get Sebastian back upstairs without pulling his arm off, where Mr. Kent, Tuffins, and his mother were waiting.

"Everyone's getting settled. You and your sister are in that room," Mr. Kent said, pointing to the one across from Laura and Emily. Then he pointed to the room next to it, anticipating what I planned. "And Mr. Braddock will be in that one. I'll take the room with the prisoner upstairs."

"Thank you, Mr. Kent," I said. "And Tuffins, Mrs. Tuffins, I don't know what we'd do if you weren't here."

"Well, we are. So please tell me if you need anything," Mrs. Tuffins insisted, looking much more composed. Perhaps Rose had managed to convince her there was nothing improper going on. "We'll let you know when the tea is ready, dear."

Mr. Kent stared at Mrs. Tuffins with the deepest appreciation. "Tuffins, if I had known your mother was such a paragon, I would have come to live here ages ago."

"How sad that I never mentioned it," Tuffins said, as dry and measured as ever.

Mr. Kent clicked his tongue and disappeared upstairs, while our hosts went down. I took Sebastian to his designated room and sat him on the bed against our shared wall. He did not protest, just looked up at me warily through his dark lashes.

"For as long as you're in here, I'll be canceling your power out. No one is going to get hurt. Just tap the wall; I'll be on the other side."

I took his hand in both of mine, like it was some sort of sacred object, and set it on the faded floral wallpaper. I slipped out of his room and into the one next door. Rose had taken the bed farthest from Sebastian's room, by the window, and was sitting with her arms around her knees, watching the street. I shoved at my bed, wincing at the screeches it made, until it bumped up against the shared wall.

I climbed atop it, running my hand along the wall, feeling nothing and more nothing, until I knocked. A knock answered back and I slid my hand over till I found the current of our powers.

It worked. I could actually feel him through the wood. The sensation was muffled to a degree lower than when we touched through fabric, but it was still there, it still caught my breath, and it was still undoubtedly Sebastian.

He didn't move away and neither did I. I held my hand there for a long moment, before the silence behind me got unnerving. I turned around on the bed, leaning my back against the spot, letting the hum warm my whole body a little.

Rose was perfectly still, gazing out the window with that same lost, vacant gaze that Laura had. I didn't know what to say to her now. I'd already promised her we'd be safe at home after we deposed the head of the Society. I'd agreed to leave London and not even an hour had passed before we had to turn back into the fray with no real plan of which to speak.

"Rose, I'm—"

"I'm sorry," she said, stealing the words from the tip of my tongue.

"No, I am. You don't need to apologize for anything," I told her, managing the same gentle firmness that I used with Sebastian.

She shook her head. "I . . . the whole time Dr. Beck and Mr. Hale and Camille held me captive, not a moment went by when I didn't dream about going home."

"Not a moment went by that I wasn't dreaming you were back," I said.

"And when I finally get back and I finally see our parents," she said, shivering. I didn't need to ask where this was going. "I ruined everything."

I stared at her, wondering if I misheard. Maybe I did need to ask. "Rose, how . . . how can you say that? You are the last person to blame. You were with me at the ball. You saw what I chose."

"A choice my power made for you."

My stomach sank; everything was so muddled up. First Sebastian holds himself responsible, now her. Her tears were beginning to spill over now, and she wiped them away with her sleeve.

"He turned all our powers off, yours included," I argued, getting up to kneel by her bed, taking her hand in mine. "That's how he was able to hurt you without any remorse."

"It was off at the moment," she said. "But I don't think that removes years of lingering effects."

"There were also years of loving you without any power, long before it developed as we got older. You're my *sister*."

"And they were our parents. And friends." Tears were rolling down her cheeks, and she wasn't bothering to wipe them away anymore. "Why else would you pick me over so many?"

Because I didn't believe Captain Goode would do it. Because I hoped someone would save us at the last minute. Because I was selfish and couldn't bear to lose her again.

There were plenty of reasons. Too many. And even if there weren't, this long and complicated chain of fault still traced back to me. I brought Sebastian and Rose back. I put them in the Society's path. The fact that they blamed themselves for my mistakes only ground my heart to smaller pieces.

I closed my eyes, feeling the familiar guilt and the grief rising inside me, filling my lungs. That same heaviness from the days after I lost Rose. That darkness that rendered every direction indistinguishable. That raw sensitivity across my entire body. The feeling that the only way I could stand the pain was to never move again. Back then, I had family. I had guidance. Mae had experienced the same loss and managed to keep living. Miss Grey gave us a hopeful and selfless purpose, despite all the horrors she had suffered. Even my parents, at the very least, helped me find my bearings by serving as a reminder of what not to do.

But now they were all dead.

I hugged Rose tightly and climbed up to my feet, thinking, breathing, refusing to let myself sink into those depths again.

"What are you doing?" she asked.

The one thing that gave me a clear sense of direction. "Figuring out how to kill Captain Goode."

Chapter Five

———

GIVEN THE INHERENT pleasantness of Mrs. Tuffins and her boarding house, not much could be done to render Mr. Adeoti's room intimidating beyond closing the drapes and restraining him to a chair. Even so, I didn't expect such a pleasant greeting from our prisoner.

"There you are. Hello!" Mr. Adeoti said when the door opened. His eyes were bright, alert, and very eager.

"Yes . . . here we are," I managed to respond.

Catherine went to the windows to let some light in, while Mr. Kent pulled Mr. Adeoti's chair into the center of the bedroom. They joined Sebastian, Miss Chen, Rose, and me in a stern-faced circle around the tracker.

"Now, Mr. Adeoti," Mr. Kent said ominously, "we have some questions for you."

"Thank heavens, finally!" Mr. Adeoti said.

"I . . ." Mr. Kent paused and gestured to Mr. Adeoti's restraints. "You do realize you are our prisoner, yes?"

Mr. Adeoti replied that he did.

"Then . . . why are you happy?"

"Captain Goode made you sound very threatening," Mr. Adeoti replied. "But you don't seem dangerous at all."

"Are you sure about that?" Mr. Kent asked, cracking the knuckles on his metal hand.

"Yes." Mr. Adeoti smiled. Upon seeing our silent frowns, he stopped smiling. After a fraction of a second, he smiled again. "Yes, I am sure. I read the restraints Miss Chen used."

Our circle couldn't help but glance at Miss Chen in confusion. She kept her gaze on him. "Ask him about his power."

"What is your power, Mr. Adeoti?" Mr. Kent asked.

"Oh, it's called psychometry," he answered. "It's how I track people. If I touch an object that a powered person has touched, I can experience some of the memories they had while they were making contact with it."

"So when we tied his hands for the ride," Miss Chen said quietly, "I used fabric from my dress to show him how miserable our last three days have been."

"I've tried to help people leave the Society myself," Mr. Adeoti explained with exasperation. "But no one ever trusts me because of my power. They think I'm a spy for Captain Goode. But you can get the truth from me. Please, ask me all my secrets!"

Again, our circle couldn't find the words. Most of our interrogations led to vicious arguments and angry answers. Not pleas for more questions.

Mr. Kent finally sighed and cleared his throat, giving up his intimidation game. "You don't want to hurt, capture, or kill us?"

"I don't. I swear it."

"Then why are you following his orders?"

"If I don't, he forces me to record the history of the Society's weapons for the library."

"That . . . doesn't sound so terrible," Catherine put in.

Mr. Adeoti shuddered. "Normally, I can only see a week into an object's past, but when he enhances my power, it gets rather . . . overwhelming. I can see much further back and the most powerful memories come first and . . . I can practically feel them myself. Sometimes they can be moments of love and happiness, but when it's a weapon, it's usually quite the opposite. One never gets used to it."

"Why didn't you run away?"

"They could recruit another psychometer like myself, or a dreamer like Miss Grey, and find me anywhere and ruin whatever life I create. So I decided to stay and work against them subtly, by tracking people too slowly or pretending to lose their trail."

"Are there other psychometers?" Mr. Kent asked.

"No, I've been the only one," Mr. Adeoti said.

"Then is there no one else with a power that can track us?" Catherine asked, her eyes bright. Mr. Kent repeated the question.

"As far as I know, there isn't."

I could feel the entire room latching onto that information. There were a few glances in Rose's direction. Sebastian looked at me with a resigned expression that hurt more than a pleading one. But he knew it as well as I did. There was a reason we stayed in London. Even if we weren't being followed, we had to stop Captain Goode.

"What are Captain Goode's plans for tomorrow?" I asked.

"I don't know much," Mr. Adeoti said, sounding more apologetic than he really needed to. "He only gave orders to those involved."

"Then what do you know about it?" Mr. Kent asked.

"The Queen is planning to address the murders at the recent ball. They are going to launch an attack during her speech tomorrow."

The room went still. So that was Goode's big plan. He got his revenge against everyone who wronged him. He took over the Society. He got the power he wanted. And now all he can think of is to *kill the Queen*?

"Since no one wants to say it, I will," Mr. Kent said, breaking the silence. "I think the Queen can defend herself, and it's presumptuous and condescending of us to plan to swoop in and rescue her."

"Right, we've got to consider her feelings," Miss Chen said. "And the feelings of her guards."

"The target may not even be the Queen," Catherine said, ignoring the quipping. "There'll be plenty of other influential people there. The Police Commissioner, the Home Secretary, the Prime Minister."

"I'm sure one of them has a useful power for defending the Queen; there's no need for us to get involved," Mr. Kent suggested.

I couldn't believe what I was hearing. "You still want to run away?" I asked.

"We know for sure that no one will be able to follow us," Miss Chen said.

"And we also know for sure that people there are going to die. Probably all of them," I said, receiving a few shocked glances. "Captain Goode wasn't just angry with us at the ball. He was furious at Lady Atherton for using him. He couldn't stand the idea of the aristocracy using powered people for their own gain."

"Evelyn, do you want your sister to get hurt?" Catherine asked. "Because that will happen if we stay."

"Miss Rosamund wanted to leave, too, as I recall," Mr. Kent said.

There it was again, all of us falling over ourselves to keep Rose safe. Making the same decision I had made at the ball, sacrificing others for her.

"Stop," Rose said. "Please stop it! Stop abandoning all common sense to protect me. It's not fair."

"If anything, we're being smarter," Mr. Kent said. "Running is for our own safety, too."

"Then ask everyone what they would do if I were not here," Rose said.

"I don't know if that's necessary—"

"Please!" Rose exclaimed. "Just . . . ask. I need to know."

"Very well," Mr. Kent said, letting out a breath. "Miss Chen, if Miss Rosamund was not here, would you stay, or would you run?"

"Stay," Miss Chen answered, looking a bit perturbed by the truth. "Dammit, I didn't think I would."

"Miss Harding, if Miss Rosamund was not here, would you stay or would you run?"

"I would stay if the rest of you were," she said, frowning.

Mr. Kent continued around the circle and repeated the question for Sebastian.

"Whichever Miss Wyndham would choose," he answered.

I didn't know whether to feel guilty or relieved that he'd tied himself to me.

"I want to stay, either way," I said. "I will never feel safe knowing Captain Goode is out there. Even if it were about Rose, leaving doesn't seem like the path to her or anyone else's safety."

"And if anyone's wondering about me," Mr. Kent finished, "I'd probably make the heroic choice and stay."

Rose crossed her arms and clenched her jaw. "Then that's what we're doing."

"But the fact of the matter is, you *are* here," Catherine said.

"Swaying you with my power," Rose argued. "I am well aware it doesn't matter what I say. You'll want to protect me however you think is best. But the best way is Evelyn's. She's right. It won't be long before Captain Goode finds another teleporter or dreamer or psychometer, and it won't matter if we're halfway across the world."

No one had an argument against that. I couldn't help but

admire the way Rose circumvented the effects of her power to get everyone's honest choice. Even when it might not have been the choice Rose wanted.

"Do you know where we can find him right now?" I asked Mr. Adeoti. "Perhaps we can catch him unprepared."

Mr. Kent repeated the question reluctantly.

"No," Mr. Adeoti said. "I'm sorry."

"How did you find us?" I asked.

"They sent us to the train stations and the docks to search for you. And when I'm near an object that has been touched recently, I can sense it. That's what happened when I went past the ticket counter at Victoria Station where Mr. Kent bought the train tickets."

"Then why can't you track Captain Goode?"

"Gloves," Miss Chen put in, hitting her forehead with her palm. "I should have told everyone to wear gloves."

"So he wears gloves and then you can't track him?" Mr. Kent clarified.

"That's part of it," Mr. Adeoti said. "And I wouldn't know where to start. He appointed Miss Quinn to occupy his position at the Society of Aberrations building while he took over for the head. He sends his orders in now, but we don't know where from."

"And everyone accepted that?" I asked.

"He said that Mr. Braddock killed the previous head," Mr. Adeoti said matter-of-factly. "And that the rest of you are traitors who want to destroy the Society, so he had to keep his location a secret."

"Oh, for God's sake, that's absurd."

"Anyone who might question it has probably had their family or friends threatened," Miss Chen reminded me. "If I were still there, I'd be tracking you, too."

"So we . . . threw an innocent man off the train," I said.

"The metal man?" Miss Chen asked, wearing a look of disgust that Mr. Adeoti shared. "No, he was always offering to make a statue garden out of England's enemies for the Society. Don't lose any sleep over him."

"I agree," Mr. Kent said, holding up his metal hand as evidence.

At that moment, there was a gentle knock at the door.

"Yes?" I called out.

The door opened, revealing Mrs. Tuffins, now wearing an apron that added yet another mismatched pattern to her ensemble. "I wanted to let you know the tea is ready downstairs," she said.

"Oh, thank you, Mrs. Tuffins. We'll be right down," I said, trying to tighten the space in the circle around Mr. Adeoti.

It did absolutely nothing. "Hello, I don't believe we were introduced earlier," Mrs. Tuffins said, looking past me, all smiles.

There was a loud squeak behind me, and I turned to find Mr. Adeoti rising to his feet, the chair still bound to his hands behind him.

He gave a short, hunched bow. "Joseph Adeoti. It is a pleasure to make your acquaintance and be your guest. You have a lovely home."

"Oh, how nice; my, what a kind group of young people," Mrs. Tuffins said with a warm smile, finding absolutely nothing wrong with a man so attached to his seat. "I will see you downstairs."

She closed the door on her way out.

"Was that invitation for me? I would love to have tea," Mr. Adeoti said. He smiled again to reveal his dimples. "If you still don't trust me, I can come down like this. Then you wouldn't have to find me an extra chair."

"Have you been telling the truth since we came in here?" Mr. Kent asked.

"Yes," Mr. Adeoti answered.

"Are you planning to betray us to Captain Goode or anyone else?"

"Heavens no."

"What would you do if we untied you?"

"I would do my best research to help end the Society and prevent you from dying against Captain Goode because your powers are horribly outmatched."

"I . . . thank you. That . . . would be appreciated, I think," I said.

"No, no, it's perfect! He won't be expecting any sort of challenge from you!" Mr. Adeoti said with an encouraging smile as Miss Chen stepped behind him and tore his restraints.

"Well, I guess there's no need for this intimidating hand anymore," Mr. Kent said. "Miss Wyndham, would you mind sorting this healing out? It's getting dreadfully heavy."

Sebastian stepped just outside of the room as I put my hand onto Mr. Kent's metal one.

"Oh, that won't work at all," Mr. Adeoti said.

Mr. Kent chuckled until he saw Mr. Adeoti's serious face. "Truly?"

"Yes, as far as I know."

"And how far is that?"

"From the Society of Aberrations library," Mr. Adeoti said. "I've read most of the information about powers, and there's nothing about healing metal back to flesh."

"Nothing *yet*," Mr. Kent insisted, watching his hand intently. "I have faith in Miss Wyndham's power."

"I'm glad one of us does," I said, feeling the cold steel. "Nothing seems to be happening."

Mr. Kent took his hand out from my hold and clunked it against a chair in exasperation. "So in order to reverse this, I have to find that metal man and persuade him to turn it back?"

"Yes," Mr. Adeoti answered.

"There's no other way?"

"I don't believe so, but perhaps we could find a way to ask—"

"What if Captain Goode were to shut off our powers?"

"That wouldn't change anything that's already been done to you."

"Could Camille transform it back?"

"Oh yes, she's quite powerful!" Mr. Adeoti said hopefully. "A little scary, though. It might be possible."

"She's dead," I reminded them.

"Oh, for God's sake, everyone's dead," Mr. Kent groaned.

"I think there is one way," Mr. Adeoti suggested. "Given the powers available to you."

"What is it?"

"Miss Chen could shatter your hand up to where the metal ends, and perhaps Miss Wyndham's healing power can regrow it. There isn't a recorded example of a full hand being grown back, but fingers have been restored. Heads can't be regrown, though. So we'll be able to learn more about where the limits of Miss Wyndham's capabilities lie, too, which is very fun!" Mr. Adeoti gave an optimistic grin.

Mr. Kent looked at his hand. Then me. Then back at his hand. "Well, looks like I'll be living with this forever."

"Oh no! Don't be alarmed," Mr. Adeoti said. "Fingers are closer to hands, so if I had to guess, it would grow back—"

"I like my hand very much," Mr. Kent interrupted. "It's my third-favorite body part and first and second would not be appropriate replacements. I'd rather not rely on a guess. Now, who wants some tea?"

After everything we'd been through, we all did.

Downstairs, our tea was a peaceful scene of domestic bliss. Mrs. Tuffins joined us in the sunlit parlor and distracted Laura and Emily with the simple activity of needlepoint, giving guidance with a motherly warmth. For the rest of us, she supplied soothing tea, delicious cakes, and happily mundane stories of her previous boarders. It was almost enough to forget about the world outside for a little while.

Until the topic turned to the Queen's speech that would be held tomorrow.

"Now, it's very unusual for her to speak!" Mrs. Tuffins said, her kind face a little troubled. "But then . . . well . . ." She hesitated, realizing that we had all been at the ball the Queen would be referencing.

"I would like to go see it," I ventured, taking a long sip of my tea.

"I think we all know that, Evelyn." Catherine gave me a slightly sour look. Out of everyone, she seemed the most reluctant to stay in London, let alone put ourselves in Captain Goode's path.

But no one could say much right now with Mrs. Tuffins here. So I pressed the advantage.

"I think some of us, at least, should go and hear her. It might be quite edifying."

I felt their glares but took a bite of cake instead. It was perfectly light, the jam was perfectly tart, and I decided to enjoy it. Tomorrow we might be able to kill Captain Goode, after all.

"It might be . . . unsafe. The crowds, you know," Catherine tried to interject.

"You know I have to. It's my duty. As a . . . proud Englishwoman. I'm sure you understand."

Miss Chen gave me a wry look at that, and Emily snorted.

"I think . . ." I stopped, wondering how to communicate the next part. We certainly didn't need Laura or Catherine there, too easy a mark with their lack of powers. And I didn't want Rose there, either, though that was less of a problem considering I did not think she would be likely to come and no one else would want her in harm's way.

"I think those of us with more . . . *unusual* pride . . . should go." Did that work?

Judging by the strange looks, no, it did not.

"Oh dear, I'm afraid I hadn't considered going; does that make me a terrible Englishwoman?" Mrs. Tuffins was fretting, looking guilty, and I immediately smacked myself—mentally, at least.

"Oh no, not at all!" I gulped, looking around the room for help. But they let me flounder out of my own mess. "I just—well, if she is going to mention the ball, and it seems she will—I think some of us, specifically, have a duty. As people who were . . . there." I finished to a solemn silence.

"Oh, my dears. Of course you want to hear your queen speak about that." Mrs. Tuffins covered my hand with a warm pat and pulled Laura to her on her other side, letting her cuddle in.

"I think we should be safe from . . . the crowds," Miss Chen began, "as long as we stay back a bit."

"Maybe we can find an obliging rooftop," Mr. Kent said, nodding discreetly toward Emily.

"And if the crowd is too disruptive, we can *break* through or . . . *float*. Away." Miss Chen frowned and seemed to mentally review what she had said, then looked around to see if we understood her reference to her and Emily's powers.

"I suppose," Catherine said finally.

"Though I don't think all of us could go," I added. "Rose, maybe you, Catherine, and Mr. Adeoti could stay here with Laura." A little part of me was disappointed that Laura did not even argue. The others just nodded.

Although no one could voice their discomfort, I could feel it around the room.

Rose stared down at her tea, sipping it slowly and carefully.

Catherine was pretending to listen to Mrs. Tuffins, but she kept glancing worriedly at my sister. Emily was subtly trying to slide bits of cake to Laura, who was focusing intently on her needlepoint. Miss Chen, Mr. Kent, and Mr. Adeoti began to speak in lower voices, whispering more concrete plans for tomorrow and compiling a list of necessary supplies.

And Sebastian was, of course, next to me, his leg touching mine, a constant reminder of his power. I snuck another peek at him, hoping to see signs that he was improving, and found myself inexplicably delighted to see him slowly eating a plain bun. That showed some sense of care. Or self-preservation at the very least.

Maybe tomorrow he would allow himself to eat a plum bun. And the day after that even a jelly cake. Perhaps all my Sebastian-pastry fantasies would come true if we found a way to stop Captain Goode tomorrow. We'd stop whatever terrible plan he had in mind, and, while we were there, we might as well stop him for good by stopping his heart.

As we finished our tea and cakes, I took Mr. Kent's list and added one final item.

Perhaps he would be so obliging as to find me a gun for tomorrow. For safety, of course.

Chapter Six

T HE SCENE OUTSIDE Westminster Abbey was a staggering
sight. It couldn't quite be described as crowded. Operas and
balls were crowded. This needed an entirely new word.

Thousands of people packed the streets to their very limits,
flooding into every open space available. Members of the ton settled into their exclusive and costly spots by the windows of every
surrounding building. Nimble children shimmied up gaslights
and climbed onto awnings. Policemen lined the street to preserve
order. The whole city seemed to be out for the spectacle.

Sebastian, Mr. Kent, Miss Chen, Emily, and I were gathered
on the roof of the Westminster Palace Hotel, watching over the
abbey's western entrance across the street from us. We had been
fortunate enough to secure our places early in the morning
without any trouble. Tuffins had retrieved the Kent carriage and
proven himself to be an excellent driver, which surprised exactly
no one. He'd let us off as close as possible and no one had recog-
nized Sebastian nor the rest of us along the way, thanks to our
disguises.

I had decided it better not to ask Mr. Kent how he came by our
elaborate costumes. He'd found simple enough secondhand dresses
for Rose, Catherine, and Laura, so they could be comfortable at

home in clothing that hadn't been worn for the three worst days of our lives. But for the rest of us, he'd concocted detailed alternative identities with rather more imagination than was strictly necessary.

For me, he'd decided I would be a world-traversing photographer, wearing a well-worn English traveling coat along with a Chinese silk scarf and Indian-style bracelets. Miss Chen was a pioneer woman from the American West in thick leather boots and a wide-brimmed hat. Emily, wearing multiple layers of blue shawls and a white bonnet wrapped around her thick dark hair, was an Irish milkmaid.

I suspected this was how he thought of each of us.

For himself, Mr. Kent had chosen the humble profession of circus owner, which he decided gave him license to wear a shockingly pink waistcoat under his black coat and an extremely tall hat. And finally, he'd given Sebastian a dark-green coat, a rather ugly orange waistcoat, and poorly matching pin-striped trousers, not to mention a scruffy beard and mustache—all part of his identity as a penniless poet.

"He's simply too attractive, and it's not fair," Mr. Kent had given for his reasoning. Sebastian had just sighed, which admittedly fit his disguise well.

We looked absurd.

But the crowds around us on the roof seemed to be an equally eclectic mix, and we fit right in among the dockworkers swearing up a storm and the delicate ladies gasping in shock. The scents of all sorts of Londoners wound around us, smoke and perfumes, spirits and bread, but the air was mostly thick with anticipation. In the distance, we could hear the roar of the crowds along the Queen's route. She was getting close. In response, the bodies behind us seemed to push in closer to get a better view.

My hand tightened around Sebastian's in a steel grip. A crowd was the last place he wanted to be, and we were forcing him into the middle of the biggest one.

"Are you all right?" I asked.

One look from him answered my question. He ruffled his hair and shook his head. "I am trying not to count the people."

I didn't ask whether his worry was Captain Goode or himself. "If you do, we'll be counting them as people saved," I said, huddling closer to him, watching the stage.

Below us, a wooden platform had been erected in front of the abbey steps for the speakers. Workmen rushed about finishing the setup. Chairs were positioned, a pathway was cleared from the carriage drop-off below us to the stage, and armed guards were standing sentry every step of the way. Guards that would be useless against Captain Goode and the entire Society.

This was the closest we could get without putting ourselves in danger. Our best hope was to spot him from up here and stop him before he hurt anyone. Though Mr. Kent, Sebastian, and I were particularly helpless in this situation, Emily and Miss Chen more than made up for it. I knew the power they had over any objects that were in their sight. And Mr. Kent had procured two pairs of opera glasses for them to get a better view of the entire scene.

"Does anyone see him?" Mr. Kent asked.

Our group responded with a series of *no*s.

My hand fiddled with the pistol in my pocket, waiting for a different answer. Mr. Kent had obtained the revolver for me without any warnings or asking any questions, and I didn't know if he believed I wouldn't use it or that I wouldn't have opportunity. But Captain Goode was down there, somewhere. He would show himself soon, and I would be ready.

"Here they come!" someone yelled.

The crowd grew less dignified and more frenzied as the speakers climbed out of their carriages and gathered up on the stage with the dramatic abbey entrance behind them. The first to take his place was Commissioner Henderson of the London Police, easily distinguishable by his muttonchops and bushy mustache. He was soon followed by the stout Home Secretary, Sir William Harcourt, and behind him, observing the crowd pensively, was our white-haired Prime Minister, William Gladstone.

The greatest roar of all rang out, and Sebastian stiffened at the sound of all these people. We both took in a sharp breath, watching the arriving carriage. It was a black so inky and dark it seemed to have every color shining brilliantly in it, each one waiting for its moment in the sun. The horses, too, were early-hours dark, and so sure of themselves, so perfectly muscled, I felt a betting man would put his life on them in a race. The driver came to a smart stop, and the guards on either side opened the door for the occupant the waiting crowd knew to be inside.

The Queen.

Victoria stepped out daintily, her small figure brimming with import. Her guards smoothly escorted her toward the stage, where she paused, and I could see a flash of indecision flit across her face. It was gone quickly, replaced with sober reflection. She climbed the steps, looked out across the crowd, and gave a small, somber wave. The roar increased, people waving hats and handkerchiefs furiously.

I looked down at the most powerful woman in the world—even more powerful than those I knew with strange abilities. The power to rule an empire spanning the entire globe, to change the course of history.

While the thunderous cheers for her proved her popularity, the silence all those people gave her was even more impressive. The crowd finally quieted. The stillness was eerie. Thousands of people, huddled together, with bated breath, waiting to be reassured about the world.

"A terrible event occurred four days ago."

The words weren't exactly discernible, but people turned to whisper them, and so they came back to us in waves, the crowd repeating her like schoolchildren at lessons.

"Make no mistake, those responsible will be arrested and brought to justice."

People murmured approvingly.

"However, there is a dangerous, vicious rumor I must quash." The air was brimming, almost vibrating with anticipation.

"This horrible tragedy was perpetrated by men. Not creatures, not something pagan or otherworldly. To believe such nonsense is the height of foolishness, blasphemy, and irrationality."

The crowd shifted a little as the condemnation was delivered.

"When the persons involved are found, their punishment will be great. They will feel the full weight of the law upon them. But heed me: They are *men*. Not some fantastical, unnatural concoction of your imaginations."

The relief rolled back, the Queen's assurances seeming to bolster the people who had begun to imagine were-men and demons.

So that, of course, was when something strange happened.

It was a rumbling. Faint at first, growing louder and more violent by the second. It seemed to be coming from the abbey. The two towers over the west entrance shook and cracked, and everything around it started to vibrate. The wooden stage rattled. All the scaffolding. Our hotel building, one hundred feet away, even shook.

Two guards didn't wait to see what would happen. They were halfway up the steps to the stage, heading for the Queen, when a sudden blaze of fire erupted in their path, sending them stumbling and falling back down. Now everyone on the stage leaped to their feet, looking for the threat, looking for help, looking for an escape. But none of those were visible beyond the five-foot-tall flames trapping them in.

The scene seemed to move in slow motion as the crowd behind us crushed me against the roof wall, straining to make out what was happening. I grasped the edges of the stone with one hand and held Sebastian's hand firm in the other as I leaned out as far as possible, unable to believe my eyes. The crowds below swelled forward as well. Some of the guards struggled to keep them back while the others jumped into action, pulling out swords and rifles to attack the unseen perpetrator. The guards closest to the Queen attempted to put out the fire, but whatever they could find to smother the flames simply got engulfed, too.

Suddenly, a wave of gasps rippled through the crowd as a figure emerged from the smoke, floated above the stage, and set down in front of the abbey entrance. He was large, dressed in an old-fashioned black cloak, and he walked with a familiar, elegant gait. He ran one hand through his sleek, dark hair, and we got a better look at his face.

He looked like every Byronic antihero come to life.

My stomach dropped when I realized what I was looking at.

Another Sebastian Braddock.

"Death will come for you!" he roared for all to hear.

Sebastian's grip tightened around my hand, sending a surge of his power through my veins and it was the only thing that kept me certain the other was an impostor. The Sebastian below looked a bit bigger and seemed to wear a more sinister expression, but they looked nearly identical. In the corner of my eye, I could see Miss Chen and Emily glancing at our Sebastian to make sure he was still here underneath the bearded disguise. What in

God's name was going on? Was this the work of another shifter like Camille?

Now with a target to focus on, some of the guards hurried past the stage and aimed their rifles at this impostor Sebastian. He did not break his stride. He gave a lazy wave, and the world rumbled around him. More cries of shock went up, and the crowd pointed upward. The top part of the cracked left tower dislodged itself, but it didn't fall. It teetered. As if someone was holding it on the very edge, keeping it from tipping over.

"Emily," I said, desperately turning to her. "Can you stop him?"

"I can't!" she whispered, her face looking especially pale. "Nothing's working."

"Miss Chen?"

"I keep trying to break the ground under him," she answered, looking grim. "And—oh, that filthy little bastard." Her eyes began to search the crowd.

"Maybe we can just grab the Que—"

"Not one move!" the impostor yelled, his voice echoing more than it should. "Or the tower will drop!"

The shadow of the tower loomed over the stage, threatening to crush the speakers along with my last remaining idea. We watched helplessly as the impostor climbed up the stage and passed through the flames without any injury.

"We have to do something," I said, trying to pull Sebastian with me.

"No." Miss Chen blocked me with her arm. "I've seen this before."

That comment gave me pause. "You've seen an assassination attempt on the Queen with someone threatening to drop the Westminster Abbey tower on her . . . ?"

"I've seen illusions like this. . . . ," she replied, scrutinizing the scene with her opera glasses.

"Sebastian Braddock, your reign of terror ends today!" a new voice yelled below. Three figures entered the tense standoff. Captain Goode was fully dressed in his navy-blue military regalia, looking the part of the hero. He stood intimidatingly tall but with a bit of noticeable bulk, like a former soldier who had only recently settled into a cozy promotion. A wave of revulsion roiled through me, and I snarled without quite meaning to. Behind him stood a tall blond woman and Miss Quinn, who extinguished the flames on their side of the stage as they climbed up.

"Captain Goode!" the impostor Sebastian shouted. "You can't stop me!"

I covered Miss Chen's glasses. "What do you mean by illusions?"

"There was a sniveling ass named Pratt at the Society who could create people and objects out of nothing," Miss Chen said, setting the glasses down. "They look and sound real, but if you try to touch them or attack them, you'd simply go through them like a ghost. There isn't anything of substance to break."

"So there's nothing attacking the Queen right now?" I asked. "What about Captain Goode?"

"He's defending the Queen from nothing—it's all a show," Miss Chen replied, putting the opera glasses back up to her eyes.

Back down on the stage, Captain Goode was putting his hands up in a peaceful gesture to the fake Sebastian, trying to slip closer to the Queen. "What is it that you want? No one has to get hurt."

"Oh, that's where you're wrong," the impostor replied, lifting his hands up, aiming his palms at the Queen. "More people must die, starting with her!"

A bright blast shot out of the impostor's hands straight at the Queen, but the surprisingly nimble Captain Goode got there first. He took the stream of attacks in the chest, yelling in pain as he shielded the Queen until the impostor seemed to run out of energy.

Captain Goode raised his chin triumphantly. "I've shut down your power, Braddock! It's over!" he declared triumphantly, nodding at his blond friend.

"No! It cannot be!" the impostor Sebastian cursed, falling to his knees.

My mind was reeling, and I smacked at the railing ineffectually. No, no, no. There were too many absurd sights at once to comprehend. It felt like a dream. The powers being put on full display to the public, Sebastian attacking the Queen—and now, Captain Goode escorting her off the stage, looking as noble as anything. This could not happen. I turned wildly to my friends.

"Emily, can you grab Captain Goode?" I asked.

"No, Miss Kane, please don't do that," Mr. Kent said, setting his hand down on Emily's. "Miss Wyndham, we aren't at all prepared to deal with that."

"But he's right there," I urged. "We have to do something—Miss Chen."

She gave me a sidelong look. "Tell me you've a better plan than lifting Captain Goode up, bringing him close enough to shut down our power, and then dying painfully when the rest of the Society catches up."

"We'd run," I said.

"Right. Run *then* die, and painfully. Sorry, but no."

Gunshots drew our attention back to the fight. Without his powers, the impostor Sebastian pulled out a pistol and fired several shots at the escaping Queen. With Captain Goode and the nearby guards shielding her with their bodies, she remained unscathed. Not that it mattered, as the bullets were imaginary, apparently.

"Miss Fahlstrom, now!" Captain Goode shouted.

His mysterious blond companion fired electric sparks at impostor Sebastian's hand from behind, knocking his gun away. She fired more shots that he managed to dodge as he floated back into the air and waved dramatically in the direction of the precarious abbey tower. He waited for a moment, and when it did not come crashing down as intended, he turned to discover that it was now secure again. Miss Quinn had frozen it in place.

The impostor gave an almost inhuman roar as he made his escape. "I will have my revenge, Goode!"

"I'll be waiting!" Captain Goode shouted back.

Mr. Kent bared his teeth, speaking tightly through them. "I believe I owe the Whitechapel penny theater a formal retraction and an apology. *This* is by far the worst acting in the entire city."

"Apparently the rest of this audience doesn't think so," Miss Chen replied somberly.

The ridiculous crowd roared as Captain Goode and his companions escorted the Queen back down the pathway toward us. Some even took up a chant of his name.

So this was what he meant by "enlightening the public." A shiver went down my spine as I took in the sheer number of people around us who believed Captain Goode to be the hero. And Sebastian the villain.

I could not let this stand. I had to do something.

I watched as the Queen, Captain Goode, and his companions made their way back toward the royal carriage, feeling ineffectual and desperate.

"This is bad; this is very bad," I said, tightening my hold on Sebastian's hand. "We need to go now."

There was no argument. Sebastian and the rest of our group followed close behind as I squeezed through the crowd and more bodies surged in to take our perfect viewing location. I burst through the stairway door and flew down one floor, two—

"It's that . . . way," Sebastian said, sounding a bit unsure of himself as I pulled him into the second-floor corridor.

"Come on," I replied, forcing him to the other end of the building. "We have to get to a window."

We burst into a crowded parlor, at which point I simply started shoving through people with all my strength. Ladies yelped and gentleman harrumphed as I slipped through gaps and made ones where there were none. Poor Sebastian was trying to keep up while simultaneously apologizing to the people I left in my wake.

"What are you doing?" Sebastian called. "Evelyn."

I pulled out of Sebastian's hold, feeling him leave my veins as I made it to the open window. One last solid push through a couple and the clear view of the abbey was there, welcoming me. I leaned out as far as I dared and found the Queen's carriage waiting two floors below. Captain Goode, his companions, and the Queen were crossing the street to their escape, heads together as Captain Goode spoke rapidly.

I reached into my coat for Mr. Kent's pistol, the metal wondrously heavy in my hand. I pointed it out the window and closed one eye, taking aim down the tiny barrel, holding my breath, ignoring the gasps behind me. One good shot and I would end this nightmare right now.

"Evelyn, no!"

Sebastian's sensation shocked me like a splash of cold water. He grabbed me from behind and reached out, his tight grip digging into my arm. The crowd around us screamed as I pulled the trigger and watched a useless hole appear in the side of the carriage, one foot to the right of Captain Goode's heart. Then I fell to the ground, the gun was twisted out of my hand, and the room was in chaos.

Most likely because Sebastian was standing above me, his beard and mustache torn off in the struggle, the gun he ripped from me fully visible in his hand, in a room full of people who'd already watched him attack the Queen once.

"He's here! It's Sebastian Braddock!" a voice cried.

"Stop him! He's tryna' shoot the Queen!"

I grabbed the gun from him and tried to reason with them. "No! It was me, not him!"

No one was listening. And there wasn't time nor space to run. The crowd converged quickly upon us, a sea of elbows, knees, fists, striking Sebastian and me all over. We landed hard and couldn't get back up. Legs knocked us off balance. Arms dragged us down. The weight of bodies kept us from moving. I tried to scream but someone was pressing on my chest. I reached out for support, for Sebastian, for anything to find my bearings.

A gunshot went off. And then another. Gasps and cries and strange clunking sounds came from above me, and finally I could breathe again.

Clunk.

"My apologies!"

Clunk.

"Sorry! You punched me first."

Clunk.

"And you *looked* like you were going to punch me. Ah, there you are. Hold on tight."

Mr. Kent was there, grabbing my hand with his ordinary one and Sebastian with his metal one, shouting for Emily's assistance. Immediately, he rose into the air, lifting Sebastian and me along with him. I felt a weight on my leg, someone from the crowd latching onto me, trying to drag me down, and then there was a loud rip and they fell away with the bottom part of my coat. We floated up to the ceiling, and I could see the astonished and terrified faces staring up at us.

"Stop them! They're the ones!"

"Monsters!"

"He's not the one who attacked the Queen!" Mr. Kent shouted back. "He just looks exactly like him. It's complicate—ow! For God's sake, he stabbed me in the ankle! Who stabs a man in the ankle?"

A window broke apart, and a hole opened up wide enough for us to float outside, two stories above the street. Gazes and fingers and shouts were aimed up at us before our trio was dropped on the crowded roof of a neighboring building. More onlookers shifted their attention from the abbey to us. More kindling on the verge of being ignited.

"We need . . . to meet . . . the others," Mr. Kent gasped as I helped him up. He winced as he took his first step. "Dammit! The ankle is now my fourth-least favorite place to be stabbed!"

"It's Braddock!" a man shouted from the building we had left. "The villain is escaping!"

And that was enough to set the crowd ablaze. One man sprang forward, then another, and in one surreal second, the rest of the roof was charging at us in service of the Queen.

"I'm not going to say go on without me," Mr. Kent said as we stumbled backward. "I'd honestly prefer we all just died together."

"I'd rather make us even," Sebastian said, then he picked up Mr. Kent in his arms and began to run, trusting me to stay close.

"Wait, no, I've decided I would prefer to die," Mr. Kent argued, looking extremely baffled as to how he came to be carried in Sebastian's arms.

"We can sort it out after," I yelled, keeping my hand on Sebastian's back, pushing him forward.

We hurried across the roof with every last bit of energy we had left, our breaths heavy and our footsteps heavier. Behind us, the shouting intensified, and the growing rumble of pursuers shook my bones. We flew by smoky chimneys and stone balustrades and hopped over roof hatches and skylights. The city skyline ahead of us melted into the smog and seemed to stretch out forever, but it was clear to see we were quickly running out of roof.

The balustrade ahead of us broke down, and I saw Miss Chen and Emily waiting on an empty roof across the street.

"Keep going, keep going," I told Sebastian and myself as we neared the edge. I sucked in a breath and forced myself forward, no matter how much my stomach turned. The last time I'd tried this alone, it did not go well, but I lifted my skirts as we reached the ledge and prayed and leaped. The street and the carriages and the horses and the crowd hummed below me. My stomach dropped for one horrible moment, and then Emily was there to catch us and carry us the rest of the way.

"Thank you, Emily," I said, squeezing her hand when I touched the ground.

"It's better not to jump off buildings," she said seriously.

"I will keep that in mind."

"Also better not to shoot in the direction of queens," Sebastian added, not bothering to hide the edge in his voice.

"I had a clear shot," I snapped.

"And we had a clear plan," he replied, looking very sulky as Mr. Kent lolled in his arms, trying valiantly to look as though this was a normal and commonplace pose for him.

I returned my hand to Sebastian's back. He seemed to bristle at my touch, but with Mr. Kent in his arms, neither of us had a choice. Emily floated us from rooftop to rooftop in silence as we made our way southwest, watching the streets get a little calmer the farther away we got from the assassination attempt.

When we were far enough away, Miss Chen broke open a hatch that dropped us into a thankfully empty stairwell landing outside a barrister's office. We stumbled down to the ground floor, opening the door to a small lane, where Miss Chen left us while she went to fetch a carriage. Sebastian finally set Mr. Kent down so he could lean against a building for support.

Sebastian pulled a handkerchief out of his coat and held it over his face, as if the smog or the stench of the streets was bothering him. But as his eyes watched every person that passed us on the street, fearing another frenzied mob, the permanence of what happened started to really sink in.

The Belgrave Ball could have been covered up as a poisoning. Only a few witnesses saw our fight on the train. But there was no going back from this. Thousands of people saw the illusions and hundreds more saw our escape. Captain Goode had once warned us of the dangers of our powers going public, and now he'd gone and revealed them himself in such an indisputable display.

A carriage finally rattled to a stop in front of us and Miss Chen threw open the door, but I barely felt any relief from our escape. It was only a matter of time before word of the powers would spread. It was only a matter of time before people would know what happened today.

And it was only a matter of time before Sebastian Braddock would be the most hated man in the city.

Chapter Seven

I T TOOK APPROXIMATELY eighteen hours for the city to go completely mad.

By the next morning, the more opportunistic businessmen were on the streets hawking charms that supposedly kept you safe from Sebastian Braddock's "demonic energies." A gossipy fashion column announced that black cloaks were the newest daring style for men. Newspapers splashed exclusive interviews with the city's hero, Captain Goode, who reassured the public that there were people using their extraordinary talents for good (of course, he included himself in this number) and they outnumbered the ones who had darker intentions. But he warned the public to watch for those with our specific powers—the one who killed with a touch, the one who extracted your deepest secrets with a question, the one who only healed other villains.

Which, of course, led to droves of people coming forward to say that they, too, had powers.

"He said he could read minds, which, really, if you are going to claim a power, I don't know why you'd claim one so entirely disprovable." Mr. Kent had joined the rest of us at breakfast, fresh from an errand to gather newspapers, gossip, and the general tenor of the city.

So far, he had told of us a woman who swore she could hear rocks speak, another who seemed to believe she was Nostradamus come back to life, and a man who claimed an ability to multiply the number of sheep in any given room—not outside, but the amount of sheep *inside a room*.

"But it's the rumors about Mr. Braddock that are the most absurd—that he's a spy or a demon or . . . *French*. I mean, really, even *I* think that's going a bit too far, and I barely like you."

"I saved your life." Sebastian sounded more affronted than I would have expected, and I saw Mr. Kent quickly hide a smile. If I didn't know better, I would think he had taken up my own strategy of needling Sebastian into talking and participating through sheer annoyance.

"You saved my ankle," Mr. Kent corrected Sebastian, whipping an embroidered napkin onto his lap and reaching for another scone. "And while I am partial to my ankle, I think we can all agree that a man's ankle is not the same as say, a lady's ankle. Not that I would turn down a man with a good set of ankles. It's all about anticipation, really. Oh, do you want to hear my Grand Ankle Theory?"

No one did.

Miss Chen tossed her napkin across the table at Mr. Kent, who caught it and wrapped it around his scone as he rose from his seat. "Fine. Remain unenlightened. Mr. Adeoti, are you ready to go?"

Mr. Adeoti was already standing, a notebook in hand, an eager smile on his face. "Yes, of course."

"Ready for what?" I asked, perhaps a bit too demandingly.

"We're going back to Westminster Abbey for clues," Mr. Kent said. "If Captain Goode or anyone from the Society dropped or touched something, we might see what they have planned."

"That's a good idea," I said, standing up. "Who's coming?"

Mr. Kent shook his head. "It'll be too conspicuous with a bigger group."

"Especially with someone who keeps firing a gun," Catherine put in tartly.

"I shot once," I said. "And it would have ended everything."

"Yes, it would have gotten you killed, and then they would have found us, too," Catherine said.

She gave a worried glance at Rose and glared back at me. I sat down; no way to argue that. She really was getting protective of Rose.

"Well, enjoy . . . sitting in uncomfortable silence for the rest of the day. We're off," Mr. Kent said, giving a nod to Mr. Adeoti. "Now tell me, is it possible that someone's power could be the ability to be extraordinarily handsome?"

"I don't know. Perhaps. Anything is possible!" Mr. Adeoti answered.

"So is it possible for someone, let's say me, for example, to have two powers?"

Their voices drifted away down the hall, and a moment later we heard the front door close. The silence was so thick that I could have sliced it and spread it on my scone. And what could we do for the rest of the day? Ahead of us were hours of nothing but drinking tea and waiting here for Mr. Kent, while Captain Goode was out there turning more and more of London against us.

The only noise for a few minutes was the shuffling of paper, the clinking of silverware, and the whispers of Emily and Laura as they fussed with a piece of fabric.

Sebastian let out a breath as he flipped through article after article vilifying his name. I patted his shoulder, and he gave me a grumpy glare. Which I deserved, considering how I'd implicated him further. But still, I would accept a grumpy glare over a vacant stare any day.

Catherine and Rose were at the far end of the table, Rose staring at her tea and Catherine frowning as she rubbed at her spectacles.

She fumbled on the table for her napkin but couldn't locate it without the glasses, until Rose reached over and pressed it gently into her hand. Catherine sent her a warm, happy look, and Rose cracked a real smile for a moment before her face fell and she turned back to her tea, seeming to shrink a little.

Next to them, Miss Chen had closed her eyes as she chewed her breakfast. At first, it seemed like she was relishing her scone with far more appreciation than I'd ever seen someone have for one. But then the image reminded me of the time I saw her at the Society. When Oliver and I had interrupted her in the middle of her training.

I banged my cup down a little more forcefully than I had intended and got up, pushing my chair away from the table with a screech that made everyone turn to me. "I think we have to train," I said.

As soon as I spoke the words, it felt like the key to everything. To Sebastian and Rose overcoming their worries about their powers. To getting us close enough to Captain Goode without feeling helpless.

"Train what?" Rose asked, looking a bit perplexed.

"Our powers," I said. "Miss Chen, I believe you have some measure of control over yours. Is that correct?"

She nodded reluctantly. "Yes. Somewhat."

Rose's eyes grew wide in the same way they did whenever she'd read about some fascinating new treatment. Sebastian was slowly lifting his head, blinking as if he were just coming back to us.

Seeing their reactions, Miss Chen grew a bit self-conscious. "But I don't know what kind of teacher I would be, either. I barely understand the idea behind it myself. I only had a little instruction—"

"I would be very glad of anything you could teach me," Rose

said, looking at her intently. "Perhaps if we were all learning, someone might stumble upon a new discovery."

Miss Chen considered that and gave a shrug. "Right. Well, nothing else to do. . . ." She surveyed the room for a moment, considering. "Don't suppose Mrs. T would let us use the parlor?"

"Yes, let's try not to break anything," I said, gesturing everyone to the door.

Emily slung an arm around Laura's shoulder and rubbed her back a little, promising that later they could find Soot the cat and see if he wanted to fly around with them.

I made a note to find Soot and hide him.

As everyone filed out of the room, I hung back and caught Catherine's hand. "I'm sorry. Is everything all right? I don't want you to be mad at me."

Catherine nodded. "I know. I'm not. I—"

"What is it?" I asked.

Her voice was higher than usual, and she scratched at her arm uncomfortably. "It's Rose—I don't want to add to her distress after all that's happened. And it's . . . just . . . well, has she said anything to you?"

I blinked a few times. "About what?"

"Um, is she perhaps mad at me?" Catherine became extremely interested in the cuff of her sleeve.

No," I said quickly, for if anything, Catherine seemed to be the one person Rose wanted to be around. "Why would you think that?"

"I think she's avoiding me." And when she said that, I did recall how Rose had wanted to room with me. Surely that was simply because we were sisters or some notion Rose had about bothering Catherine?

"I think Rose is glad to have a friend here," I said, but something made me look again at Catherine. Wild curls of hair were tumbling around her face, not willing to be tamed into a knot. But that was always the case with Catherine, who cared little for appearances. It was the sadness and tension in her eyes that seemed out of place. "You don't normally worry about what anyone thinks about you."

"Yes, well, she's not anyone," Catherine said. "She's your sister and I want to help. I hope I haven't done anything to upset her."

"I truly don't think you have," I assured her. "It's everything else in the world that's so upsetting. You're the one other person she knows from before all this powers nonsense. When she first came back, I could tell you were the best person to help her. She just needs time. We all do."

She squeezed my hand once and shook out her skirts. "You're right. I'm being silly. There's a lot going on." She stood up straighter, and we followed the others to the parlor.

Everyone settled in, and I looked for Sebastian, hopeful that maybe Miss Chen's teaching would be able to help him.

Only Sebastian was nowhere inside.

There was a soft creaking from the ceiling, and I paused, realizing Sebastian's room was right above us. What did he think? We would forget that he was supposed to join us? And was it progress that he was annoyed enough with me to be out of my presence?

Silly, silly man. I padded up the stairs and found his bedroom door closed.

I knocked loudly. "Hiding, again?"

No response.

"Don't you wish to control your powers?" I asked.

Apparently not.

"It's the only way we'll be able to deal with Captain Goode," I said, hoping it would provoke him into responding. "Well, except shooting him, perhaps. But you seem intent on making me miss my shot."

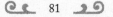

The door opened a crack. "I didn't want you to take a shot at all," he argued.

I was there before he could close it. "Why not?"

He sighed, his not-inconsiderable bulk useless against my well-placed foot. He let the door open, greeting me with his stormy face and crossed arms. "Because I didn't want to make everything worse. That's all I ever seem to do. It doesn't matter what our intentions are. We have to consider the effects."

He had a point.

"You are right. I'm sorry. But that shouldn't stop you from training." He frowned and said nothing. "You cannot possibly be against training. It is the opposite of a harebrained plan." I knew he was annoyed with me, but I was truly unsure what he could have against learning to control his power.

He sighed again before beginning to speak haltingly. "What if I . . . what if I accidentally heighten my power in the attempt to lower it?" He leaned against the doorjamb, his body forming a curved bow, full of tension. He really did have to worry about the worst case in every situation.

"I . . . don't know," I said.

His face was turned down so I could only see the curl of hair on his forehead, his lips pulled tight against his teeth.

I stepped forward so there was very little space between us. His lashes lifted a little, and there was something entirely unreadable in his eyes for a moment. My skin began to itch, and I felt a blush coming on. So I pressed on, ignoring the way the air felt suddenly warm and heavy.

"I promise you don't have to do anything. We can just listen to what she has to say."

He pushed himself away from the door. Sebastian had never been one for broad smiles, but as he ran his hand across his face for a long moment, I thought I would do anything—anything in the world—to see Sebastian smile again. And I had to continually swat the little voice inside of me that suggested maybe kissing him would make everything better, when I knew very well it would only make things worse. So I offered the one thing I had to make it better.

"I promise I will be right there with you—no rash or impulsive actions," I pressed, holding out my hands innocently.

He eyed me carefully. "And if my power raises—"

"I'll be training, too. And I'd raise mine to match yours," I promised. I would raise my powers to the heavens if it meant Sebastian taking on a little less guilt.

He didn't smile, but his shoulders finally slumped in defeat. "Fine." He gestured down the hall and waited for me to go before him.

"If anything happens, I am leaving."

"I will go with you," I said. "And if you ever get sick of me, I'll remove my hand and give it to you."

"Please . . . don't do that."

"Very well, we'll try it this way," I conceded, feeling him take my hand protectively as we entered the parlor.

Rose was sitting on the floor, her skirts arranged artfully in front of her as she gave Miss Chen her full attention. Laura was settled between Emily and Catherine on the sofa, looking small and scared. Catherine reached out to give her arm a little pat, then pulled her over so Laura was leaning against her.

Sebastian and I settled onto the rug near Rose, and Emily floated over to us.

"Here," she said. The bit of fabric she and Laura had been fiddling with at breakfast landed in Sebastian's hands. He slowly uncurled it to find inexpertly sewn initials at the bottom corner in a bright yellow thread.

"It's for your crying," Emily added, giving him a tentative smile.

"I . . ." Sebastian struggled with how to accept this very kind and bluntly given gift. "Thank you, Miss Kane," he said finally, carefully folding it.

Emily's smile became a wide grin and I had to curb my own as Miss Chen began her lesson.

She cleared her throat and leaned on the fireplace mantel. "Now, I can't promise everyone here that I know all there is to know about this," Miss Chen began, rubbing her hands together briskly. "I've been doing it for a year and I still can't get my power as high or low as Captain Goode could, but I'll try to tell you some of what I learned from those bastards."

And so she did. She started by leading us through a series of odd breathing and imagination exercises. "First, everyone close your eyes. Try not to think. Breathe. Concentrate on this room. Listen to my voice, the sounds around us."

The logs snapped and popped in the fireplace behind her. The windows rattled from the winds outside. Soot purred softly from Laura's lap.

"I want you to remember what it felt like when Captain Goode took control of your powers. Mr. Braddock, Miss Rosamund, there's a chill that runs through your body when he takes it from you. Try to remember how that felt the first time. Try to remember the cold that settled in the pit of your stomach. The strange lightness, the feeling that something was gone."

Her voice wrapped around us as she paced about the room. "Miss Wyndham, Miss Kane, try to remember that warmth your heightened power gave you. The power you felt running through your veins. Try to remember all the possibilities that opened up to you."

I closed my eyes and breathed, imagining the blood beneath my skin warming, letting my healing power grow in my gut, pooling into a shimmering orb. The memory of the last time slid into my mind. The desperate fury flowing through me at the ball. The strangeness of Captain Goode's intrusive touch. The satisfaction of seeing his throat slit and bleeding.

"Miss Wyndham, I can tell you're thinking about Captain Goode," Miss Chen said. "Focus less on murdering him, more on the power."

Right. A heavy breath left me. My fists relaxed into gentle non-strangling hands. I peeked open one eye to check on Sebastian. His eyes were shut, his eyelids fluttering as if he were dreaming of something better. He was trying. Despite all his fears, despite London's opinion of him, despite the vivid memories of Captain Goode and Mae this dredged up, he still found the courage to try.

And he trusted me to help him.

I closed my eyes, trying to focus on Miss Chen's other approaches.

"Some people try to recreate a moment when they've had their powers raised. They recall the smell of the room, the objects they were looking at, the thoughts they had. Others think about the actual experience of using their enhanced powers—the urgency, the strain. I've heard others describe it as a switch. I realize how absurd this sounds, but do try to imagine a switch inside your chest, and pull it up or down."

I tried again and again, settling into a calm state of mind, letting images, sensations, and switches run through until my mind grew quite agitated, forcing me to start over. Memories of healing my friends did little until the thought of Sebastian stirred something inside me. My heart leapt, my eyes shot open, and then I realized it was my stomach growling.

Dammit. I should have known I'd be terrible at this.

At the end of a frustrating two hours, I felt sweaty, numb in my buttocks, and ready to declare the whole endeavor a waste of time. But there was a soft giggle from behind me, and Emily was floating

Laura's embroidery hoop in the air, telekinetically stitching. Her needlework was still rather clumsy and imprecise, but it was the most skillful use of her power I'd seen.

Next to me, Sebastian was still concentrating, but his grimace was slightly less pronounced. I grasped his warm hand and the current still flowed between us, but it did feel slightly fainter. I looked up to ask what he thought and saw his lips press hard together, as though he were suppressing a sob or smile. I could not say which. His eyes were dark and full of that emotion again, the one I could not discern.

"Miss Rosamund, are you all right?" Miss Chen asked.

Those words wrenched me around to find my sister standing by the fireplace, her eyes closed, a shy smile slowly taking form.

"Yes, I think so. . . . I felt something small. I thought it was a typical chill, but then I got another and it's staying there even when I'm warmed." Rose opened her eyes and met mine. "Ev, I think it might be lessened."

I couldn't help the silly grin that spread across my face, nor the hug I gave her. "That's wonderful! Though you will have to test it on someone else. I still think you're the best sister the world has ever known, so I'm not sure it's really working that well—"

Rose smacked my shoulder playfully, a giddy smile on her face, color high on her cheeks. "Can't you just say you hate me a little bit?" she said, giggling, and I was bowled over that such a simple thing could bring such good cheer—especially to my naturally serious sister after everything she had gone through. I had missed her smile almost as much as Sebastian's.

"We shall have to ask Catherine," I said, pulling Rose's arm under mine and marching her to my friend, determined to cheer everyone up. "Catherine, isn't Rose quite suddenly less pleasant to be around?" I tried to sound severe.

Behind her spectacles, Catherine's eyes went perfectly round as she darted her gaze between us, her tongue poking out to wet her lips.

"I—"

"She thinks she might have controlled her power!" I bumped my hip to Rose's and we both beamed at Catherine.

"I, well, of course. Yes, much deteriorated." Catherine gave her a tentative smile. Rose turned a little, blushing, and I laughed.

Finally, there was a break in the heavy clouds that had been following us since the ball. Miss Chen had warned us this would take some years to perfect, but that didn't matter. For the moment, at least, my friends were together and feeling a measure of hope, of lightheartedness, a play, at least, at normalcy.

Then the door slammed open, revealing a dour Mr. Kent and Mr. Adeoti. "There's been a murder," Mr. Kent said. "And the word is Sebastian Braddock is to blame."

Chapter Eight

N OT A HALF-HOUR later we were standing in front of a non-descript building, our large, strange group—consisting of Mr. Kent, Sebastian, Miss Chen, Mr. Adeoti, Emily, Laura, and me—receiving plenty of stares. Laura had stubbornly refused to stay at home, saying she was worried her brother would hurt his ankle again. She had looked so terrified to be away from him and Emily that Mr. Kent decided she could come if Emily helped keep her out of the way. And with Tuffins driving the carriage, we could always send her home in a pinch.

"Oh! I forgot to mention this is a brothel." With that advance warning, Mr. Kent knocked loudly on the door.

That explained the stares. "You brought your little sister to a brothel?" I hissed.

"Kit, you are not to touch anything."

From the moment the word *brothel* left his lips, Laura seemed to regain some of her missing sense of mischief. Her eyes brightened a touch, and I am sure thousands of sensational novel plots tumbled through her head. "This, why, this is . . . scandalous." She looked almost delighted. And had never been more right in her life.

Finally, a voice called out from inside, "Yea?"

"Hello, I heard someone was murdered here last night. Is that true?"

"Yes," the man said and then let out an audible growl. "That's no business of yours! Get on!"

"Miss Chen, your assistance would be invaluable," Mr. Kent said.

There was a snap on the knob and the door cracked open. Mr. Kent pushed in past the blustering guard.

"You can't come in—"

"We are paying customers!"

"No, we bloody well aren't," I said.

Mr. Kent smiled at the furious guard and continued inside. "Now, where did the murder occur?"

"The second floor," the man answered before he muttered curses and escaped into what appeared to be the brothel equivalent to a morning room or parlor. As we reached the stairs, a lovely older woman emerged from the room, frowning at our group and frowning even more at Mr. Kent.

"Mr. Kent, what is the meaning of this?" she barked.

"Ah, good afternoon, Miss Molly," Mr. Kent said as he ascended the stairs. "Heard you had a murder." Of course Mr. Kent knew the proprietress.

Miss Molly followed us up. "You misheard. The body was found farther down the street."

"Right where you moved it, I presume."

She pursed her lips. "And what is it you want? To blackmail us, I suppose."

"Of course not, blackmail is abhorrent. I would never," Mr. Kent said, his metal hand to his heart. "I've come to do good. I was hoping to see where the crime occurred so we might look for clues."

"The police were already here, making a fuss and scaring off the gents. I won't have you further disturbing my . . . my tenants. Now be on your way."

"Deeply sorry, that wasn't a question. You'll know when it's a question," Mr. Kent said with a chuckle.

"The police were here, Kent! Get out before I call them back."

"You wouldn't want me to start rumors about the health of your girls, now would you?"

"No." Miss Molly grayed a little at that.

"Good. Then which room did it occur in?"

"The one at the end that is labeled *The Truthseeker*." Miss Molly glared at him as she answered.

We all looked baffled by that. "Why does the room say that?" Mr. Kent asked.

"It's these powers," Miss Molly replied, waving the notion off. "My girls thought it would be amusing to dress up like some of those powered folks and play with the patrons. The men last night went wild for it."

I pulled Laura to my side and put my hand in front of her eyes as we made our way along the second-floor landing, passing rooms labeled *Death*, *The Enhancer*, *The Snow Queen*, and even one that said *The Healer*. Oh goodness gracious.

My face went hot as that door opened and a painted girl stuck her head out. "Oy, Miss Molly, what's the racket?"

"Nothing to concern yourself with, dear," Miss Molly said. "Get some rest."

"Which power is the most popular?" Mr. Kent had to ask.

"*Death*," Miss Molly answered. "I had a line down the stairs for that one."

Mr. Kent let out a heavy sigh. "Of course it is. People love brooding fools." Sebastian just looked miserable, and Laura piped up with a series of inappropriate and fantastical questions:

"Have any dukes fallen in love here and rescued someone to become their duchess?"

"What about a girl who was disguised as a man and found a runaway sister here?"

"Do you have a mysterious past and broken heart and are you waiting for your long-lost love?"

As Mr. Kent was not repeating these questions, Miss Molly did not answer, preferring to glare at all of us.

At the end of the landing, a blackened door was already half-open. The inside of the room was a mess. Half the contents, along with the walls and floor, were charred black. There was no denying a fire had erupted and been contained in here.

Mr. Adeoti put his hand on a wall. "Aha. Jarsdel."

"Who?"

"Mr. Jarsdel. He has a fire-based ability."

"Where would we be without you?" Mr. Kent asked drily.

"Dead, probably," Mr. Adeoti answered, sounding relatively unconcerned. "He didn't really touch anything else in here. From what I can tell, he simply came in, seized the victim, and killed him. He was in another room, however. . . ."

"Which room?"

"The healer's room," he said blithely, then looked a little guilty as he turned to me.

Mr. Kent looked at Miss Molly and raised his eyebrows without asking the question.

She answered anyway. "That man, he paid for her services first. Then came in here to attack another patron. A gentleman it was. Thomas Cox was his name."

We turned back around and knocked on the healer's door. Miss Molly had some words with her and then we were let into the dim bedroom. Two women were in there, one dressed like a nurse, albeit an underdressed one, the other a pretty redhead adjusting her smart little hat in the mirror. "Be a good gent and tell me all your secrets," she practiced to herself.

"My God, it's the perfect woman," Mr. Kent uttered. "But the attire, it's all wrong."

As Mr. Kent went to go flirt with the female version of himself, Laura and Emily giggled at the bed. Oh Lord. We were corrupting poor Laura. What was Mr. Kent thinking?

Mr. Adeoti gingerly touched the bed frame and then various places on the wooden floor. He slowly made his way over to a small pile of soiled bedsheets in the corner of the room. His face turned even redder as he set one finger on the edge of a sheet and stared steadily at the ceiling. No one needed to ask what he was seeing because it was written all over his face.

"For the love of England don't repeat anything . . . indecent," I said. "But do you have any sense of where he'd go? Or what else he wants?"

"Well, he killed that Thomas Cox last night for Captain Goode, and they did intend for it to be blamed on Mr. Braddock," Mr. Adeoti said, shaking his head sadly.

"What motive were they going to ascribe to him?" I asked.

"Well, the man seems to have been some minor aristocrat—" Mr. Adeoti began.

"Baronet." Miss Molly crossed her arms and stared at all of us suspiciously.

"Indeed. And they, well . . ." He looked sheepishly at Sebastian. "They want to make it seem like Mr. Braddock is especially dangerous to aristocrats."

"But . . . *Captain Goode* is the one who feels that way!" I was shaking with anger, my fingers vibrating against my skirt, clenched in my fists.

"Bastard," Miss Chen said, her jaw tense and eyes furious. "Burned the man alive for nothing."

"On the bright side, he was probably in the worst agony for only a few seconds," Mr. Adeoti offered. "And then he likely felt nothing."

"I don't suppose this Jarsdel happened to leave anything behind here?" Mr. Kent asked.

"He did," the girl pretending to be a healer was compelled to say, looking unhappy about it. She looked nothing like me, of course, but knowing that she was pretending to be . . . well, me, in a way, was still disconcerting.

And knowing that the general public was titillated by that was far worse. My stomach gave a little roll.

"And what wonderful piece of evidence did he leave behind?"

"The watch," she answered, looking at Mr. Kent's pretender.

The girl sighed and reached into her reticule, pulling out a watch.

"He didn't tell me the truth," she explained boldly, putting up her chin a little, as though daring us to challenge her.

"You must not have asked the right questions." Mr. Kent chucked her chin and handed the watch over to Mr. Adeoti.

"The British Museum, a Lord Lister," Mr. Adeoti said, eyes closed, then they flew open. "He's planning to attack a board member this morning, making it look like Mr. Braddock is on a killing spree."

"If he hasn't already," Miss Chen said, glancing out the window for a sign.

"This Mr. Jarsdel," Sebastian asked. "Does he have red hair, a rather bushy beard? A scar?" Sebastian sounded far too knowledgeable about this person.

Mr. Adeoti nodded throughout. "On his forehead."

I turned to Sebastian. "You know this man?"

"I do. The Society sent six of us to capture him," Sebastian replied. "And that was when he wasn't enhanced."

It took twenty\minutes to reach the British Museum, most of which Mr. Kent spent persuading Laura to wait for us in the carriage with Tuffins and that she wouldn't be missing a secret brothel hidden inside the reading room.

As we crossed the open courtyard toward the grand portico entrance and the imposing Greek columns, Sebastian turned to Mr. Adeoti.

"Mr. Jarsdel's power isn't fire, exactly, is it?" he asked.

"Indeed, Mr. Braddock, it's connected to the sun."

"And that makes it worse, I assume?" Miss Chen asked.

Mr. Adeoti nodded. "He's stronger in the sunlight. He can also emit a flash that temporarily blinds anyone looking at him, so be sure to cover your eyes."

"And how do we not get set on fire with our eyes closed?" I asked.

"Oh, you'll likely be set on fire!" Mr. Adeoti said. "But hopefully we will learn something new today."

"I suggest hiding," Sebastian said, his lips pursed.

We reached the front door, where Mr. Adeoti paused for a moment as he held it open for us, his eyes seeing something beyond us. "Mr. Jarsdel's here. I don't think he knows exactly where his Lord Lister is, though."

"Then that gives us the advantage," Mr. Kent declared as we entered the main vestibule. He stopped at the first attendant we saw and asked if he knew a Lord Lister who was on the board and currently somewhere in the museum. The attendant had no idea.

"A very slight advantage," Mr. Kent clarified to us.

We moved from room to room, ignoring the thousands of years' worth of priceless manuscripts, artifacts, and sculptures. Instead, we headed straight for the attendants with the same question ready. Our path took us through a vast library, the Egyptian wing, and a few Greek and Roman rooms until we reached a staircase where Mr. Jarsdel had touched the banister on his way up.

"He didn't find him on this floor," Mr. Adeoti said. "He's just a few minutes ahead."

"Then we will just have to find him first," Mr. Kent said, as if it were the simplest thing.

We climbed the stairs and passed through a room dedicated to oriental artifacts and into another Egyptian room.

Before crossing the threshold, I turned around to find Miss Chen looking at something in a glass curio cabinet. By the time I came upon her, she was pulling jewelry out of a perfectly round hole in the glass front.

"You can't steal things from the museum," I whispered.

Miss Chen snorted. "How do you think they got here in the first place?"

"I . . . fine, steal them after we're done," I said, quickly plastering a smile on my face as a passing lady gave us a strange look.

"Excuse me, miss, what is it you have there?" a voice behind us asked with the tone of someone who definitely knew what we had there.

Standing by a cabinet at the entrance was a short, dapper man, squinting at us in shock through his monocle.

"What is it *you* have there?" Miss Chen shot back, giddy bewilderment on her face. "I didn't think you English actually wore those. This is incredible."

The man looked affronted, especially when his monocle cracked from Miss Chen's thrilled gaze. He spun around to seek help and found it in Mr. Kent and the rest of our group.

"Ah good, you found him. Lord Lister, yes?" Mr. Kent said.

"Yes, that's me," the man answered, looking confused. "But these young ladies, we must fetch the police, they are thieves and—"

"Miss Wyndham, Miss Chen! I never would have thought you had it in you. I am thoroughly impressed." Mr. Kent winked at us both.

"Now, sir!" Lord Lister began blustering.

"Oh, right, yes. I have some news for you, Lord Lister. Someone is trying to kill you, so I suggest you come with us."

Lord Lister stared at us, trying to suss out the joke, then frowning when he saw everyone's serious faces. "Who are you? Who is . . . trying to kill me?"

"Imagine a sun," Mr. Kent said. "But it's grown arms and legs and a torso and has decided it doesn't like you very much."

Lord Lister stared helplessly. "I . . . don't have a son. . . ."

"Mr. Kent, you're confusing him more," I hissed, pushing our group into the Egyptian room, toward an exit. "Let's go."

"If I were told the sun wanted to kill me, I'd be on my way and save the questions for later."

"I can't imagine you ever saving questions for later," I replied.

"Is that the sun . . . man?" Lord Lister interceded, pointing to the other end of the room.

We followed his gaze to a red-haired man walking straight for us, flames rapidly growing in both his hands.

"Oh, very likely, well done, you!" Mr. Kent said.

"Get Lister away," Sebastian told me, cracking his knuckles. "And keep him healed."

He took a deep breath and a slow step away from me. Then another. And then he turned and darted around the edge of the room toward Mr. Jarsdel.

"Emily, be ready," Miss Chen said. And then the loudest crash I'd ever heard filled the room.

As the windows along the wall shattered one by one, flames poured out of Mr. Jarsdel's hands. They rushed toward Sebastian like a massive ocean wave of fire, but Jarsdel was forced to stop, ducking as Emily sent the broken window glass toward him. Sebastian was able to dive behind a sarcophagus, the last bits of flame snaking by him.

Mr. Jarsdel shifted one hand in our direction, sending out more fiery waves as he closed in on us. I pushed Lord Lister behind a display case for cover, while museum visitors screamed and desperately scrambled for the exits.

As the room emptied, more glass cases shattered from Miss Chen's gaze, and Emily picked up the glass debris to send a vicious storm straight at Mr. Jarsdel. His fire managed to burn some of it, but there was too much. The glass cut across his face, and he copied Sebastian, diving for cover behind another sarcophagus.

Sebastian took this as his chance to rush our enemy, but Mr. Jarsdel's flames encircled and shielded him from Sebastian, forming a five-foot-tall wall of fire. A quick swerve and Sebastian dove out of the way, his jacket catching most of the blast. He landed behind a reconstructed tomb wall and hastily discarded his burning jacket.

Miss Chen picked up the assault, climbing a cabinet to get a clear view. The floor around Mr. Jarsdel started to crack, splintered wood exploding into the air in a circle around the flames. Within seconds, the floor fully collapsed and Mr. Jarsdel disappeared from sight, falling down to the floor below.

And immediately rocketed back up. His palms aimed downward, Mr. Jarsdel propelled himself back up to our floor and straight at Miss Chen before any of us could react. He tackled her through a glass case and a marble bust and nearly into the brick wall, but Emily caught them and flung them apart.

I rushed over to heal Miss Chen, pulling Lord Lister along with me. She had cuts and burns along her face and arms, but she groaned and shrugged off the pain, rising back to her feet. I helped her up, trying to heal her as much as possible first. Emily had Mr. Jarsdel pinned to the wall, but he was struggling to break free. Flashes of flames escaped from his hands, his aim slowly getting closer to Emily. She held on, sweat breaking on her brow as she fought to keep him in place.

The flames grew around Mr. Jarsdel. He seemed to shake with anger and panic, primed to explode. I crouched behind a cabinet, bracing myself when Sebastian yelled, "Close your—"

The room turned a searing white as I remembered the blinding power a moment too late. I could make out nothing but a sense of brightness, of fire in my eyes as I clutched Lord Lister's hand and pulled him away, my other hand in front of me, grasping at nothing as we stumbled forward. I prayed that the others had closed their eyes, for if Mr. Jarsdel was the only person who could see, we had no chance of fighting him like this. Not that the chances of outrunning him were any better.

I groped ahead of me, running into display cases, stumbling over artifacts, and expecting a wave of fire any moment. Then something dark broke through the white haze. My vision was returning. I thanked my healing power and scrambled forward, ignoring the broken glass stabbing into my palm. Behind me, the blurry, stumbling outline of Lord Lister slowly came back into focus, but I couldn't see past him. The rest of the room remained hazy, as if it were filled with smoke.

Because it was. Display cases and chests were smoldering around the room, more smoke rising from the ruined room below us, keeping us hidden.

"Mr. Kent!" I yelled. "If you can hear me, ask Mr. Jarsdel a long question!"

A blast of fire flew straight at us in response. I barely managed to pull Lord Lister away.

"Mr. Jarsdel, what are your thirty favorite things to light on fire?" Mr. Kent shouted.

"Birds, riverboats, gardens, soap factories . . . ," Mr. Jarsdel answered, firing off more blasts in our general direction.

We dove behind a cabinet for cover, but one blast struck Lord Lister in the back, knocking him to the ground. I hastily tried to smother the fire on his jacket, but his yells only made things worse, narrowing down our location for Mr. Jarsdel. His voice and his long list of combustibles came closer as he assaulted our wooden hiding spot, which wasn't the best defense against fire.

"Wheat fields, trains, windmills . . . ," Mr. Jarsdel continued.

"Stay here," I whispered to Lord Lister as I pulled out my dagger. I was the only one who could survive Mr. Jarsdel by running straight through his blasts. It'd be painful but better than waiting, watching him slowly cook my friends to death.

"Bridges, schools, and, finally, spoiled rich girls," Mr. Jarsdel said, smugly ending his list. But his eyes widened in surprise as I leaped out and dashed toward him.

He raised his glowing hands to fire, and the next moment, Sebastian was behind him, forcing his arms downward, the flames flickering harmlessly to the ground. Sebastian's eyes met mine, and I could see the plea in them as he grappled Mr. Jarsdel into submission. I slid to the side, scrambled back away from them, and started the count.

One, two, three . . .

Mr. Jarsdel started coughing, but he continued to put up a fight. He struggled to bring his arms up, and when that proved impossible with Sebastian's hold, he turned his palms downward to take flight. Sebastian held on, and the blast propelled them both through the air, out the window, and down into the courtyard below.

Seven, eight, nine . . .

I shot back up to my feet and raced for the window, refusing to be left behind. I leaped out and dropped down a floor, hitting the stone ground hard. I couldn't let Sebastian down.

Twelve, thirteen, fourteen . . .

Mr. Jarsdel's energy left him, and his fire sputtered out a few yards ahead. After crashing to the ground, they had toppled and rolled along the stone. I chased after them, running harder than I'd ever run before. Please, please, please.

Eighteen, nineteen, twenty.

Their momentum slowed, and Mr. Jarsdel's body pinned Sebastian down. I dropped by their sides as Sebastian groaned and coughed and gasped for air. His eyes opened, and he lost what little breath he had left, panicking as he realized he was still touching Mr. Jarsdel.

"I'm here . . . Sebastian," I managed, grabbing his hand, letting the sensation convince him if my words couldn't. "I'm canceling it out."

I pulled Mr. Jarsdel's body off him and felt for his pulse. He had blue splotches on his skin, and he was unconscious, but that was it. We'd timed it correctly.

"It's all right," I told Sebastian. "He's alive."

He let out a sigh of relief and winced as he shifted his weight to one of his several injuries. I wished I could heal him, but I simply had to settle for helping him to his feet.

The rest of our group found us a minute later, still walking hesitantly as they blinked away the haze from their temporary blindness. In the distance, I could see Lord Lister making his escape. We could hear alarms ringing and people shouting frantically on the other side of the building, at Great Russell Street. The fire was still raging and doubtlessly destroying some of the museum's prized possessions. The streams of water from the firemen seemed to be doing very little to help. I cringed at the thought of explaining this to Catherine.

"Did they put out the fire?" Miss Chen asked, averting her gaze from the museum.

"No," I said, my eyes, along with everyone else's, sliding up to the smoky sky.

"See?" She fingered the bracelet she'd stolen. "We should have saved more."

With the panic centered around the fire, we were barely noticed among the fleeing museum guests. Mr. Kent and Miss Chen helped carry the unconscious Mr. Jarsdel out the gates and to the carriage. Laura looked a bit stunned as Tuffins opened the door for us. He, of course, seemed to notice nothing unusual.

Next to me, Sebastian sighed. I couldn't help the pride I felt for him, and I squeezed his hand a little. He managed to use his power, it had only incapacitated the man, and he wasn't catatonic right now. He looked concerned, yes, but he was still here with us.

"I think the count is down to fifty-two," I said. Sebastian looked at me blankly. "You saved us in there. Lord Lister, Mr. Kent, Miss Chen, Mr. Adeoti, Emily, me, yourself—I think you're down to fifty-two."

"I'm not counting myself," Sebastian said stubbornly.

"I don't believe that was ever against the rules," I said, pulling him into the carriage with the rest of the group so he wouldn't be able to argue.

As the carriage took us away, we followed Mr. Adeoti's instructions to suppress Mr. Jarsdel's powers. Using Sebastian's necktie, we bound his hands together, palms inward, so his fire could not be released.

Within minutes, the carriage stopped in front of the police station, where Sebastian and Mr. Kent unloaded our prisoner, and I followed them in. With our scorched clothes and sooty faces, we looked completely wretched, but I couldn't ignore the feeling of triumph coursing through my body.

"Hello. I've found the man you're all looking for," Mr. Kent declared. "He's here to make a confession."

Mr. Kent unceremoniously dropped Mr. Jarsdel, leaving Sebastian with the weight. He set him down on the ground and stepped away, giving me space to heal him.

"Who are you, sir?" the thin booking officer yelled. "What division are you with?"

"Z division," Mr. Kent said. "They formed one just for me. Now I have here a man responsible for a recent murder you're investigating. He has one of those powers you've no doubt heard about."

The booking officer snorted. "So do my wife and my sister," he said, earning the easy laughs of a few other policemen.

With the effects of Sebastian's power healed away, Mr. Jarsdel finally came to after a sniff of smelling salts. He looked rather dazed and then panicked. He struggled with his restraints, his hands glowing a bright orange that cut all the laughter short. A room full of suspicious eyes watched us.

"Thank you for the quiet," Mr. Kent said before turning to our prisoner. "Now, sir, please tell these good men, is your name Mr. Jarsdel?"

"Yes," Mr. Jarsdel said, his face reddening with anger as he realized where he was and what we had planned.

"Now Mr. Jarsdel, are you responsible for the murder of Sir Thomas Cox at the brothel on Leman Street last night?"

"Yes."

"And who told you to murder the poor baronet?"

"Goode."

"What is the man's title?"

"Captain."

"So it was Captain Goode who ordered this murder?"

Mr. Jarsdel tried to muffle the words in his shoulder, but the affirmative reply was heard anyway. "Mmph."

As Mr. Kent lifted Mr. Jarsdel's head and forced him to answer, brilliantly building his case, the curious detectives were warily striding forward, looking more and more intrigued.

"Did Captain Goode also plan the attack on the Queen at Westminster Abbey?"

"Yes."

"Then how do you explain Sebastian Braddock's appearance there?"

"It was an illusion. To blame him."

"And Captain Goode is responsible for both the Westminster Abbey event and the murder last night?"

"Technically."

"Wonderful. And now, gentlemen, I leave this filth in your hands."

The men were staring among themselves, slack-jawed, as we backed away.

"I suggest you grab him," I said, as Mr. Jarsdel worked at the necktie with his teeth, his breath coming in angry hisses. "And keep his palms together unless you want to be burned to death."

That finally snapped the room into action, the men surrounding Mr. Jarsdel as we backed away toward the exit.

"Wait! You are not to leave yet!" the booking officer called after us. "Who are you? Who is your superintendent? Stop!"

But we were already out the door, hurrying back to the carriage.

We'd done enough. They could sort out the rest without detaining us.

When we got back to Mrs. Tuffins's, I ran to tell Rose and Catherine. Rose was thrilled and Catherine was pleased until she learned that the British Museum was no longer looking its best.

"The entire room of jewels from the Far East?"

"Well, Miss Chen saved one piece," I said, nodding at her. We had taken over the parlor again and were sitting on the floor together, sharing a bottle of wine.

"Yes." Miss Chen held up her wrist, showing off her bracelet.

"Ah. Well, fair enough. The architects and curators who have been building the museum's collections are terrible thieves," Catherine said, sounding as though she were about to start a much longer and angrier diatribe. But she stopped and sighed. "All those beautiful pieces, though."

"It's worth it," I said firmly. When Sebastian's name was cleared and Captain Goode's was in the mud, he wouldn't be able to hide. I looked behind me to see if Sebastian was paying us any mind. He looked up, then, and seemed to instinctively soften as our eyes caught.

Yes. It was worth a few ruined rooms, a few antiques. I would knock down buildings if it meant Sebastian had a chance at happiness.

Chapter Nine

"GOOD NEWS," Mr. Kent said, entering the kitchen the next morning with the latest newspaper in one hand and a buttered roll in the other. "The world finally knows the truth: Mr. Braddock is a vampire."

The newspaper dropped onto the table in front of me. Sebastian, Rose, Catherine, and Miss Chen stopped eating their breakfasts and waited as I scanned the article, finding only nonsense implicating Sebastian in the baronet's murder.

"*An eyewitness says,*" I read aloud, "*she saw Mr. Braddock climbing up the building's three floors with his bare hands, breaking through the window, draining the life out of the poor Sir Thomas, burning him, and throwing him down to his death.*"

Mr. Kent tut-tutted. "You really must be more discreet with your blood cravings, Mr. Braddock."

"What nonsense," I said. "We did every bit of work for the police! Really, all they had to do was move Jarsdel from the lobby into a jail cell. It couldn't have been that difficult. When will they announce Sebastian's innocence?"

"It's . . . possible they might not be planning an announcement," Mr. Kent said.

"What do you mean?" Rose asked.

"When I went out, I saw new police notices for Mr. Braddock blaming him for the Belgrave Ball, the attack on the Queen, and Sir Thomas's murder."

Sebastian sighed, taking the paper from me before I could crumple it up. I wasn't sure if it was a good sign that a mild sigh was now his reaction to more false accusations of murder.

I dropped the rest of my cake. "But you made him confess in full view of several policemen," I said, struggling to take this as calmly as Sebastian was. "They can't ignore that."

"Perhaps Captain Goode's influence reaches further than we thought," Miss Chen put in. "He did save the Queen, after all."

"Then maybe we should overreach him," I said, jabbing at the newspaper. "They'll want to hear the truth."

Mr. Kent snorted. "They most definitely will not. They want a good story."

"Then we'll give them that, too."

Two hours later, when Mr. Kent, a disguised Sebastian, and I entered the office of the *Daily Telegraph*, we found ourselves stopped at the front by an assistant. He wouldn't let us speak to the editor, despite our use of the magic words: "We have information about Sebastian Braddock."

"So do ten others this morning," he told us. "You can tell me first, and I'll bring it to Mr. Warren when he's not quite so busy."

Mr. Kent tried another set of magic words. "But if you take us to him now, then we won't tell Mr. Warren about . . . what was that awful thing you did?"

Suddenly, Mr. Warren was no longer busy.

We were let into his cluttered office. He was a slight man with spectacles and a thin mustache. He looked buried by the amount of stacked books and papers around him.

"What is it?" Mr. Warren barked without even the politeness to look up. "We're very busy here, there's a great deal—"

"We have the truth about Sebastian Braddock for you," I said. "And it's not that ridiculous story portraying him as a vampire."

Mr. Warren finally gave me his attention. His disdainful attention. "There have been many ridiculous stories that have been proven true this past week," he said. "What is your rational explanation then for the horrible murders?"

"He was framed for the murder," I said. "Because he is already wanted by the police, he is being blamed while the true murderer goes unnamed."

"And who is the true murderer?"

"His name is Mr. Jarsdel. He was brought to the Brunswick Square police station yesterday and provided a full confession of his involvement in the murder, and not a single report has been made about it."

Now Mr. Warren looked at us with actual interest. "And you know this because you were the three who brought him in and left."

"So the police would actually do their job."

Mr. Warren put his pen down and folded his hands. "From what I've heard, they did. They questioned him extensively and found he'd been threatened and coerced into making these confessions. At the end of the day, an order was sent down to let him go due to insufficient evidence."

I felt my rage grow, and I resisted the impulse to destroy the editor's office. Not that it could be made messier. "They what? He just lied to them, and they let him go?"

"Do you have any proof that he did what you say he did?"

I glanced at Mr. Kent.

He took his cue. "Mr. Warren, do you believe in the existence of the ridiculous powers that Captain Goode has so recently informed the world of?"

"I believe so."

"Have you ever cried because someone didn't love you back?"

"Yes," Mr. Warren answered, disconcerted.

"Did you want to answer that last question?"

"No."

"Why do you think you did?"

Mr. Warren's eyes widened as he realized it. "You have a power."

Mr. Kent nodded in approval. "I do, indeed. The power to ask a question and receive an honest answer. Which is what I used to question Mr. Jarsdel when we brought him to the police after cornering him at the British Museum. Anything that I asked him was his true confession. Anything he said to the police after was likely a lie."

Mr. Warren took a heavy breath and leaned back in his chair, taking in everything that we had said. He looked between the three of us as if he might figure out what we were thinking.

"You know, before Captain Goode made his announcement, I heard a strange story about a man who managed to extract secrets from three policemen in C Division and blackmail them to help Sebastian Braddock and an unnamed woman escape arrest."

Mr. Kent's face remained impassive. "That does sound rather strange."

Mr. Warren looked at Sebastian closely, seeing through his disguise. "Can you ask Mr. Braddock whether he murdered Sir Thomas Cox?"

Mr. Kent chuckled. "Oh, we didn't introduce ourselves. This is Mr. Haddock—"

"Just do it," I said.

He frowned at me for not playing along, as if changing to a rhyming name would completely fool everyone. "Fine, Mr. Braddock, did you kill the baronet two nights before?"

"No," Sebastian answered.

"Now ask him if he attacked the Queen at Westminster Abbey."

Mr. Kent rolled his eyes. "Did you attack the Queen at Westminster Abbey?"

"No."

Mr. Warren sniffed, still looking stern. "I see. One last question. Ask him if he killed those people at the Belgrave Ball."

Oh dear. That was not a question I wanted him to answer. "We told you he did not," I said.

"Then allow me this one question, otherwise I will call for the police right now."

A moment of silence reigned.

Mr. Kent sucked on his teeth and cleared his throat. "Fine. Mr. Braddock, were you responsible for the deaths at the Belgrave Ball?"

"Yes," Sebastian said, his voice a broken whisper, his face wretched.

Dammit. Even with the slightly rephrased question. "It's more complicated than that," I said. "Captain Goode is the one who orchestrated it—"

But Mr. Warren was already up and out of his chair.

"I'll handle this," Mr. Kent said, blocking Mr. Warren's path to the door. "Mr. Warren, what is the worst thing you've done?"

"I've missed church several times because I wanted to sleep longer," he said.

Mr. Kent scoffed. "Fine, what is your deepest secret?"

"I wish I'd had more fun in my youth rather than work so much," Mr. Warren sputtered out.

"Yes, you really should have. Bad choice there. Is there anything at all that I can blackmail you with?"

"No." The answer hung in the air as Mr. Warren sneered at us. "Do you realize you're not even the first person to attempt to blackmail me *today*? I run a newspaper."

Mr. Kent looked at us sheepishly. "I must admit, I don't know what to do next. This hasn't happened before." His eyes lit up with an idea, and he turned back to Mr. Warren. "Oh, do you take bribes?"

"I do not!" Mr. Warren declared. "So I will tell you what we will do next. I will write the story of your arrest right after the police arrive."

He tried to rush to the door, but Mr. Kent was expecting it. He seized him by the arm and asked Mr. Warren for his eighty favorite foods, interrupting his shout for help.

"Call the—porridge! Mincemeat pie! Strawberries!"

"We should probably let Mr. Warren get his lunch. He sounds hungry," Mr. Kent said, hurrying us out of the office.

Mr. Warren's shouts got louder and more frantic behind us as he grabbed members of his staff and pointed at us, cursing us with various food names. "Pork roast! Cucumber sandwiches! Milk!"

Mr. Kent paused for a moment. "I don't think milk qualifies as a food—"

I shoved him forward. "We'll write a letter to the editor later."

"Thank you," Sebastian said politely to the assistant by the front.

As we left the building, the last thing I saw was Mr. Warren by the window, frantically writing a message even as his mouth continued to move against his will.

Then we were outside and safely in our carriage, our breaths heavy and the only sounds the fading exclamations of a man sharing his appreciation for various types of tarts.

Chapter Ten

"IT COULD BE WORSE," Miss Chen said as we stared at the next morning's *Daily Telegraph* headline.

BRADDOCK & COMPANIONS: BLACKMAILING CRIMINALS, it read.

"At least he didn't know who you were," Catherine said.

"*Underneath their poor disguises, I could see they matched the witness descriptions of the three assailants at the Queen's speech,*" I read aloud.

"But he must admit you did some good, too," Mr. Adeoti said hopefully.

"*In their attempt to convince me of their innocence, they all but admitted to setting the British Museum on fire in an effort to capture the man they claimed to be the real culprit.*"

"That's . . . a little of your side of the story," Rose offered.

"*Given this pattern, it is very likely that they had some involvement in the two fires last night that each claimed a victim.*"

The dining room sat silent; the words of encouragement drained away.

I took solace in a piece of cake, silently thanking Mrs. Tuffins for her breakfast choices on the worst mornings.

"Well, it can't get any worse," Miss Chen said, sipping her tea.

I held up the newspaper for her. "Also there are pictures."

She spit out a little tea back into the cup. "Oh no, I take that back," she said, dabbing her chin with a napkin. "Those drawings are supposed to be you?"

"Yes, that is me, the healing harlot." I indicated my own crude depiction. The artist had rendered me as a wily seductress, emphasizing my features so it was mostly curled lips and sneaky eyes. My brothel double was probably refining her costume accordingly.

"It'll be impossible to recognize you, at least," Catherine said.

"Why don't you show me his office?" Miss Chen suggested. "Just tell me where to look."

I shook my head. "No, he still seems to be a good and honest reporter."

"I would not call the man 'good' exactly," Catherine said, picking up the paper to read the end aloud. *"They are as cunning and cruel as the heroic Captain Goode suggested them to be. What do they want? We do not know. But this reporter is sure they will stop at nothing short of complete chaos. My gentle readers, take care. Be wary. We do not know enough about these extraordinary powers, but I can tell you that, like all power, in the hands of our new Constable of the Tower, it can keep us safe, but in the hands of the wicked Braddock, the effects are only ill."*

"Bit overdramatic," Miss Chen snapped.

"'New . . . Constable'?" I asked. "I hope that's not what I think it is."

Catherine and Rose were already turning through other newspapers, trying to find an explanation. Catherine stopped at one article, bit her lip, and read, *"They are honoring Captain Goode with the position of Constable of the Tower of London."*

"That's . . . absurd," I said. "He hasn't done anything."

The position was reserved as an honor for high-ranking and successful military officers like the Duke of Wellington. Captain

Goode was no Duke of Wellington. Did they just hand out constable positions willy-nilly to anyone with a positive adjective in their name?

Rose skimmed through another paper. "I think they are considering his work at the Society. They say he's been protecting England secretly for years without any recognition."

"I think there's a lesson to be learned from this," Catherine said.

"Never hope for anything good?" Miss Chen asked, biting into a biscuit.

"We can't keep doing bad things for good reasons," Catherine continued. "All it does is make us appear worse."

"What if we wrote a letter to the editor explaining everything?" Rose asked. "Tell him this is a misunderstanding. He would appreciate the truth."

"I don't know what we'd write. 'Our deepest apologies. We got nervous and Mr. Kent's tongue slipped and he accidentally attempted to blackmail you.' I wouldn't even believe it myself." I paused for a moment, realizing the house was quieter than usual. "Where is Mr. Kent, anyway?"

"He was gone when I woke up," Mr. Adeoti said, looking up from his notes.

"Trying to avoid us, I assume," Miss Chen said.

"Knowing him, he's already gone to blackmail a competing newspaper," Catherine said.

I glanced out the window to the yard in the back. Sebastian was just outside, apron-clad, helping Mrs. Tuffins ready her garden for the spring. He didn't exactly look joyful as he knelt and dug into the hard soil, but he didn't look quite so lost, either. And he didn't look for me every few seconds for reassurance.

Better to tell him about the newspaper later. When we had a plan. When I didn't feel quite so lost and helpless myself.

"I think we're wasting our time with these tangents," I said. "There must be some way we can deal with Captain Goode directly."

"We still don't know how to find him," Miss Chen said.

"If he's a public figure now, he'll make appearances," I said. "There's probably a ceremony for that Constable position."

Miss Chen shook her head. "You are not going to try to shoot him in public again."

"No, I thought we would follow him and do what you suggested for the reporter," I said. "Wait until he goes into a building or a carriage and break it from afar."

Miss Chen seemed to consider that, but my sister looked concerned.

"He's never going to be alone," Rose said. "There will always be servants in houses or drivers in carriages."

"Not to mention the fact that he may have his own body-guards like Lady Atherton had," Catherine said. "Given that his power is not particularly useful in a fight."

"What's your solution if we don't go after him?" I asked Catherine. "We sit here and wait for him to make a mistake?"

"We save lives," Catherine replied. "What was the name of the man you saved at the British museum?"

"Lord Lister," I said.

Catherine looked back at the newspaper for confirmation. "Neither of yesterday's victims are a Lord Lister. Which means he listened to you. He hid and he's still alive because of you."

"Or his body hasn't washed up yet," Miss Chen said with a shrug.

Catherine ignored that and continued, "The more we save, the more our reputation will improve. People will appreciate it."

"How will we know whom to save?" I asked. "We had to wait for Mr. Jarsdel to kill Sir Thomas before we knew of Lord Lister."

"Leave that to me," Catherine said confidently. She peered

back down at the newspaper. "We know of four targeted men so far. Cox, Lister, Snow, and Bell. That should be enough to find a pattern—oh, there it is. The next victim will probably be a man named Pasteur."

Rose snorted and giggled at that, while Miss Chen and I exchanged confused glances.

"A little . . . germ-theory humor," Catherine explained to me. She shared a quick smile with Rose. "Anyway, I think we need to take the time to research. That may give us some insight into whether he has more plans."

"We already tried this with the head of the Society," I said.

"And it nearly worked," Catherine argued. "I figured out the pattern. Only, Lady Atherton ruined it."

"If we went after the attackers instead, we wouldn't have to guess who would be on the list!" Mr. Adeoti suggested, setting his pen down. "I have a list of the Society members, and we could find them individually before they are given more terrible orders."

"And we ask them to refuse their orders?" Miss Chen asked. "At the risk of their loved ones?"

"Oh, well, we'd have to rescue and protect all their family members and friends," Mr. Adeoti said optimistically. "So with thirty Society members . . . that's only a few hundred people."

Miss Chen gaped at him and his notebook for a moment, then shut her eyes and turned away before accidentally breaking it apart. "Sometimes I can't tell if you're joking."

"Not at all!" Mr. Adeoti said, showing us his notes. "I'm sure we'd get it done quickly with our determination!"

"And where exactly are we going to keep them?" Catherine asked, looking around the cramped dining room. "And how are we going to keep the angrier ones from trying to kill us?"

"Out of all the powers we have, Miss Rosamund's power would be the safest way to convince the reluctant," Mr. Adeoti said.

Rose's face blanched at the suggestion.

Miss Chen's, however, brightened at the idea for once. "We'd have to find another place for them to stay. But they would be more cooperative—"

"No," Catherine said firmly. "No, we're not doing that. Rose doesn't want to be using her powers like that."

The defense did not seem to help, though. Rose only went whiter at Catherine's words. Her chair squeaked loudly against the wood. "I must take a walk" was all she said before she hurried out of the room.

"Rose!" Catherine called, trying to follow, but I stayed her. "I'll go."

I hurried upstairs to find hats and veils. By the time I was downstairs and outside, she was already halfway down the street, and by the time I caught up to her, I'd lost half my breath.

"Rose . . . wait," I said, holding her hat in front of her.

She stopped and snatched it from me. I glimpsed tears on her cheeks for a second before they were covered by fine netting. "Thank you," she mumbled.

I put my hat and veil on and took her arm. We walked in silence while my breath and her tears slowed.

The ground was dusty and the buildings drab, but the streets were filled with life. Energetic men unloading carts and women leaning out the windows, collecting their hanging laundry. Flower girls and newspaper boys off to ply their wares. A few children seemed to be playing a game of tag down one alleyway, and I could have sworn I heard one of them declare themselves Sebastian Braddock.

I cleared my throat as we turned a corner. "You should know I don't like the idea, either. Catching Society members and charming them to help us. I think it'd be too slow."

Rose didn't say anything.

"So don't feel obligated to do something you don't want to do. I know you don't want to use your power on anyone. No one is going to force you. Did you see how quickly Catherine spoke up?"

"I did. That's the problem," she mumbled, not looking at me.

So there it was. Catherine had been right to be concerned. "What happened? I thought you felt better around Catherine because she didn't have a power. Why do you keep avoiding her?"

"I'm not avoiding her!" Rose flashed me a look full of pain, and I patted her arm, holding it more securely.

"Just because you have a power, it doesn't mean you can't have a friend. I would have thought you would get along. . . ."

"We do!"

"But you act so oddly with her . . . different than with anyone else here. . . ." Rose looked so panicked and miserable I stopped. "Darling, I am not trying to force you to be friends with her. It is perfectly all right if you do not like her; I just don't want you to worry about your power so much—"

Rose stopped and looked at me full-on. "The problem is that I do like her, Evelyn. I like her too much. I like her more than anyone I've ever met." She refused to drop her eyes as my mind went blank, her response so unexpected.

"Oh. . . ."

"Yes." Rose's firm nod and terrified expression confirmed what had never occurred to me. It wasn't a friendship with Catherine that concerned my sister. It was a romance.

"I—uh—since . . . when?" I managed.

"Since the first time I met her."

"I . . . see. I don't remember. . . ."

Rose's thin shoulders dropped along with all her defenses, and she shrugged, laughing a little, sounding ever so slightly hysterical. "That morning after the two of you went to Haymarket to see *The Valkyrie* during your Season. You came back to the drawing room, and when she looked at me I had to hide behind my book. There was something about her eyes. . . . I wanted to stare at her forever, but I felt like she could suddenly see everything about me and it was terrifying and wonderful. She kept on saying brilliant things about Wagner, and I didn't know anything about opera, so I couldn't decide whether to stay quiet and look foolish or say something and sound foolish. And then you turned the topic to the singer's voice and anatomy, and thank goodness you did for I finally had something interesting to contribute."

"I . . . don't remember any of this."

"Of course not. It was a perfectly normal day for you," Rose said. "It was . . . a revelation for me."

I couldn't help but think back to the night Rose was taken from Bramhurst. When I had been completely wrong about her feelings about our neighbor Robert. When she didn't even want to think about marriage. Had I been equally as unobservant about Catherine? Memories of all my outings with Catherine flooded my mind, but she was always the one needling me about suitors. I never managed to turn it around on her. She was friendly with everyone but never paid anyone particular attention. At least not until this past week with Rose.

Rose leaned her head in closely, trying to read my expression through our veils.

"Does it make you uncomfortable? I know she's your best friend."

"No, no—not at all. I always knew you would like her," I said. "I just . . . wondered . . . do you know if Catherine feels the same?"

Rose's gaze turned to the ground. "I used to hope so. I used to even think it might have been. But that was before I knew about these powers. So it doesn't matter."

"Of course it matters," I insisted.

She shook her head, her voice thick. "Not if I want her to have a choice. I don't want to put her under a spell."

"As hard as it is to believe, there are people who love you for reasons other than your power."

"There's no way of knowing for certain," Rose replied. "Not for anyone I've met in the last two years."

"But it's not as if you chose this, either," I said. "None of us did. How is it different from every suitor simply falling in love with your beauty?"

"It's different," she insisted. "It's very different."

"These powers are as much a part of us as anything else."

"Then Mr. Braddock should simply let everyone near him die because it's a part of him?"

I opened my mouth. And closed it. I knew when to concede a point.

"But there are ways of controlling it," I said.

"They clearly aren't working fast enough," Rose said. "Catherine is more protective than she was even a few days ago. And it's going to take me years to get it right. Unless Captain Goode offers to help."

We turned another corner, circling back toward the boarding house.

"I don't mean controlling it that way," I said. "You should keep training, but there are other things Sebastian did. He found out how his power worked. How close someone had to be to be affected, how long the sickness lasted. Granted, it was from horrible experiments with Dr. Beck but . . ." I trailed off, a spark sending my mind whirling too fast for my mouth.

"Ev?" Rose asked. "But what?"

After that awful night I lost Rose, Dr. Beck's words had burned themselves into my brain. I replayed our conversation, hating myself for remembering it all so well. Now I almost wanted to thank him.

"Dr. Beck's experiments," I said. "I'm sorry to bring this up but . . . he—he hurt you because he wanted to find your healing power. Despite your charm."

Rose's voice went very quiet. "He apologized a lot."

"But he still did it," I said. "Even horrible people like Mr. Hale and Camille did everything to keep you from getting hurt. What did he do differently?"

"I don't know. I don't like to think about it."

"I know. You don't have to. Just remember that there's an exception. Maybe we need to ask Mr. Adeoti what he knows about your power's specifics. Or we'll have to find a way to do research in the Society of Aberrations library one day. And if there's nothing useful there, then we'll have to observe how it works ourselves. In any case, there has to be a reason and it has to be deducible."

"Evelyn, be careful. You're starting to sound like a scientist."

"I know, it's disconcerting. So disconcerting that I've decided to retire. Please continue my work."

"Thank you," she said, hugging me as we walked. "I will."

Our final turn brought us back to the front of the boarding house, where Mr. Kent was trying to drag a large trunk from the sidewalk.

"Did you . . . have an enjoyable vacation?" I asked him, lifting my veil.

"Indeed, I saw some wonderful sights and brought all of you some lovely souvenirs," he said.

I gripped the other end of the trunk, and it took nearly all of my strength to lift it up a mere few inches off the ground. "Good Lord, what's in here? A dead body?"

"Ha! Don't be ridiculous! What an outlandish joke to make! Ha!" Mr. Kent said before shooting me a scowl to keep quiet.

Step by step, we lugged this definitely-not-a-corpse up the stairs and into the safety of the boarding house.

"Is everything all right?" Sebastian asked, finding us by the door.

"Yes, I'm just trying to decide whether I really want to know what Mr. Kent has been doing," I said.

"I went to get Mr. Jarsdel," Mr. Kent said.

"You found him?" Catherine asked, the entrance starting to grow very crowded.

The trunk rumbled loudly in response, startling us all back a step. A pounding and muffled noises came from inside.

"Oh, he's awake," Mr. Kent said. "Mr. Braddock, would you help me show him to his room?"

Chapter Eleven

"Where did—how on earth did you find him?" I asked, following them up the stairs.

"I wondered to myself where I would go if I was released from the police after committing a murder and I had some free time before committing my next one." They reached the first-floor landing, and Mr. Kent looked back at me for an answer.

"Mr. Kent, with you, I really couldn't even begin to guess."

"Why thank you, Miss Wyndham," he said, taking it as a compliment. He looked past me at Catherine and Rose to see if they had an answer. "Someone must have a guess."

"Just tell us," Catherine said.

He spoke slowly so we could join in when we'd figured it out. "I'd celebrate at . . . the brothel . . . where my captors are being impersonated . . . and are at my complete service. Exactly."

"He went back to Miss Molly's?" I asked.

"Indeed," Mr. Kent said, picking up the trunk again. "I simply asked her girls to slip some laudanum into his wine if he returned. Much easier than burning down a museum to capture him."

They brought the trunk up to the empty bedroom on the second floor and dropped it in the center. Miss Chen and Mr. Adeoti filed in behind Catherine and Rose before Sebastian went over to close the door.

Mr. Kent pulled a key out from his pocket and unlatched the lock while the rest of the room watched in tense silence. "Don't worry, he's been bound alread—"

A white blinding light filled the room and my sight was gone. Shouts and scuffling filled the air.

"Dammit, someone grab him!" Mr. Kent yelled.

I felt my body shoved to the ground, and footsteps pounded past me toward the exit. And then there was a definitive thud as another body hit the ground beside me.

"I have him pinned down," Sebastian said over the sounds of Mr. Jarsdel grunting. "Everyone stay still and keep your eyes closed. Your sight will return in a few minutes."

The sounds of struggling continued as I heard Sebastian drag Mr. Jarsdel back against the far wall. Wood screeched across the floor, and as I stood back up, my sight slowly returned to see the blurry shape of Sebastian tying our prisoner to a chair.

"Evelyn, would you stand by the door?" Sebastian asked, dragging Mr. Jarsdel to the other corner.

That would put me out of his range. "Are you sure?"

Sebastian kept his eyes closed, only opening them for brief moments. He took a deep breath before answering. "Yes, I just need fifteen seconds."

I groped my way along the wall, keeping my eyes closed in case Mr. Jarsdel tried to blind us again. "All right, I'm here."

"Starting now," Sebastian said.

I started my count. After five seconds, Mr. Jarsdel's muffled yells and squirming grew louder. After ten seconds, they turned into coughing. After fifteen seconds, I stepped forward and opened my eyes.

Sebastian had let go of him and stepped away. Mr. Jarsdel looked as ill as he had at the police station—pale face, blue splotches, a sheen of sweat on his brow. He was still conscious, and for a brief moment, he gritted his teeth and his body glowed like he was going to bathe the room in light again, but he let out a heavy breath and started coughing, too weak to follow through with it.

One by one, I pulled my friends to the door, out of Sebastian's range, where they could keep a hold on me. Within a minute, their vision began to return.

"Another intimidating start to an interrogation," Miss Chen drawled, rubbing her eyes.

A knock sounded on the door. "Is everyone all right in there?" Mrs. Tuffins asked, entering before I could stop her.

"Yes, Mrs. Tuffins," I said, stepping in front of her. "We just dropped something."

"I see," she said, glancing past me. "If your new guest needs anything, please let me know."

I turned around to find that Mr. Kent had hastily draped a blanket over Mr. Jarsdel in his chair. "Oh, uh, no. He's feeling rather unwell right now."

"How unfortunate," she said. "Would a bowl of soup help?"

"He only needs rest for now, but thank you," I said. "Perhaps we'll bring him down later if he's feeling better."

"I do hope so," Mrs. Tuffins said with a smile and proceeded back downstairs, singing to herself. "So many guests!"

I closed the door and saw everyone had gathered around Mr. Jarsdel. I found a spot next to Sebastian by the window, took his hand, feeling the buzz from his skin, and squeezed it. No matter how many times he did it, it looked like it didn't get any easier. "Thank you," I whispered.

He nodded and squeezed back. No smile on his face but at least a hint of relief.

Meanwhile, Mr. Kent was busy removing the cloth stuffed into Mr. Jarsdel's mouth. "All right, Mr. Jarsdel, first question. Would you like a bowl of soup?"

"No," Mr. Jarsdel huffed. "Not from you."

"Well, I'm out of questions," Mr. Kent said.

"Ask him where Captain Goode is," I said.

Mr. Kent looked at me skeptically, but he asked anyway. "Where might we find Captain Goode?"

"At his home," Mr. Jarsdel said with a contemptuous, or woozy, tilt of the head.

"And where is that?" Mr. Kent asked.

"37 Lowndes Square."

Belgravia. So close to my parents' home. I unconsciously balled my hand into a fist.

"I think we have everything we need then," I said.

"Evelyn, no, we already discussed this," Catherine said firmly.

"Discussed what?" Mr. Kent asked.

"Her idea is to find Captain Goode and attack him from a distance," Catherine answered.

"Oh." Mr. Kent frowned. "We're definitely not doing that again."

"We'll have an actual plan," I argued. "The other ideas are worse."

"Ask him about the murders," Catherine said. "There's a connection."

"Who have you killed in the past week?" Mr. Kent asked.

Mr. Jarsdel raised his head and answered with a smile, as if he were remembering fond memories. "Thomas Cox and Laurence Snow."

"That's it?" Catherine asked. "Lord Bell was killed in a fire at the colonial office. That wasn't him?"

"Who killed Lord Bell?" Mr. Kent asked.

"I don't know and I don't care."

"Fine, why did you try to kill Sir Thomas, Lord Snow, and Lord Lister?" Mr. Kent asked.

"Captain Goode sent an order," he answered simply.

Mr. Kent sighed. "Why did he order you to kill them?"

"Said he wanted to kill aristocrat types to protect the Society."

Of course. "That clears things up for our list then," I said pointedly. I knew I was sniping at Catherine, but I couldn't help it. Not when we could actually do something.

Catherine glared at me. "Is there no other connection between them?"

"Yes. They're men," Mr. Jarsdel answered Mr. Kent unhelpfully.

Mr. Adeoti cleared his throat and approached the prisoner. "Perhaps I can find something more. Miss Chen, would you mind tearing off his collar?"

Miss Chen took a few steps closer to see the collar clearly and ripped along the seam with precision as Mr. Adeoti pulled it away. He sat on the bed and closed his eyes to read the piece for information.

"You should see if there's a way he'll join us," Miss Chen suggested to Mr. Kent. "Maybe he's being coerced."

"Do you want to kill us?" Mr. Kent asked Mr. Jarsdel.

"I do," he said groggily. "I'll do it one day."

Mr. Kent rubbed his brow. "Would you consider joining us against Captain Goode?"

"No," he answered. "The lot of you can go to hell."

"Do you have any friends or family?" Mr. Kent asked.

"No, they're all dead," Mr. Jarsdel answered.

"Is there anything we can do to persuade you to help us?" Mr. Kent asked.

"No, nothing," Mr. Jarsdel replied.

"Why are you so committed to working for Captain Goode?" Mr. Kent asked.

"He keeps my power high," Mr. Jarsdel answered. "Higher than it's ever been."

"And what if I said you could achieve the same thing on your own with hard work?" Mr. Kent asked.

"I'd say I don't care," Mr. Jarsdel growled, the white glow radiating off his skin and dying again as he started coughing.

"Ah, yes, I see, very effective power there," Mr. Kent taunted.

"It will be," Mr. Jarsdel said. "When I am burning you from the inside out."

Mr. Kent's eyebrows shot up, and he turned to us. "I think he would be a very negative presence on this team."

"Mr. Adeoti, did you find anything?" Catherine asked, tapping his shoulder. "Mr. Adeoti?"

That snapped him out of the trance. "Only . . . confirmation," he said, taking long blinks, shaking his head, trying to collect himself. "He was taken to Captain Goode's residence after the police released him, so that is accurate. And he's . . . quite angry at us."

"He's made us aware of that," Mr. Kent said. He paused and sniffed the air. "Does anyone else smell that?"

Sebastian was the first to react, pushing Mr. Kent out of the way and diving down behind Mr. Jarsdel's chair. Thin plumes of smoke had risen in the air. He had been trying to slowly burn through his restraints.

"One of his fingers got loose," Sebastian said, covering Mr. Jarsdel's hands with his jacket, smothering any errant flames. "I need more rope."

I handed him the remainder, which he used liberally to wrap each of Mr. Jarsdel's fingers together, along with his whole hand. Even between Mr. Jarsdel's weakened state and the extra precaution, sleeping in the same house as this killer didn't seem any safer an option than my proposal.

"We can't start our own prison up here," I said. "It's too dangerous."

"We can't let him go," Sebastian said, tightening the ropes.

"We're not giving him to the police again," Mr. Kent said.

"Then we should act now while his information is still accurate," I said.

"What information, Evelyn? All we have is an address," Catherine said. "Mr. Kent, ask him how close Captain Goode needs to be to shut off your powers."

"I don't know," Mr. Jarsdel answered Mr. Kent.

"Ask him whether he needs to see you or whether he can sense your power."

"I don't know," Mr. Jarsdel answered again.

"Ask him who Captain Goode's bodyguards are."

"Miss Fahlstrom is always with him," Mr. Jarsdel answered.

"And anyone else?" Mr. Kent asked.

"I don't know" was the refrain. "I only saw them once."

"And you want to go attack him without knowing any of this?" Catherine asked, barely concealing her exasperation. "We all stayed behind to stop the murders. Not to take unnecessary risks and be the next victims."

"I'll help," Rose said.

The room was silent for a moment before protests came from Catherine and me, our other argument forgotten.

"Rose, you don't need to—"

"I said we'd find another way."

"Please, I want to," she said, quieting us. She glanced at Sebastian. "This is the only way to learn how it works."

She took a few steps closer to Mr. Jarsdel. I felt myself moving closer in case he tried to do something again.

"Mr. Kent, will you ask if I might change his mind?" Rose asked.

Mr. Kent nodded. "Mr. Jarsdel, Miss Rosamund very much hopes you'll join us. Would you help us for her sake?"

"I—No . . ." Mr. Jarsdel said, with the slightest hesitation.

Mr. Kent pressed on it. "How do you feel about Miss Rosamund?"

"She's the only one of you I can stand," Mr. Jarsdel said.

"Then why won't you reconsider?"

"Not going to trade that power even for a pretty girl!" Mr. Jarsdel replied.

"Perhaps it needs a lot more time," Mr. Kent said, glancing back at Rose.

"There may be a way to speed it up." Mr. Adeoti cleared his throat. "There isn't much specific information about the charm power, but there are general patterns to how all the powers operate. I suspect there's a weak effect with presence, but perhaps speaking or direct contact will be stronger."

"I see," Rose said, biting her lip, thinking to herself. "Mr. Jarsdel, do you not feel any guilt for the lives you've taken?"

"They were a threat to us," Mr. Jarsdel answered, even though Mr. Kent wasn't asking the question.

Rose paced a few steps back and forth in front of our prisoner. "I understand, but I . . . I can't help but imagine one of them having a fight with his wife that morning. Maybe they parted furious at the other, but it softened over the course of the day as they both realized the misunderstanding and their mistakes. By the time it was evening, they would have been counting the minutes, eager to see each other, to apologize, to appreciate each other. But then you found the man on his way home and ended his life, while she spent the night awake, waiting. It makes me sad to imagine there might have been things that were never said."

"I hope that wasn't the case," Mr. Jarsdel said, his voice breaking a bit. He still looked angry, but it wasn't directed at anyone. "I don't wish to make you sad, Miss Rosamund."

Rose glanced back at Mr. Kent for his assistance. He took a moment, clearing his throat multiple times. I could feel a lump in my throat on Rose's behalf myself.

"Mr. Jarsdel, the invitation still stands. Would you like to join us now?" Mr. Kent asked. "To ensure Miss Rosamund's happiness?"

Mr. Jarsdel looked genuinely torn. "No . . . I'm sorry, my loyalties are elsewhere." He turned to Rose. "Perhaps you may be able to join the Society of Aberrations. Then we might protect you."

Rose closed the distance and stood over Mr. Jarsdel. She held her hand out and circled him, trying to find the most harmless place to make contact. She finally stopped behind him and settled her palm on the top of his red head. It would have made a very strange portrait.

"Will you join us now?"

"I . . . I don't know. I'm sorry."

I gaped at Rose and Mr. Jarsdel. He wasn't a convert, but the progress was astounding. How much more time until he would do anything for Rose's sake? Until he wanted to protect her so badly he would give his life for her, like Mr. Hale and Camille did?

"This may take some time," Rose said. "Would someone fetch me the newspapers from downstairs? I'd like to read them aloud to Mr. Jarsdel."

We spent the rest of the day like those quiet ones in Bramhurst with Mother in the morning room. The ones where Rose and I would spend hours doing needlepoint, drawing, or whatever else a young lady was required to learn to charm a man. Except here, we were skipping straight to the point.

Catherine and Sebastian stayed in the room to help watch over Rose, while Mr. Adeoti and Miss Chen moved to the parlor to study more objects of Mr. Jarsdel's. I spent the time attempting to practice Miss Chen's techniques to raise my power, but it was impossible to concentrate as I imagined Captain Goode escaping us again and again.

Rose's reading and contact made more progress. Every hour, Mr. Kent returned to ask a series of questions testing our prisoner's loyalty, and by lunchtime, Mr. Jarsdel agreed to join us in protecting Rose. By teatime, he would kill anyone to protect Rose. By dinnertime, he was quite certain that he would die to protect Rose. And by bedtime, Mr. Jarsdel was adamant that he would do anything for Rose.

Mr. Kent seemed to enjoy testing the limits of what anything meant.

"Would you live out the remainder of your life in the wild among a herd of goats if it would keep Miss Rosamund safe?"

"Of course I would."

"Would you put on an angry expression, dress in multicolored clothing, wear a pastry on your head, and rob ships at sea, calling yourself the Irate Pied Pie Pirate for Miss Rosamund's protection?"

"Yes."

Rose trembled next to me, politely trying to contain a massive yawn.

I took her arm away from Mr. Jarsdel. "All right, even that isn't keeping you awake. It's been a long enough day; you should rest. Catherine, will you take Rose down? Mr. Kent, these pressing questions can wait for tomorrow."

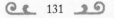

"We need to be prepared for all possibilities," Mr. Kent argued.

"Right. Such as Miss Molly's girls being mad at you for stealing their trunk. Do you still need it?"

"Oh no. I guess I'll have to go back to the brothel again to return it. What a shame," Mr. Kent said unconvincingly. "Mr. Braddock, help me with this."

Sebastian glanced at Mr. Jarsdel and me with concern.

"I'll lock the door and be right behind you," I said. "Mr. Kent, ask Mr. Jarsdel if he plans on hurting me."

"Mr. Jarsdel, are you planning on hurting Miss Wyndham?"

Mr. Jarsdel shook his head. "No, of course not, she's helping protect Miss Rosamund."

"There you are," I said.

That seemed enough to satisfy Sebastian. He took up the other end of the trunk and headed down the stairs with Mr. Kent, behind Rose and Catherine. I wrapped a blanket around Mr. Jarsdel as I waited for all the footsteps to recede all the way down to the next floor. The room finally empty and silent, I whispered a final question to Mr. Jarsdel.

"If I told you I had a plan to get rid of Captain Goode tonight and keep my sister safe forever, would you help?"

Mr. Jarsdel looked at me as if there was only one obvious answer. "Of course."

"Good," I said. "Then be ready."

Chapter Twelve

———————

I STARED AT the ceiling, listening to the creaks and aches of the boarding house, waiting for everyone to fall asleep.

Rose did almost instantly. It was understandable—she had had a brave and exhausting day confronting her power and trying to understand it. I could just make out her form on the bed across the cramped room, her limbs neatly tucked into a little C shape. Her slow, deep breaths barely ruffled the hair splayed on her pillow.

Sebastian took a little longer. I traced patterns on the wall, feeling the sensation move lower and lower as our hands tired. I could picture him on the other side, his eyebrows scrunched down low, hooding his eyes that wouldn't shut. Nightmares were waiting for him, but I hoped there were dreams slipping in to remind him of the good he was doing, of the people who still cared for him.

As the buzzing finally left the wall, I removed my hand and shoved my thin sheet off, restless and anxious to finish this. It would be for the best. No one else's lives would be risked. Captain Goode would be less prepared in the middle of the night. The least amount of people could get hurt. All this really would take was one shot and one person to take it.

I slung a leg out of bed before I could lose my nerve. Rose's even breathing skipped and I froze. Slowly it found its rhythm again and I slid gracelessly out of the bed, landing louder than I would have liked. Rose did not even stir. She had always been a heavy sleeper. I padded across the floor and eased our cabinet open, pulling out my traveling coat, my veil, and my hat. I picked up my boots in one hand and continued to tiptoe to the door.

I gave her one more look. Even in the relative darkness I could see her forehead furrowed, her lips tight. I hoped when Rose and Sebastian woke up, all our problems would be solved. I hoped I'd see them smile again.

Slowly, I creaked up the flight of stairs to the second floor, pausing and listening intently to the odd snuffles and night noises coming from the bedrooms to be sure I was not marked. With the click of my key, the door opened on Mr. Jarsdel, sitting where I left him, his eyes blinking and adjusting to the dark room.

"Be very quiet," I whispered, unlatching the blade to my dagger fan. I started cutting the rope that confined him to the chair. "You will do anything to protect Miss Rosamund?"

"I will," he answered, nodding sluggishly, still sick from Sebastian's effects.

"Including killing Captain Goode?"

"Yes."

"Very well. If you're lying to me, I'll kill you."

The ropes loosened and he stood up slowly. No flashes of light. No mad dash to the door. I lowered my dagger from his neck and draped my traveling coat over his shoulders to cover the hands bound behind his back. I didn't trust him enough to remove those restraints yet.

I locked the bedroom door behind us and kept a hold on Mr. Jarsdel as he led us back downstairs, the faintest glow from his body telling us where to step in the darkness. Stair by stair, holding our breath, we made it to the ground floor. The front door was in sight, a few paces down the corridor. A sigh of relief escaped me.

And got caught in my throat. Mr. Jarsdel shut off his glow upon seeing a faint light coming from the parlor. Someone was still awake, and we had to cross the threshold.

Dammit.

I squeezed in front of Mr. Jarsdel and signed for him to wait there. I got to my hands and knees and crawled, trying to envision the layout of the parlor. One settee was right by the door, facing away from it, but the other was positioned perpendicular, so they would see something in the corner of their eye. Unless I was hidden by the first settee. When I reached the door I paused for a long moment. I lay down fully and began to inch myself across the floor, using my heels to propel me, while Mr. Jarsdel stared down at me.

I inched some more. Finally I was across and no one had spoken or called out. They were either facing the other way, engrossed in a book, or simply not looking down, as I had hoped. I got to my feet so slowly, it reminded me of the child's game where one pretended to be a living statue. I was about to wave Mr. Jarsdel over when Miss Chen spoke, stepping out not from the parlor but from the darkened dining room.

"You are very odd."

"Erm—oh, I didn't realize you were awake! I was . . . getting a glass of water," I fumbled, trying to keep her eyes on me.

"Hmm. And getting a glass required slithering along the floor?" Her American drawl was more pronounced at the late hour. I could just see her arms folded as she leaned against the wall in the dark.

"I was . . . inching."

"Oh, my mistake." I could feel more than see her raised eyebrows that accurately indicated she believed nothing I was saying.

"All right, if you must know, I was off to have a tryst." The lie burst from me in the hopes of embarrassing the both of us and cutting the conversation awkwardly short. Of course, it had the opposite effect on Miss Chen.

"With Mr. Jarsdel?" she asked, stepping out into the corridor. Already knowing he was there.

"How did you know—"

"His room is right above ours."

Damnation and double damn. "Did Catherine wake up?" I asked.

"Not yet," Miss Chen said vaguely.

It wasn't hard to decipher her meaning. She'd keep quiet if I had a good plan. Unfortunately, in all the time I'd known her, Miss Chen had considered every plan terrible. How could I make this one sound detailed and well thought out?

"Well, I—"

"I'm coming with you," she interrupted. "Let's go."

"You don't . . . want to hear my plan first?" I asked.

"You're going to blind Goode," she said. "Simple, smart. Just give me the gun this time."

"Oh, I . . . all right," I said, handing her the pistol.

"Thanks." Miss Chen tucked it away in a small space in her boot.

While I put on my boots, she disappeared into the kitchen and returned with a rag, which she used to blindfold Mr. Jarsdel as a precaution. I put the hat and veil on him to make the blindfold look less obvious, and when we were done, we guided what looked like a strangely shaped woman outside.

The night air was cool, soothing, and freeing after the long day in our stuffy rooms. The streets were slick and shiny from an evening rain. We walked briskly to find a busier road, but I didn't quite have the same fears of thieves and cutthroats leaping out of dark alleys as I used to. Not when I had an actual murderer on my arm to worry about. Within a few minutes, a hansom picked us up, the driver barely giving Mr. Jarsdel a second glance. I gave him the Lowndes Square address, squeezed into the tight space meant for two, and we were on our way.

"Do you know which house it is?" Miss Chen asked.

"Not exactly," I said. "But I know the square well enough. We'll be able to see everything from the garden in the center."

"And where are you planning to attack him?"

"It depends. Captain Goode's Constable ceremony was tonight. If he's not home yet, we'll have to wait for him to return and Mr. Jarsdel can catch him as he gets out of his carriage. If he is home, I think Mr. Jarsdel will have to meet with him in the drawing room. Either way, Mr. Jarsdel, can you think of a matter that would be too urgent to wait for the morning?"

"Information about you or Mr. Braddock," Mr. Jarsdel said.

"Perfect," I said. "And you wouldn't be lying."

"Yes, not lying is the most important part," Miss Chen quipped. "So once he's blinded, how long until his sight returns?"

"Two minutes to see outlines," Mr. Jarsdel said. "Five minutes to see fully."

"Ah, then here's the most important question," Miss Chen said. "Who gets to do the honors?"

"That also depends," I said. "I am fairly certain if Captain Goode has bodyguards, they will be in the room and be affected by Mr. Jarsdel, too. In which case, Mr. Jarsdel would have no trouble killing him. But if a bodyguard happens to close their eyes or look away for some reason, we need to be ready to assist. In which case, you do the honors."

Miss Chen scrutinized me as passing gaslight hit my face. "Maybe you should take the gun. I feel guilty about taking that from you."

I shook my head. "It'll be satisfying enough to have planned this. As long as you don't miss."

"I won't," Miss Chen said. "But you should at least kick him once or twice."

"Of course," I said. I cleared my throat. "And uh—thank you for coming. I know you wanted to leave London and get away from Captain Goode. And now we're heading straight to him."

"I like simple plans," she said with a shrug. "Less places where they can go wrong."

We spent the rest of the ride in silence. I watched the city go by, watched as we crossed the Thames and passed Victoria Station. My heart weighed a little heavier, my breath came a little faster as we passed my parents' home.

I knocked on the roof before we got too close. The hansom came to a stop a street east of Lowndes Square. Miss Chen paid the driver while I pulled Mr. Jarsdel out and led him to the sidewalk. As the cab trundled away, I removed my hat and veil from Mr. Jarsdel and untied his blindfold. The three of us continued onward through the dark, empty street.

We entered Lowndes Square at Number 50, where Miss Chen broke apart the gate to the communal garden in the center of the square. Using the bushes for cover, we crept down to 37 and watched it through the fence. It should have been an obvious blight on the neighborhood, looming over the street, horrifying the square with its dark inhabitants. Instead, it was tucked in among the neat little row of elegant houses that all shared a likeness with the ones in Belgrave Square. And Captain Goode's residence looked like a simpler version of my home.

I hated it.

We stared for a long moment at the white stucco. Wind began to ruffle the hem of my night rail and the hair at the nape of my neck.

"Shall we?" Miss Chen's voice cracked through the silence, as sure and capable as a well-swung whip. She did not look nervous, just determined.

"I suppose we should." I eyed the house, wondering if he was in there, sleeping peacefully. "Mr. Jarsdel, are you ready?"

"I am."

I removed his traveling coat and put it on myself. His body had completely healed during our trip. Miss Chen knelt down and eyed his hand restraints. One by one, his fingers were loosened and then his hands were apart, his flame power free and strong. I took a deep breath, trusting in Rose's power. Miss Chen stayed kneeling behind him, one hand by her boot. He stood up, nodded, and didn't burn us to death.

Miss Chen turned her attention to the fence in front of us, breaking apart a small hole for Mr. Jarsdel. As the metal cracked and fell to pieces, a loud clacking came from down the road. A carriage. It turned toward us and slowed to a stop in front of 37 Lowndes. A footman emerged from the shadows and opened the door for Captain Goode to step out. Dressed in uniform, he looked striking and far too proud of himself.

"Good timing," Miss Chen whispered.

Mr. Jarsdel left the garden and crossed the street as Captain Goode started to make his way to the front door. "Captain Goode," he called. "A moment! I have something urgent!"

As much as I wanted to watch, I shut my eyes and waited for the flash of light. I counted to five. To ten. Nothing came.

"Captain, what's happened?" Mr. Jarsdel shouted.

My eyes opened to find the street empty, save for Mr. Jarsdel. The carriage, the horses, the driver, the footman, and Captain Goode had all vanished.

"That . . . was an illusion," Miss Chen said in disbelief. "Dammit, this is a trap, we have to—"

She was interrupted by a loud rumble and a massive blast of water that struck us from behind. The force propelled us through the hole in the garden fence and onto the street. I coughed out the water and tried to climb to my feet, but there was a sizzle behind me and then a searing pain that sent my body into convulsions. Thrashing and crawling away did nothing except earn me more horrible shocks. The weight of the attacker pinned me down, and then they seized my neck, lifted me up, and spoke in a sweet voice.

"I wonder if I eat your skin, will it grow back?"

The girl from the prison. The cannibal. Her hair was bright white as if moonlight was hidden in her locks, and her hand around my throat seemed to buzz with energy. She toyed with me like the dead frog in an electric current experiment.

Mr. Jarsdel was on the ground, eyes open, unable to move, two more familiar faces standing over him. A gaunt, frail man, another one we'd questioned in the prison, the one who nonchalantly talked about the murders he'd enjoyed committing. And a bearded man with a whip of water encircling him. The former bodyguard. Captain Goode had released the whole blasted prison.

I looked to Miss Chen for help, but she had problems of her own. A tall blond man had her in his hold with a knife to her throat. "Fei, so lovely to see you again."

She elbowed him in the gut. "You too, Pratt."

He kicked her legs from behind, bringing her to her knees. "I say, no need for that, my dear. I can put in a good word for you."

The door to 37 Lowndes Square slammed, and Captain Goode marched to us with Miss Fahlstrom by his side.

"Miss Wyndham, I see you received my invitation," Captain Goode said, seizing my arm. His gaze was severe and stern, the welcoming, fatherly side of him gone. "Do you really think Mr. Jarsdel's knowledge of my address was a mistake?"

My rage rose along with my power. "What are you doing?"

He pulled his left arm out of his pocket to reveal a new hand growing back and taking shape. He'd been hiding it since the ball. "I wanted my hand back."

I felt a chill as my power was suddenly cut off when he was done. It was all a trap. He knew we'd go after Mr. Jarsdel and question him again. How stupid could I bloody—

"Ah!" a yelp came from behind me.

Miss Chen had her gun aimed at Mr. Pratt's head now. "You hurt her, you lose your illusionist."

"Fei, please, look at the future I had envisioned for us," Mr. Pratt pleaded.

An illusion of Miss Chen appeared in the middle of the street. She was wearing a lavish wedding gown and speaking her vows lovingly to Mr. Pratt.

"There's a gun to your head," Miss Chen said. "What part of that suggests I want to marry you?"

"There's no need for that," Captain Goode barked out. "I don't plan to kill any of you if I can help it."

"And you expect us to believe that?"

"It will make things simpler if you do. You're incredibly valuable. Everyone with a power is. I hadn't realized how rare we are until recently. There's only one of you."

"We're well aware of that," I replied.

"What I mean is that there is only one healer," Captain Goode said. "There's only one enhancer, one illusionist. As far as our records show, each power is gifted to only one person at any given time. There's never been two living people with the same power. If you die, I will have to wait fourteen years for your power to emerge in another healer."

I gaped at him. "You mean to say . . ."

"Your power will be reincarnated," he said with a nod. "I'd suspected that to be the case, but I could only confirm it when we had enough detailed records from our recent recruits. There, we found the date of death of the predecessor always matched the date of birth of the successor."

The only one. I was the only one. How had we not known that before? A flurry of emotions boiled over and I gritted my teeth as it overwhelmed me. How dare Captain Goode keep this from us and then attempt to collect us like rare prizes? How dare—ah. Yes. The realization smacked me across the face. This was about more than just powers.

"You're doing this for your brother," I said. "You're going to find Mr. Redburn's successor."

Captain Goode gave a stiff nod. "By then, all our powers will be gathered, and England will be keeping the world at peace."

"With your daily murders and blaming of others."

"I told you before, Miss Wyndham. You can't save everyone. You always have to make difficult choices. And when you do, people look for a villain. If you don't want it to be you, then you must give them one."

"All right, stop, I don't care anymore," Miss Chen said. "I don't even know why you're still talking."

"Because I want you to know that it is in my best interests to keep you and your friends alive," Captain Goode said. "And I needed to give Mr. Seward time to put water in your gun."

With a growl, Miss Chen aimed at Captain Goode and pulled the trigger, but the gun misfired. Mr. Pratt picked up his blade and slashed her as she tried to fight him for it. A heavy blast of water knocked her to the ground.

Taking advantage of the distraction, I reached for my dagger fan, tied to my wrist. But by the time I swung at Captain Goode, he was ready.

"Mr. Dunn, your assistance," he yelled, my hand again in his grip. He glared at me as the cannibal girl's grip tightened briefly around my throat. "The wonderful thing about your power is that I don't even need your cooperation or permission to use it. I can lock you in a box, raise the power, and send you to the sick and wounded without any fuss. You'll be much more useful."

The frail Mr. Dunn approached, removing his gloves. He set his papery hand on mine, and I lost all feeling in my arm. It fell limply to my side, paralyzed.

The wind was picking up now, swirling the group's clothes and hair till they looked almost comically evil. And then to complete the scene, thunder rumbled and lightning cracked through the sky. Striking the house right next to Captain Goode's. Repeatedly.

They all turned for a moment, distracted by the sudden attack, while I could hear Miss Chen fighting Mr. Pratt again. "Miss Wyndham! Watch—"

Her warning was drowned out by the winds from what looked like a tornado flying down the street, straight at us. I kicked and yelled and clawed at Captain Goode's hand, trying to pull out of his grip, out of the cannibalistic girl's hold on my neck, but it did nothing. The winds tore through our group without a care, hurtling us in every direction.

I hit the ground hard and rolled into a fence at the end of the square. As the world kept spinning, I clumsily lifted myself up, ignoring the aching in my head. My hands shook relentlessly, and I realized Captain Goode's glove was still in my fist. At least that was something. Winds and lightning continued to rip through the streets, shattering stone and flinging debris all over, before descending on the house next to Captain Goode's. It stood no chance, as a growing fire consumed it and the winds scattered its remains.

"God dammit—" Miss Chen's voice gasped behind me.

I tried to find her in the dark, but she was nowhere on the street. The sounds of her struggling led me into the garden, which suddenly looked wilder, untamed. She was trapped in a wall of green, struggling against vines that wound themselves around her ankles. Her power off, she let out a vicious curse and dug her fingers into the thick plant.

My left hand instinctively reached for my dagger, but I stopped. I knew this power. I had seen it at the Society of Aberrations last month, while Oliver was training. That boy would be somewhere here. Indeed, his head was peeking out of a shrub a few feet ahead of me, only a shock of brown hair and mournful eyes visible. He was too young for this. Just as Oliver was. I felt the fury rise higher in me.

I ran to him, watching Miss Chen, who had managed to rip off one plant but was now struggling with the errant vine that was wrapping around her neck instead. Still, the boy was so focused on her, he did not notice me until I was right behind him.

"George, please!" I whispered. "I know you; you're Oliver's friend."

Immediately, half his vines curled up defensively around him, the other half, sharp with thorns, aimed at me. "I'm sorry. I don't want to hurt anyone."

"You don't have to do this." I tried to be gentle even as I spoke the words as rapidly as possible. "Come with us."

He shook his head, eyes wet. "My friends . . ."

My heart broke a little. Dammit. "Just . . . just say we overwhelmed you. We'll come back for you. For all of you."

He gave the faintest nod as a shout came from the street.

"Find them!" Captain Goode shouted over the roaring winds.

I raced over to Miss Chen, her expression confused as the vines released her.

"Come on," I said and grabbed her with my working hand. She was bleeding from several wounds, but she still had the strength to walk, barely. I dragged her through the junglelike garden, creeping under trees and in the shadows until we reached the hole she'd made in the gate. As we crossed the street out of the square, I looked back to catch an elaborate lattice of thick and leafy vines covering our exit.

The loud destructive storm boomed and crackled behind us, our breathing and footsteps the only sounds echoing down the long street that I hoped would lead us somewhere safe. Instead, we turned at a corner onto a narrow mews and found ourselves facing Mr. Pratt. Or rather, one hundred Mr. Pratts filling the street.

I stopped and backed away, looking for another exit, but Miss Chen slipped out of my hold.

"I knew you missed me," the hundred Mr. Pratts said at once, each armed with a knife.

She kept limping toward him, refusing to back down. Her right hand curled into a fist, and she charged at the center one. But at the last moment, she veered to the left and struck Mr. Pratt across the face.

The illusions all vanished as he fell to the ground, his nose bleeding.

"The real one's not as handsome as he thinks he is," Miss Chen said as I caught up to her.

Mr. Pratt scrambled back to his feet, ready to fight the both of us. I didn't know whether the two of us, this wounded, could manage it. Fortunately, I didn't have to find out.

A heavy wind blew Mr. Pratt back, and a bolt of lightning struck the ground between us, propelling him into a wooden stable house door. Thunder rumbled, and he looked up over our heads in fear. The mews filled with twenty copies of him, and they all scattered and ran away as more lightning crashed down upon them.

Miss Chen and I climbed back up to our feet and turned to find a goddess floating down toward us.

Or at least that's how my dazed mind took in Radhika Rao, her bright skirts and shawl fluttering as she landed, fog growing and swirling around her.

"I . . . Miss Rao . . . how did you know we were here?" I managed to ask.

"I did not, healer," she said, hurrying past us into a clear path through her fog. "This way."

I slung Miss Chen's arm over my shoulder and found her expression matching my own as she stared openmouthed at the formidable woman. We hurried and stumbled after her, toward the busier Knightsbridge Road. As we passed under a gaslight, I could see Miss Rao looked tired, her arms and face covered in patches and bruises. Her right arm was wrapped in a makeshift sling.

"You're hurt," I said.

"I am aware," Miss Rao said. "That's why I saved you. Heal me."

"About that . . ." I said. "Captain Goode just took my power away."

Thunder rumbled as she stared at me. "Very well. I'll wait with you."

I felt relief fill me, knowing she wouldn't be leaving us here. Soon enough, a hansom pulled over to pick us up. Miss Rao and Miss Chen stayed in the shadows, hiding their injuries, while I gave the driver our address. The three of us squeezed into the cramped space and the carriage rattled forward. Fog filled the streets behind us to cover our escape.

"How did you get injured?" I asked.

"Which time?" she asked back.

"I . . . all of them?"

She pointed to a patch on her leg. "A man shot at me when I was destroying ships coming from the East." She pointed to some of the bruises and cuts peppering her skin. "These are from the guards at the India office." She pointed to her black eye. "Colonial office." She held up her arm in the sling. "Your Society sent children to catch me and one caught my arm."

I gaped at her, recalling Oliver's story from before the Belgrave Ball. When he and his friends had been sent after her. "You've had a . . . you did all of that . . . with a broken arm?"

"My other arm was well enough," she said, nodding to the one in my grasp.

"You were the one who killed Lord Bell at the Colonial office?" Miss Chen asked.

"I did," Miss Rao said.

"And tonight was . . . ?"

"The India Secretary," Miss Rao said.

I felt my stomach twist. "I thought you didn't kill people."

"Your Society changed my mind."

"But . . . that . . . isn't going to get Britain out of India," I said, reluctant to anger the most terrifying person I knew.

"What is it you were trying to do?" she asked.

"That's . . . different," I said. "Captain Goode killed my family and friends and a hundred others. And there's going to be more."

"You are right. That is different," Miss Rao said, thunder rumbling as she looked out the window. "Far more people are dying in my country. Your reasoning is nothing in comparison."

I shook my head. "No, that's not what—I just mean, if you kill the Secretary, they will find someone to replace him."

"Then I will kill him, too."

"And when does it end?"

"When everyone in this country is too scared to hold that position," Miss Rao said simply.

The carriage creaked to a stop down the street from our lodgings. We climbed out, and Miss Chen gave me the money to pay the driver. As I helped her up the stairs and searched for my key, I felt a lump in my throat, wondering how I was going to explain this to everyone. At least I had a couple of hours until they woke up. To them, it'd almost be like I never even le—

The door opened.

Catherine, Rose, and Mr. Kent were at the entrance, red-eyed and not at all happy to see me.

Chapter Thirteen

"Ow. Ow. Ow."

Rose's needle was apparently dipped in some kind of terrible fire-liquid. Every stitch stung, the pain clear and bright without any numbness or excitement from the fight left to stave it off.

"And this is what happens when you act recklessly," Catherine continued. She was pacing Rose's and my bedroom, what little length there was, her hair unbound and riotous, her tone as sharp as a schoolmarm's, even as she endeavored not to wake the rest of the house.

"Look at poor Miss Chen. Now she will have to wait for that leg to heal until your powers come back in three days' time. It will be extremely painful! Wounds like that could fester and—"

"Please discuss the pain and festering in another room," Miss Chen groaned from her place on Rose's bed. She and Miss Rao had already been administered to, as I was deemed both the least injured and the least deserving of nursing.

I closed my eyes, trying to summon the warmth and raise my power. Memories of my Society healing missions flashed through my head, reminding me of the confidence, the peacefulness, and the sheer invincibility I felt at the time. None of which I had now.

Shivers ran through me, as if a window had been left open inside my gut, a cold draught rushing in.

I opened my eyes to find Miss Chen sighing. "Any hint of your powers returning?" I asked.

"Nothing." Lines of tension feathered out from her mouth, held in a tight grimace. As she maneuvered to face me, her hands clenched the thin sheet, a wave of pain rolling over her body. "What about you?"

"I'm sorry," I said for possibly the thousandth time. I bit down as Rose continued stitching my cut closed, the black thread slowly laddering up through my raw, red skin.

"I simply don't understand what you were *thinking*!" Catherine was going to make a very good parent someday; she wielded the tone of disappointment perfectly, like a weapon.

"I was also there—" Miss Chen tried.

"I know an Evelyn plan when I see one," Rose muttered.

"I'm sorry," I said again, feeling faintly frustrated. Even though Captain Goode deliberately revealed his address, there was still a part of me that thought it a good plan. Was it a little . . . rash? Yes. I regretted my impetuousness, but I did not particularly enjoy this lecture, not when Captain Goode got lucky with the timing of our attack. I couldn't imagine his plan was to keep all those people waiting there for days to ambush us.

"We did learn something new about the powers, though. . . ." I said.

"Yes—the only healer in the world is astonishingly irresponsible and selfish," Catherine replied.

"And Mr. Adeoti will find something on Captain Goode's glove."

"Which was worth losing Mr. Jarsdel?" Catherine asked. "After all the hard work Rose and Mr. Kent did to persuade him to work with us?"

"I'm not one to call anyone selfish." Mr. Kent was lounging against the doorway, his arms crossed lazily in front of him. "But it was not your best idea."

That Mr. Kent should say such a thing stung almost as much as Rose's needle. I was tired and feeling irritated and probably a little feverish, so it shouldn't be any wonder that I snapped back at him.

"Really? This is coming from someone who finds every excuse to leave while the rest of us try to actually fix things?"

He pierced me with a long look and slowly slipped out of the room, his usually warm eyes dulled with a sadness that told me how beneath me the comment was.

That was unfair. Mr. Kent had been brave and gallant, staying with the group even after I had told him there would never be anything between us. He could have left London with his sister at any time. He had been anything *but* selfish.

My sister jerked the thread a little harder than was necessary and I winced. She did not even react.

"Very nice," Catherine said. Her hands were on her hips now, and she was eyeing me with almost contempt. Knowing that I deserved it did not make any of it better, and I wished they were all out of the room. I wanted to be alone.

"Can you just let me sleep? You can be as mad at me as you would like tomorrow," I said.

"We are all tired. Your sister hasn't slept one wink and here she is, stitching you up as neatly as any doctor could do." Catherine looked admiringly at the handiwork, then at my sister in full. Rose's cheeks pinked a little, and I remembered her confidences.

I closed my eyes, a cold swirl of guilt roaming my stomach, and all I wanted to do was sleep, forget everything that had happened for a few dreamless hours.

"Done." With one last pinch, Rose snipped the thread, and I felt the bed move as she shifted back. "I can't do much for your paralyzed arm."

"That's all right; it'll come back. Thank you." I did not open my eyes. "Please get some rest."

I heard a little scoff from Catherine, then a long sigh.

"Fine. But you should at least apologize to Mr. Braddock." Catherine had softened a little when I caught her eyes.

"Why?"

"He has taken himself off to the attic. He doesn't want to be near anyone without you to cancel his powers out."

Rose dropped her tools into a borrowed medical kit from Tuffins and gave my hand a squeeze.

"Rest," Rose said kindly. Then, with one more baleful glare in my direction from Catherine, the two of them left, and the door softly clicked shut.

I could feel Miss Chen's eyes on me.

"Blast, blast, blast." I kicked the covers off, jamming my feet into slippers.

I hadn't thought about how this would affect Sebastian.

"He's fine. He will just have to stay apart for a bit—" Miss Chen began. She tried to raise herself up a bit but winced.

"You don't know him," I muttered, wrapping a robe around me and letting the flash of pain as it brushed my stitches act as a useful reminder: I had been careless and selfish. "He is going to find some way to blame this all on himself."

"Well, I still don't see how it's all your fault, but it's certainly not his."

"No," I agreed, "not his at all."

"I am sure he is sleeping," Miss Chen tried again.

"He is not sleeping. He is brooding," I corrected her and left the room, padding up to the attic.

My stomach sank as I thought about his fragile progress, the progress I took from him. He was only beginning to come back to us, to find some purpose and endure his power. And by losing my power, I'd isolated him from everyone else again.

Not to mention the rather daunting information I now had. That no one else in the world shared his power.

The attic room was not hard to find. I just continued up until I could go no farther, and at the top of a narrow set of stairs was a small door.

When I gently pushed it open, my breath actually caught.

Illuminated by a circle of warmth from an oil lamp, Sebastian lay on a thin camp bed, his shirt slightly parted, his legs crossed at the ankles as he read a book, licking a finger as he flipped a page. From across the room, I could make out a slight stubble and a smudge of dark lashes.

He somehow managed to look terribly romantic, terribly tragic, and yet ready to leap into danger at any moment.

"Do you put effort into looking like that?" I called.

He looked up, fumbling as he almost dropped his book. Very correctly he came to his feet, only he misjudged the height of the ceiling and hit it with a solid smack.

He held the top of his head, wincing, and I hurried toward him before I could think.

Just before I reached out to touch him, his eyes flew open, panic swirling inside, and he stumbled back. "No!"

I stopped, feeling the faintly thicker air. So this was his power.

"Get back! Get back!" Sebastian was huddled as far from me as he could get, though he was eyeing the window in a way that had me thinking he would jump out if necessary. I fell back till ten feet of space lay between us.

"It's all right; it's all right," I said, hoping my composure would help his. "I am perfectly well."

"Stay there," he commanded, his hand shaking as he clutched at his shirt. "For God's sake, Evelyn—"

"I am fine!"

"You could have been killed."

"Do not be so theatrical. I would have needed to stand there for twelve hours, and boredom would have taken me first."

He groaned and half started a new sentence a few times before finally sighing. "Just . . . stay there."

"I'm not moving."

"I know, I just . . ."

"Sebastian. Get back to your bed. I won't move. I promise." I finally took pity on him.

Slowly, he inched back to the bed, and I gingerly sat on the dusty floor. A lash of pain flew up my injured arm as I tried to rearrange myself with one hand. I must not have concealed the pain well, for Sebastian was staring at me, frowning.

"How badly injured are you?"

"Nothing Rose couldn't take care of."

He slumped back. "He could have killed you."

"Actually, he only would have captured me and kept me in a cage for the rest of my life. He told me so himself." I tried to smile, but it seemed like too much effort right now.

We sat in silence for a while.

"I am sorry." I blurted the words out without really knowing I was going to apologize. But I was sorry that my actions had landed Sebastian in this room and sorrier still that he would undoubtedly find a way to make this all his fault.

"At this point, I am not even surprised you acted as you did."

"Oh. Is that . . . better?"

"No."

I scrutinized him thoroughly, looking for a hint that he was taking this on himself, but he seemed nothing more than irritated. "You are not going to do that thing you do, then?"

"What thing?

"The thing where you make everything all your fault?"

He snorted and raised one eyebrow, looking as imperious and arrogant as I had suspected him to be when we first met. "I have killed a lot of people, Evelyn—or at least my power has, but I cannot claim responsibility for when you act stubbornly. That is as certain as the sun rising in the morning."

I could feel myself gaping but was unable to stop it. "That is . . . I am . . ."

He crossed his arms, making his shirt part again at the neck so I could make out a little golden skin beneath.

"Sorry," I finally pronounced.

"No, you aren't. If you were, you wouldn't keep doing this. You wouldn't keep acting like some sort of . . . of . . . Byronic hero."

I did not hear him clearly. "Excuse me?"

"Your behavior, it's everything you've ever accused me of. Your short temper, your cynicism, your brooding, your violent obsession—"

I glared at him. "You're joking."

"And most of all, this solitary revenge path. This foolish, self-destructive need to do everything on your own."

I stood up, done with everyone in this house. "Fine. I acted rashly and made a mistake. I admit it. But please never call me—"

"It's not just now!" He jumped off the bed, coming slightly closer. "You almost got yourself killed by Dr. Beck, you almost got yourself killed by the Society, and you've done it twice with Captain Goode. There's a pattern. I have been thinking it for ages but didn't want to say it, but it is here, and it is assuredly Byronic."

I stepped forward as well, so we were as close as we could be without his powers affecting me. "You, of all people, have some nerve saying that. I rescind my apology."

"I did not accept it anyway, as it was false."

"Fine," I growled. "Even though you are as wrong as . . . as . . . as something very wrong, I can't change how you see me or how I am, for that matter. I won't suddenly be a paragon of virtue or whatever it is you think I should be. I'm not ever going to be like . . . like . . ." *Mae*, some dark part of me wanted to scream.

Sebastian looked up so sharply I thought maybe I had said it out loud. But his jaw tightened and he pressed on. "I don't want you to change. I . . . I just need you to talk to me."

"I've done nothing these past weeks but try to get you to talk."

"And you haven't been telling me everything. You have to tell me when there's bad news."

"There is bad news all the time! It would be easier to tell you when there is *not* bad news!"

"And when you're feeling frustrated."

"Also, all the time!"

"And for God's sake, stop trying to nobly protect my feelings by keeping things from me!"

"Fine!" I broke. "Captain Goode is smarter than us! And his power is stronger than our useless training! And we're the only ones with our respective powers! There's no one else! Happy?"

We stared at each other, both of us breathing heavily, a tension different from our powers snaking across the room, ensnaring us both.

"What do you mean . . . only ones?" He was white-lipped, tense, and edgy as a rabbit surrounded by wolves.

"Captain Goode told me there is only one person with each power at a time. That when we die, our power is passed along to someone else to be born with it. So I am the only living person who can heal, and you—you are . . ."

"The only person whose touch kills," he finished. "Could he have been lying?"

"Mr. Adeoti confirmed it with a glove we got from him."

"I see," he said numbly, taking a few steps back to sit down hard on his bed. The protesting creaks were the only sounds between us for some long seconds. Our argument had blown through the room, leaving us awkward and vulnerable.

"Tell me what you're feeling," I said.

Sebastian stared out at nothing, as inscrutable as a curtained window.

"This talking rule works the other way, too," I said. "I can get Mr. Kent to help."

That got his attention. "It feels . . . lonelier." He frowned. "I'm glad to know there aren't others out there with this power. I am. But I . . . there's a part of me that hoped maybe someone had learned how to fully control it. Or there were enhancers other than Captain Goode, who would take it away."

"Right." That same weight sank deep in my gut—for Sebastian and myself. The sudden loss of people who I had assumed would be out there, somewhere. I had friends with powers, sure, but I had felt a special comfort reading about the healers in the Society of Aberrations library, thinking I might one day see if others shared my particular experiences. The strange freedom and recklessness our bodies gave us. The constant urge to fix things. The worry that I'd outlive everyone I knew. But it was only me now. One person.

"Your turn," Sebastian said.

"Pressured," I said slowly. This was the conversational equivalent of edging out onto a tight rope, uncertain if it would hold my weight or send me crashing to my death. But Sebastian had been brave enough to try. I could, too. "If I'm the only one in the world with this power, then doesn't it make me responsible for every person's health? Even though I can barely keep myself alive. I don't know how I'm expected to keep the entire world alive at once."

"I don't believe that's expected of you," Sebastian said.

"How can you know that?" I asked. "Dr. Beck treated the powers like a new scientific breakthrough, mainly to justify his experiments. Captain Goode makes them sound like some destiny in service of the Empire to justify the Society of Aberrations. All I can see is that no one has any idea what the point of these powers is and they are simply making something up."

"Right," Sebastian said, his brow furrowed. "Then I will simply say that *I* don't expect you to heal the world."

"What do you expect?" A strange sense of comfort filled me as I realized I would trust his judgment over any grand explanation.

"The same of anyone with power," he said. "To do what they can to protect the ones without it. It doesn't matter how many, as long as you keep doing it."

"Says the man counting the lives he needs to save."

"You've made me lose count."

Something loosened in my own body, some tenseness I hadn't known I was holding in until it began to melt away. "Then you don't think we have roles to fill?"

He turned to me then, his jaw set, his eyes snapping. "If we were making assumptions like that, then I would be responsible for killing the entire world."

A scoff escaped my mouth at that thought. "And we would have to be mortal enemies instead of . . ."

I trailed off, cursing myself for adding those two words to the end. Not quite friends. Not quite . . . whatever it was that was more than friends but also not. Possible-beyond-friends-if-it-weren't-for-the-Mae-shaped-guilt-in-our-hearts. That didn't quite roll off the tongue.

"Halves," Sebastian finished for me.

"Yes, that is the word." I slid forward to the edge of his range, ten feet from his bed.

His eyes flickered away and of course he blushed, because he was Sebastian and he always blushed.

The attic was silent around us, but I could hear my blood responding, burning my ears, rushing to my cheeks, prickling in my palms. Sebastian ducked his head, his eyes closed, his hands clasped, elbows loosely planted on his knees. He was back to training his power.

"Miss Chen couldn't raise hers back up," I told him. "It's no use against Captain Goode."

"It will be useful after him," Sebastian said.

We sat in the musty attic until long after the sun rose, streaming in through the slanted window, slowly inching closer and closer to each other.

And I felt no pain.

Chapter Fourteen

"Underneath that ridiculous description is yet another drawing of what one assumes is Mr. Braddock, but it really does not do him justice." Mr. Kent tossed a fourth newspaper in the fire. "So, to sum up, Mr. Braddock killed the India Secretary, attempted Captain Goode's assassination, and has committed two other murders in three days."

"*I* killed the India Secretary," Miss Rao grumbled next to me.

"You may need to leave a note next time," I said, squeezing the arm I was already holding.

I was squished between her and Miss Chen on the parlor couch so I could heal them with my very slowly returning powers.

The rest of our group was spread around the room; Mr. Adeoti pored over Captain Goode's glove and recorded every detail at the writing desk; Rose and Catherine reviewed his notes and the newspapers near the window; Mr. Kent paced in front of the fireplace while Emily and Laura practiced their needlepoint, telekinetically and manually. Sebastian had finally deemed it safe enough to leave the attic as long as he stayed far away from the rest of us, which landed him in a very feminine, frilly armchair in the farthest corner of the room, where he peered at one of Mrs. Tuffins's novels with skepticism.

"*We must be taking much more drastic actions now,*" Catherine quoted Captain Goode from one of the few papers Mr. Kent had not managed to burn. "*The longer Sebastian Braddock and his accomplices are free, the more and more people are going to die.*" She balled up the paper, and it followed its friends into the fire.

"More scaring the populace," I said feebly.

Catherine shook her head. "I think he's threatening us. He's going to keep killing more and more. Unless we turn ourselves in."

The words settled thickly over the room, souring the air.

Suddenly, glass shattered.

My heart leaped as I turned to Miss Chen, hoping she had regained control of her power.

But she only groaned. "Sorry," she announced. "I just threw a glass figurine at the wall. Everything is still miserable. Carry on."

I felt my jaw tighten and wished that it was rage that fueled our powers, because I had an endless supply after almost three days of waiting. No matter how much we tried, Miss Chen's training techniques did nothing to speed up the process. Captain Goode's effects couldn't be reversed.

"Dammit, we need to do something," I said.

"Even when you two get your powers fully back," Mr. Kent said, "I wouldn't think it's a good idea to investigate like we were before. It will almost certainly lead us into another trap of Captain Goode's. He knows how we'd investigate and track another murder."

"So what do you suggest?" I asked. "We run?"

"Of course," Mr. Kent said. "That's what I'm always suggesting. Running away is my favorite solution. I like it even more than hiding, believe it or not."

"And do you think he's going to get bored without us here and stop?" I asked.

"Maybe we need to fake our deaths," Mr. Kent muttered. He turned to Miss Chen. "Perhaps that illusionist friend of yours can stage our dramatic fall from a cliff."

"He's her illusionist suitor," I corrected.

"Regardless of what he is," Miss Chen said, "I'd rather push him off the cliff first."

"Fine, then we'll have to die in a horrific fire that renders us near unrecognizable," Mr. Kent declared. "Captain Goode is killing these people because he knows it's bothering us. But if we simply act like we don't care, he won't have any other recourse."

"We do care," Sebastian said from his chair.

"And it doesn't matter if we don't care. He cares," I put in. "You saw how much he believed in the Society when he first recruited us. He believes in it even more now that he's in charge. It's not just us he's concerned with. It's anyone whom he sees as a threat."

"Besides, he doesn't want us dead. He wants us captured," Miss Chen joined in. "And I know none of you are thrilled with Miss Wyndham and me at the moment, but I still think we could cause some damage."

"What do you mean?" Mr. Kent asked.

She looked steadily ahead. "We destroy everything of Captain Goode's. We keep reminding him we're here. Every building he comes from, we destroy the moment he leaves. The Tower of London. The Society of Aberrations. His homes. His carriages even. We can do it from a distance without ever being depowered again."

"It's a good idea, but that's only going to escalate things," I said. "He's going to kill more people and we're going to destroy more buildings . . . until?"

"I don't see an end to it, either," Sebastian said.

Miss Chen sighed and picked up another little figurine from the table, eyeing the window. I took the little fox from her, turning it over and over, the ceramic cool beneath my hands.

"I think we need to fight him a different way," Catherine finally declared. "There's a good reason Captain Goode went public with the powers and the Society of Aberrations. He knew he'd have more power with the public's support. But if we can turn the public against him, he'd be more vulnerable."

"Yes, that worked splendidly when these three visited that newspaper," Miss Chen countered.

"But the public loves a good story, especially a true one," Catherine said. "What if we found a way to publish it elsewhere? Or distribute it in pamphlets?"

"We could drop them out of a balloon over the city," Mr. Kent said, an eager glint in his eyes.

"It doesn't matter as long as the illusionist keeps framing Sebastian as the villain," I said.

"And none of this is going to stop Captain Goode from hurting people," Sebastian said. "That should be our main priority."

"Of course," Mr. Kent said. "But we are definitely not doing your idea."

Sebastian frowned and crossed his arms. "I haven't said my idea."

"I barely know you, but I'm sure you want to turn yourself in to Captain Goode," Miss Chen said.

"And we all think that's a brave, noble, terrible idea," Mr. Kent added.

Sebastian looked between them, at a loss for words.

"Was that your idea?" I asked.

"Yes. . . ." he mumbled.

"Someone else must have an idea," Mr. Kent said to the room.

"Miss Rosamund, you wanted to leave before. Perhaps you still wish to. . . ."

"I don't know," she said. "What do you think has happened to Mr. Jarsdel?"

"He's probably in Captain Goode's prison," I said. "And if he's still under your spell, I doubt he'll be released anytime soon. Not that he knows how to find us. Miss Chen had him blindfolded."

Rose looked a bit relieved at that. Until my next words.

"We could try it again," I said. "We have Mr. Adeoti's list of powers. If we find the most effective ones, track those people, and sway them to our side . . ."

Catherine didn't leap to Rose's defense again, but from my angle, I could see her hand take Rose's under the table.

"I don't want to start another Society of Aberrations," Rose said, moving her hand to pour herself a cup of tea. A flash of hurt crossed Catherine's eyes. She rose to her feet to take a turn about the room. There was . . . something, at least, between them. I hoped it was more than Rose's power.

"We'll capture a couple of people," I said. "Murderers that we will only use to stop Captain Goode. He is forcing children to fight for him. Kids Oliver's age, who are scared out of their wits."

"Then why not help the children?" Rose asked.

"Because Captain Goode will figure out what we're doing after the first one or two," I said. "We'd need to get the most effective powers on our side."

"Mr. Adeoti, what's this?" Catherine asked, peeking over his shoulder. She shook him harder, breaking him out of his trance, and pointed to his notes. "Mr. Adeoti."

He glanced at her finger and his eyes widened. "Oh, it's . . . it's nothing."

She looked at it closer. "Miss Fahlstrom's power doesn't sound like nothing."

"It's just that I'm not finished," Mr. Adeoti said. "I'm only halfway through the last week on the glove. I was hoping to find a solution first. I didn't want to start another argument after you've all welcomed me here—"

Their conversation had caught the attention of the rest of the room.

"An argument over what?" Catherine asked.

His glance darted to me for a moment, and I didn't like where this was going.

"What is it? I thought her power was electricity." But as I said it, I knew that was wrong. The cannibalistic girl had used that power and there couldn't be two.

"That may have been an illusion," Mr. Adeoti said.

"*Miss Fahlstrom's power is the ability to foresee a powered person's death*," Catherine read. "How is that possible?"

"I don't know. It's a power I haven't seen before," Mr. Adeoti said. "It seems all she has to do is look at someone, and she'll have a vivid vision of their death. That's what she did for Captain Goode the days before Miss Wyndham's attack."

The pieces started to shift into place. "What did she see in her vision of Captain Goode?"

"She saw Mr. Jarsdel blinding him on the street, Miss Chen shooting him, and you stabbing him in the heart."

The room sat silent, everyone's gazes shifting to me. Even Soot seemed aware of the revelation.

So that was how he knew the exact location, the exact time, and the exact plan of our attack. He wasn't that clever or cautious or even lucky. He cheated.

"Then what you're saying is . . ." I said, trying to wrap my head around the phrasing. "My plan failed because it would have succeeded wildly."

Mr. Adeoti nodded. "In a sense, yes."

"I knew it was a good plan," Miss Chen said.

"No, it wasn't," Catherine insisted. "Your plan failed because you didn't take Miss Fahlstrom's power into account. And come to think of it, you're lucky Mr. Braddock diverted your shot at the Queen's address. Otherwise, Captain Goode would have been prepared for you there, too."

Sebastian gave me a sheepish look at that.

"But now we know," I said, excitement pushing aside the guilt. "Mr. Adeoti, what does Miss Fahlstrom see after a death is averted?"

Mr. Adeoti flipped through his notes. "Once Goode seems to be on a path where he's no longer in danger, she warns him of his next death."

"That sounds like a fun way to live," Mr. Kent put in.

"And she knows of nothing in between?" I asked.

"No, that's all," Mr. Adeoti said.

"So if our intentions are solely to capture him," I said, "our plan won't be predicted."

"Theoretically, yes," Mr. Adeoti said. "Assuming there were no accidents."

"We'd have to find the right trap," Catherine said, pacing by the writing desk.

"I will see if I can make a list of places he regularly visits," Mr. Adeoti said.

It felt like floodgates had been opened in my mind, ideas pouring in faster than I could manage them. There was a new energy crackling through the room. We could finally get Captain Goode.

"We can do it safely, carefully," I said. "If we keep our distance with Emily, Miss Chen, and Miss Rao—"

"No." Miss Rao smoothly stood up from the couch and removed the sling around her arm, her injuries finally healed.

"I—Miss Rao, is something wrong?" I asked. She did not turn as she headed to the door. "If you were to help us, we might both get what we wish."

"No." Miss Rao's voice cut like a knife. "Not with you."

"What do you mean?" Mr. Kent asked, which was good, as I was feeling extremely offended and might have been ruder.

"The healer only cares about what affects her." She turned to me. "You don't care about what happens to anyone else."

"I'm trying to help everyone."

"No, you're using that as an excuse when all you still want is to kill the power remover. You align your goals with others and pretend to be fighting for everyone, for change, but when the time comes to make a decision, you will choose what you want. You will choose your revenge."

"I want to stop him without killing if we must. We all have the same goal."

"No, we don't. Because you don't care about the people under his power. You don't care about preventing another Society, preventing your country from repeating the same evils. Everything has to change or nothing will. It doesn't matter what you're saying now about capturing him alive for the sake of the plan. It's entirely about what you'd do in that moment he's at your mercy. And you've already proven what you care about. Your friends should not trust you to resist killing him. They cannot trust any plan you are involved in to remain a secret to him. If you truly want to help, you would leave, too." And with that damning, truthful statement, she slid out the door.

The room sat in shocked silence except for a lone voice of protest in the corner. I turned, the world a little off-kilter, my thoughts moving too quickly, or was it too slowly?

It was true.

She was right.

"No!" Laura yelled. "You can't leave, Evelyn. We have an idea, too." Emily floated the both of them across the room.

Mr. Kent looked at his sister with indulgence. "What is it, Kit?"

"You find a person with the power to bring back people from the dead. This way Captain Goode will have his brother back, we'll have Miss Grey and Oliver and Mama and Papa, and there will be no need to keep fighting over all of this." She looked at Mr. Adeoti. "If someone can see deaths, someone has to have the power to bring them back. It must exist."

"The plant boy can grow a magical fruit," Emily suggested.

Mr. Adeoti looked at them with pity and then to Catherine for help.

She didn't have any to offer. "We haven't found anything like that."

"Then maybe it's part of Evelyn's powers," Laura said, grasping for anything. "If her powers got raised *all* the way—"

"I tried, Laura," I said. "I'm sorry. It wasn't enough. I . . . I think Miss Rao's right."

I *knew* she was right.

"No, that doesn't mean that you have to leave," she pleaded.

"Everyone should stop leaving!" Emily added.

"But I can't be involved," I said. "I can't trust myself to make the hard decision when it's in front of me. I was selfish at the Belgrave Ball. I chose Rose over everyone else."

Rose was shaking her head. "Evelyn, no, you didn't."

"What do you mean?" Miss Chen asked.

"When Captain Goode entered the ball, he had already hurt Rose. And after he raised all of your powers and you were shot out of the room, he gave me a choice. He turned up Sebastian's power and said if I let go of Rose, let her die first, he'd let everyone else live. But I couldn't. Even . . . even when Rose was begging me to, I still refused to give her up. And I let everyone else in the room die for it."

"Because of my power!" Rose argued to the rest of the group.

"Your power was off," I said. "He turned it off the moment he found you."

"And the effects lingered," she said.

"And I made the same choice I would have made anyway," I said. "In that moment, I didn't think about anyone else in that room. I didn't think about protecting you, Rose. Mr. Kent, ask me what I was thinking about."

He bit his lip. "Are you certain?"

"Yes."

He took a breath. "What did you think about when Captain Goode gave you that choice?"

"I thought about myself and how I couldn't lose Rose again," I said. "I made that awful choice for myself, and it got everyone killed. And I'm not going to do that again."

There it was: the truth. No one could deny it. I marched away from the circle of stunned silence and out of the house. I felt nauseated even thinking about Sebastian and how he must have looked at me, knowing what I'd done to Mae. I couldn't bear it. I never wanted to face that again. And for better or for worse, I could finally say that I truly understood what was going on in Sebastian Braddock's mind all those times he ran away.

Chapter Fifteen

I WALKED.

I walked far, weaving through alleys, crossing thoroughfares, not really certain of my destination.

I needed to think.

I needed time away from everyone who knew the decision I had made at the ball.

Unfortunately, I could not run away from myself.

Miss Rao's words swarmed inside my head, the truth in them stinging me over and over. She was right. It didn't matter what I said I would do. If you asked me in advance, I'd always pick the noble decision, the right one you're supposed to make. But the Belgrave Ball was proof that I'd be selfish when it came time to actually make the decision. And if there was even the slightest chance I'd do the same thing when it came to Captain Goode, then I was putting everyone at risk.

Even this damn walk was selfish. My friends would be worried about me. I took to touching street poles as I passed, so Mr. Adeoti might be able to track my wanderings. I tried to convey that I wanted to be alone, to come find me only if there was a real need.

It was growing darker. The sounds of laughter brought me down a narrow street, where a young man in a striking red suit drew eager crowds into a penny theater shop. He tempted them with exhibitions centered around these horrifying and extraordinary powers: photographs of curiosities from all over the world, waxwork statues of every known powered person, "authentic" items from the Belgrave Ball, including pieces of the ballroom and Sebastian's bloody gloves.

There was even a long line forming for a play premiering in an hour, recounting Captain Goode's heroic defense of the Queen against the dastardly Sebastian Braddock and his gang of villains. Of course, a poster listed all the powers to make special appearances, including the harlot healer.

I turned away and sighed. How had it come to this? I was the only living healer, the one meant to save lives against all odds, not put them in danger. It was absolutely ridiculous that I'd had these powers for four months and I'd saved, at best, ten lives—half of which I'd lost at the ball. Heavens, I didn't deserve these powers. I was fairly certain if I asked Mr. Adeoti about other healers in the past, he'd probably say they saved more lives in a single day.

Soon I hit the Thames. Through the smog and fog I could see the dark reds and purples of the sunset melting into the night. I wound through streets aimlessly, hoping I might be able to lose myself down a cobblestoned alley.

But as I turned down an empty one, I felt my body freeze midstep. I couldn't go forward; I couldn't turn around; my limbs couldn't even flail in panic. I floated upward, my eyes searching for who or what was doing this to me. Had Captain Goode found me?

"Evelyn! We found you!" a voice very unlike Captain Goode's said.

As I was set down on a roof, my body was finally adjusted so I could see my captors. Laura and Emily were both frowning and ready to argue.

"How did you find me? You two shouldn't be out here," I said, struggling as Emily held me in place.

"We followed you! From the rooftops!" Laura grinned, clearly enjoying her adventure. "And we're not going back until you are."

I stared at their stubborn gazes. "Even after what I said? It's my fault your parents are gone."

"No, it's not," Laura said. "It's Captain Goode's."

"But I should have—could have saved them. I have this amazing power, and it's still not helping anyone."

"So help them," Laura said rather bluntly, pointing to the building behind me across the street.

It was long and massive. Its tall gate seemed to stretch down the road forever, disappearing into the fog. St. Thomas' Hospital. Rose had told me about this over the years, saving every little mention from our father's newspapers. It was still being built, and it was already ten times larger than the hospital Miss Grey and I had visited to find Oliver.

I stared for a long while. Months before, I'd thought about walking into a hospital and healing everyone, though Captain Goode had discouraged me from doing it, on the grounds that it would draw too much attention to the Society. The entire city would be talking about the miracle.

Which made it such a simple, perfect idea now. They already knew about miracles.

"That is a . . . brilliant notion," I said. "Emily, will you bring me back down?"

"Only if you let us come with you," she said.

"You should go home, both of you."

"It's not a home if everyone leaves," Emily said stubbornly. There was a note in her voice of deep sadness, and I looked at her more fully. Emily was constantly trying to keep us together, keep everyone safe and happy. So unlike her own family that had abandoned her to a wretched asylum.

"We will stay up here all night." Laura sat down to demonstrate, reaching into her overly large coat and pulling out a handkerchief-wrapped bundle that turned out to be a muffin.

I sighed, wished for a muffin as well, then decided it would not hurt to take them into a hospital.

"If you promise to be very quiet," I began.

"Evelyn! When have I ever let you down?" Laura's tiny hands were on her hips and her eyes were blazing, and I loved her irrepressible heart so much in that moment.

"Never," I conceded and pulled her in for a hug.

Emily floated us down gently into a dark, empty alley below. We crossed the street toward the hospital, and I touched a gaslight to let Mr. Adeoti and Mr. Kent know that we were all safe if they were to track us this far.

After my thoughts were imprinted on the cool metal, Emily proceeded to toss us one by one over the iron gate into the foggy courtyard. We crept quietly, staying in the shadows until we reached a ground-floor window to one of the hospital wards. It took Emily a moment to peer inside and unlatch the window, which brought us into a dim room full of twenty sleeping patients.

"Emily, can you keep watch by the door?" I whispered. "Warn us quietly if a nurse or an orderly is coming."

"I can put them all on a roof," she offered.

Not ideal. "I don't want to alarm them. We're doing this so the newspapers won't keep treating us like the villains. We need to hide."

"Fine," Emily said, looking a bit disappointed.

"And Laura, remember, we have to—"

"Hello," Laura cheerily greeted a pale patient.

"Stay quiet," I finished for no one in particular.

"Water," the patient rasped. He was an older man—thin, graying hair, a thick beard. I crept over to them while Laura poured a glass of water and gave it to the man. He sipped it slowly as I glanced at his chart, wondering what ailed him.

"Thank you, nurse," he told Laura.

"Oh, we aren't nurses," Laura proudly declared. "We are here to cure you."

The man coughed and hacked loudly at that, answering my question about his condition. Consumption.

When he finally finished coughing, he took a deep breath and fell back onto his pillow. "You'll cure that?" he asked skeptically.

"Of course. Evelyn can cure anything. She has one of those powers you might have heard of . . ."

As Laura regaled the patient with everything there was to know about the powers, and some things that were embellished, I took a seat between his bed and the patient to his left, took a breath, and took both their arms.

I held on for a few minutes. The man had a coughing fit in the first minute, and once I was certain that would be his last, I let go. "There, all cured," I said.

The man chuckled, like we were silly little children. "You two are funnier than the other nurses."

"Thank you," I said, not particularly wanting to correct him. Not with so many others to heal. He'd figure it out on his own sooner or later. Or at least a doctor would.

I proceeded to the next two beds along the line and took the hands of both sleeping patients, while Laura struck up a conversation with another one nearby.

"I should like to get a puppy." Somehow, Laura's whisper was still carried halfway across the room. "I would let him do whatever he wanted. No rules. He would be the happiest pup in the whole—"

A loud bell interrupted Laura and rang through the hospital nine times. Perhaps that was time for the nurses' rounds.

Sure enough, after about ten minutes, I felt myself lifted a couple of inches off the ground and shaken silently as Emily's warning.

"Out the window," I whispered.

As Laura and I climbed out, Emily held the door to the ward closed tightly against the nurse's best efforts. The moment we were out of sight, Emily let go, and the nurse burst in, out of breath and perplexed about her strength and the door's.

With the nurse checking the patients in that ward, we crept over to the next one free of nurses.

"I like this," Laura whispered louder than most people shouted.

And despite the fact that we were creeping through bushes in the middle of the night like criminals, I had to agree. "Me too."

We should have done it sooner. There was something simple and uncomplicated about it all. No worries about whether I could trust someone. No doubt about whether I was doing the right thing. Just helping people through a painful night so they could return to their lives in the morning.

We slipped into the next ward, a children's one, which only seemed to be half-filled. I checked one boy's chart to make sure a nurse had already been in here, and then I proceeded to take his hand, along with the swollen hand of the boy on the other side of me, and started healing.

Laura made several turns about the room, looking for those in the most pain and unable to sleep, keeping them company until I could move on to them.

We improved the routine smoothly over the course of the night as we realized how many patients the hospital held. Eventually, Emily started floating beds closer to me, while Laura would maneuver the patients' hands so I could make physical contact with four or five people at once and heal a ward within thirty minutes. We slowly worked our way through, slipping out the windows when the clocks rang out and the nurses did their rounds and circling back when they were done. We tried to find the most severe wards first—the ones with terminally ill or contagious patients. Then we floated up to the first and second floors, finding the wards with patients recovering from surgery and non-life-threatening ailments.

A silent trance soon settled between the three of us as we worked through the small hours. Both Emily and Laura looked exhausted by the time the clock struck four, but they were harder, more determined workers than I ever expected, continuing without complaint.

As dawn broke, we started to hear fragments of hushed commotion in the hospital corridors. Patients were waking up perfectly healed and attempting to leave the hospital despite the protests of the bewildered nurses. Soon, the number of healed patients outnumbered the staff, and they were demanding the hospital send for their families. This helped keep the nurses distracted as we moved down to the last and busiest ward: the emergency ward.

There was no avoiding the nurses in here, which is why we saved it for last. But there were only a few of them, all busy helping a doctor perform surgery on a patient in the corner. No one noticed us enter, so we simply proceeded to close the curtains around patients and heal two at a time without causing a scene with floating bodies.

It worked surprisingly well as we made our way around the room without being caught. I started to feel a giddiness and excitement until we reached a bed with a young, incredibly skinny boy with a broken leg. I couldn't help but feel transported back to a few months ago when we found Oliver. My stomach turned as I took his hand, wondering if I was healing another innocent just so he could meet an awful fate.

But there was really no alternative. I couldn't leave this boy to suffer. I couldn't leave any of these people to suffer. And I couldn't leave Oliver's friends to suffer under Captain Goode for the rest of their lives, as I hadn't been able to leave Oliver ignorant of his power, to continually get hurt. I had needed to save him.

No, he would have hated that word. He hadn't needed saving. Just the power to make his own choices.

And as it started to dawn on me how wrong my approach to Captain Goode had been, a nurse slid open the curtain to find three strange and suspicious girls gathered around her patient.

"Miss! Ladies, you can't be in here," she announced.

"We'll be finished in a moment," I said.

I set the boy's hand down and brushed past the nurse toward the last patient I needed to heal: The man currently undergoing surgery. He was covered in bruises and cuts and had broken a number of bones. It looked like he'd fallen from some high-up place multiple times.

I squeezed in between the doctor and a nurse and took the man's hand.

The doctor stared at me, aghast. "Miss, what are you—you can't be here. Nurse! Fetch an orderly! What is going on in this damned pla—argh!"

Emily lifted him and the three other nurses into the air. Her breathing was heavy with exhaustion, and she held them only an inch above the ground. But that was still enough to keep them from running.

"I'm sorry. We'll let you down in a moment," I said, trying to soothe the doctor. I didn't want this to turn into another crime story. "My name is Evelyn Wyndham. You may have heard of me in the news. I have the power to heal others, but I have been named a villain. I am here to prove that wrong. The entire hospital has been healed. We only want to save lives. When the newspapers come to ask you about this, do you think you can deliver a message for us?"

The doctor nodded reluctantly, fearing the worst. "W-what message?"

"That members of the Society of Aberrations are being kept against their will through threats and blackmail. We want to help them escape. And if they want help, they are to take the stairs down into Paddington Station, take off their gloves, hold on to the rail, and think about who they are and how they are being threatened. Can you remember to say that?"

They all looked rather confused, but collectively they managed to repeat the message back to me.

"Thank you," I said, then turned to Emily. "It's all right now, Emily."

She set them down with a sigh as I let go of the now-healed man. The doctor stared at him and then us with a glazed look in his eyes.

"Please, deliver this message," I implored the nurses. "They go into Paddington Station, hold a staircase railing with bare hands, and only need to *think* about their situation. If you do this, then I may be able to come back and help again."

"Yes, miss," one of them managed.

They stared at us as Laura and I took each of Emily's arms and helped walk her out of the ward, out of the crowded lobby, and out of the hospital gates behind a wave of healed patients and their astonished loved ones.

Outside, the air felt warmer. I could swear that it smelled a little cleaner. The girls' energy was infectious as they giggled about grand plans for healing all of London. It was enough to make me think maybe we had found the right track, the way to cast doubts against Captain Goode and help the Society members without anyone else getting hurt.

And help me make amends.

At the front gate, we found Mr. Kent and Rose waiting for us. From atop an idling carriage on the street, Tuffins gave us a nod and Mr. Adeoti gave us a wide smile as they watched our approach.

"Here you are with your selfish behavior again, Miss Wyndham," Mr. Kent said with a smile. He put his arm around Laura, clearly relieved she was well. "And dragging my sister down to such depths. Shame."

"I'm sorry. I promise to take her to a brothel next time," I told him.

"It's the least you could do," he replied, leading Laura and Emily to the carriage.

Rose gave me a hug. "This will be a nice change in the papers."

"It's what I'm hoping," I replied. "I left a message for the newspapers to relay to the Society of Aberrations members being held against their will. I told them to go to Paddington Station and hold on to a stairway railing, telling us who they are. Mr. Adeoti can check at the end of every day and find out who wishes to leave. And Captain Goode can't spare enough people to watch every stairway of the whole station at all times."

Rose's nose wrinkled a little. "That's quite brilliant of you."

"I needed to do . . . something, after everything that happened."

"No one blamed you." She had her serious voice on.

"I couldn't even look at Sebastian. He knows now that I am the reason Mae died. . . ."

"Stop. Look at me." Her eyes gleamed in the dawn light, and

she did not flinch. She stayed steadily with me. "Darling. No one thinks Captain Goode would have stopped if you had chosen to let me go. As awful as everything is, there is not a soul in this house who thinks that night was your fault. Or Sebastian's. Or even mine, though they probably should."

"Don't say that—"

"I know. I know Captain Goode did this to us. It's the most insidious part. He thinks his power entitles him to everyone else's. Yet we're the ones who feel responsible when he uses us. And I believe he would have found a way to cause as much terror and death without me. Or you. It was about him, not us."

I touched her cheek and tried to smile, her words either breaking or healing my heart a little; I couldn't say which right now.

"I am sorry I keep wanting him dead."

"I am not. We will find a way around it." She nodded firmly and squeezed my hand.

"How did you decide this?" I asked.

She glanced back at the carriage. Catherine had stepped out and was listening to Laura and Emily's tale of our night.

I did smile then.

"She's quite certain there's a solution. Which somehow makes me quite certain, too."

"She is a wonder," I agreed.

"She is. It's terrible." Rose's smile slipped a little, and I nudged her with my shoulder.

"I know you think she only likes you because of your power. But you must realize how well you get on, in a way that has nothing to do with her being charmed. You share jokes and interests and even a similar practical turn of mind."

She turned to lead me around the carriage. "I do see it. But I could never know for sure."

"We'll find a way," I said and squeezed into the carriage with my sister and my friends.

When we arrived back at the house, Sebastian was waiting alone outside, and a flutter ran through my chest, like I'd opened a gift. He took my hand, led me into the sitting room, and didn't let go.

"You aren't to blame," he said. "And if I could tell you that a million times and chip away at it, I would. But I think we both know from experience that it isn't that simple."

He fixed me with a stare. "You once found the kindness to forgive me for your sister. If you could do that, then you must allow yourself a fraction of that unfathomable kindness. Promise me you'll try. And I'll do the same."

"I will," I managed.

Sebastian's power hummed through me, and though it was supposed to be weakening me, I couldn't help but feel stronger. There was so much sadness, and we weren't out of the woods yet. But maybe not everything needed to be forgiven and forgotten completely. Maybe it wouldn't all heal. Maybe it was enough to share the pain, the guilt, the burden. Maybe that's how we keep going.

Chapter Sixteen

"MR. KENT, if you are quite done—"

"Honestly, I've not even started yet."

My message for the members of the Society had made the evening headlines. It was embellished, slightly.

Largely, it referred to me as Sebastian Braddock's mistress. This was apparently extremely humorous to Mr. Kent, and I was resisting kicking at him across the carriage as we made our way to Paddington Station, heavily disguised.

"If you continue, I'm not going to heal your metal hand," I threatened.

"I've actually grown quite fond of this fellow, so your threat means nothing," Mr. Kent said, clapping his hands together. "Now, I have so many questions for the two of you."

"And you shall ask none of them," Sebastian snapped. He was wearing a pair of extremely thick muttonchops and a large floppy hat that belonged on a farmer, not a young gentleman. This seemed to amuse Mr. Kent almost as much as the newspaper's little misprint, and he reached over to stroke Sebastian's furry jaw.

"Don't worry, Braddock, I am a gentleman. I won't tell anyone."

"There is nothing to tell!"

"Sure, sure." Mr. Kent nodded knowingly and winked. "Nothing at all. And to think, Miss Wyndham, you could have had a scandal-free life with me, but you chose the indecent path with the roguish Mr. Braddock."

"Yes, it's all very amusing," I said bitterly.

Mr. Adeoti was watching everything between us with a polite smile. "But on the bright side, everyone will be talking about your message now."

That much was true. And for that, I was happy enough to take Mr. Kent's teasing. As long as the message encouraged Oliver's friends and any other unhappy Society of Aberrations members to seek our help and planted a seed of doubt about Captain Goode to the public, it was worth it.

The carriage came to a sharp stop. "All right, Tuffins?" Mr. Kent called.

"I am not sure, sir. I . . . I think not." The reply was muffled but understandable. I strained to see through the grit-covered window, but all I could see was another stopped carriage in front of us. We shared worried glances and Sebastian tentatively opened the door, looking around. We were on the bridge, not far from Paddington Station now. In fact, we could see it.

For it was smoking.

"It was Braddock! He derailed the trains!" The shouts came from all around us. We could see two trains lying on their sides, the metal cars buckled—twisted and broken in jagged angles. We watched, helpless from the bridge, as the bodies of passengers were pulled from the smoking wreckage. Alarm bells pealed out as the fires were doused. Frantic footsteps fell down the bridge as people rushed to find their loved ones. Madness swirled around us, and there was absolutely nothing we could do.

"I . . . I should follow them to the hospitals," I said numbly, moving without realizing how or where.

"I don't know, Miss Wyndham," Mr. Kent said, giving me a worried glance. "Captain Goode may retaliate there, too."

"I'm sorry," I said, my voice small. "I keep underestimating how far he is willing to go."

Sebastian clenched my hand, sending a rush of shivers up my arm. "It's not your fault. It's Captain Goode's," he insisted, our endless refrain.

"Hope that Braddock fella hangs!" a passerby shouted.

"Aye, my train's been canceled. I've got half a mind to go do it myself," his companion remarked, unaware he was brushing past the man himself.

"Ignore them," I whispered, clutching Sebastian's hand back. "They don't know a thing." A few deep breaths gave me a moment to think, to find a way to salvage this failure somehow. "Mr. Adeoti, do you see any messages here?" I asked.

Mr. Adeoti gave a cursory look around the bridge. "Nothing."

"Then let's make a round."

My arm remained locked to Sebastian's as we navigated through the packed crowd to find our way off the bridge. With the station shut down, we circled the area in the hopes that some Society members had left messages on nearby walls. As we wove our way back and forth down each of the surrounding streets, newspaper boys shouted speculation about where Sebastian might strike next. Hastily drawn handbills offering rewards for Sebastian were being hung up on walls. One man wearing a sandwich board advertised that Sebastian had enjoyed a pie and a beer at a corner public house before committing his horrible crime.

I could feel it wearing Sebastian down. I could see it wearing all of us down. There was a growing heaviness to our trudging and a reluctance to hope for anything. It seemed Captain Goode had an answer for everything we did.

"Wait," Mr. Adeoti said, a rush of excitement in his voice. "I believe I see something."

We crossed the street to the brick wall of a rather mundane building, searching for signs of anything suspicious. Deeming it safe, Mr. Adeoti made his way to the message and leaned his back against the wall, his hands touching the bricks. He closed his eyes for only a few seconds before he snapped out of the trance.

"That was quick," I said. "What did it say?"

"It's . . . short," Mr. Adeoti said. "It's from Captain Goode. All he said was 'Your turn.'"

We decided it best to leave then.

Our route was unnecessarily long to escape from anyone following us. We wound through a few alleys, down into an underground station, and out another gate before emerging back up on the street. Mr. Kent made sure to ask loudly if anyone was following us before we found Tuffins and took the carriage straight home.

The boarding house fell into a somber, helpless silence when we returned. The crash was reported in the evening papers, ten dead and eighteen injured, and the blame was, again, placed entirely on Sebastian, who had been seen running from the trains. We tried to regain the hope we all had the other day. Mr. Adeoti, Catherine, and Rose continued their research; I came up with plans and Miss Chen explained why they were ridiculous; and Sebastian went back to gardening moodily, while Mr. Kent tried to explain that he could brood just as easily at a brothel. But even by the end of the long day, no one had a single idea. The problem was dreadfully simple now. We didn't know how to find Captain Goode, and anything we could think of would result in more and more retaliatory deaths.

The problem kept me awake long into the night. The ceiling provided little in the way of answers and the walls proved equally unhelpful. The blankets, my night rail, my skin were all too hot and I tossed and turned, fighting the urge to visit another hospital, to wait outside the Society of Aberrations, to do anything.

Finally, I rolled out of bed, settling on a secret trip to the best place I could think of: the kitchen.

Rose's voice stopped me at the door. "You're not sneaking away again, are you?"

"No, even I have run out of reasons to sneak away in the middle of the night," I reassured her. "I just need some thinking cake."

"Mmm, thinking cake," she said sleepily. "Save me one with . . . brilliant-idea . . . jam."

"If we haven't run out already," I said, creeping out the door.

The stairs brought me down with quiet creaks, shafts of moonlight guiding the way. Downstairs was darker, but I knew the path well enough by now. My steps were slow and careful, and my eyes were on the ground watching for Soot, not at all expecting the body that rounded the corner and collided with me.

My scream would have shaken the house had the shock of his power not taken my breath away. The tiniest gasp came out instead, muffled into Sebastian's chest. "Oof."

His arms steadied me, and my legs valiantly resisted the urge to turn to water.

"Um, Evelyn" was all he managed. I looked up into eyes of guilt.

Not just the usual Sebastian guilt he carried around, but something far more immediate. I stepped back, taking in more of him. Fully dressed, a quick tick of a pulse at his throat, and now avoiding my eye.

I settled my hands onto my hips. "And where exactly were you planning on going, Sebastian Braddock?"

"Uh, for a smoke—"

"You do not smoke."

"You don't know—"

"Sebastian. You would not know which end of a cigar to light."

"I—" He stopped as he thought about it. "I suppose I don't." He admitted it quietly, like it was shameful that he was not, in fact, a worldly smoking gentleman.

"I'm sure Mr. Kent can tell you. But now, tell me where you are going."

He looked so much like a dog who felt guilty about tearing up a beloved pillow that I began to worry myself until all at once, I realized what he was about.

And I was *furious*.

"You were going to give yourself in to Captain Goode."

He looked up. Nothing like a guilty animal anymore. His chin was set, his shoulders were broad, and he looked every inch formidable. "I am still going."

I shoved at his absolutely nonformidable chest. He could not deceive me any longer. "You are not. What happened to your insistence on talking to each other instead of acting like brooding fools?"

He leaned down the scant inches between us. "We have talked. Just now." And then he had the gall to continue past me.

"Don't you dare!" I grabbed at his coat, swinging him around and me into his chest yet again.

"Oof." He repeated my earlier exhale.

"You are not going to turn yourself into Captain Goode because that will do nothing except get you killed and then he will continue killing innocent people!" My words came out in such harsh whispers, I would have been surprised if he heard more than the vowels. But he seemed to have gotten the gist as his brow knit together.

"He cannot keep killing innocent people once his supposed killer is in custody." He sounded so assured of such a naïve statement. No one would have blamed me if I had simply died of embarrassment for him thinking such a ridiculous possibility.

"He will just blame someone else!" I said. "The only way he gets to keep playing hero is by finding villains."

His lips were thinned enough that I could practically see the outline of his teeth beneath. "He won't be able to keep that up. Not if I turn myself in and tell the truth." He was so willfully, horribly stubborn.

Thankfully, so was I, as people liked to remind me. Constantly. "I forbid it."

He blinked a little. "You . . . no, you can't for—"

"I just did. I forbid you."

He frowned. "Well, I . . . no." And pushed past me again. I scurried in front of him and ran to the door, throwing myself in front of it.

"Evelyn, you're being childish."

"It's the right reaction to your juvenile determination to get yourself killed." I stuck my tongue out for good measure. If he was going to be ridiculous and dramatic, so would I.

He did not seem to know what to do with this. Awkwardly, Sebastian reached around me for the doorknob. I batted his arm aside. He reached again, giving me a quelling look. I shoved his arm and stretched my body across the doorway. There.

He sighed and grumbled. "I hate when you force me into being ungentlemanly." That was the only warning I received before he snagged me by the waist and spun me behind him. He grabbed the doorknob and pulled it open. He was so fast when he wished to be.

But I was willing to make a fool of myself, so I dove at his legs. The door shut as he knocked into it. I crawled up his legs until I had his torso in my arms, where I clung like a burr. He sputtered and tried to detach me, but I latched on as he sank down to the floor against the door.

I caught words like "impossible" and "ridiculous woman," but I countered them with my own, like "noble ass" and "absurd."

Finally, he stopped attempting to remove me from his person, panting a little. I crawled farther up his body and planted my full weight on his torso to keep him there.

"Evelyn, please, I have to go." He looked at me full-on, confidence shining in his eyes, the words determined and steady. He had convinced himself thoroughly that this was his best plan.

And he thought I was Byronic.

"I'm sorry, Sebastian," I said finally. "I know you want to leave. And you know I can't let you."

He scrubbed a hand across his forehead. "Please, you don't understand. I have to do this."

My heart felt like a great block had been placed on it. I thought about all the things between us we could not say, even with our new policy of talking about things. All the crimes for which he thought he needed to atone.

"It won't bring them back." I barely whispered the words, but he heard them and blanched.

He did not look at me, but his jaw worked a little and he swallowed. "I . . . I know that. But I still owe them something more than inaction."

"You owe me, too," I said, surprised at how fiercely the words came out. "Don't do this to me. Don't leave me and get yourself killed. It helps no one at all."

He did not seem to pay me any mind. I pushed at his chest lightly. He still didn't look at me.

"Evelyn, you don't understand—"

I reached down to grab his face and turn it to me. He couldn't keep avoiding my eyes forever. "But I do. I know what you are trying to do, and this is not the way. It helps no one, and especially not the child who will get your power next."

Finally, his eyes landed on mine, that deep green that always seemed a little too dark. Like maybe they would be lighter if things had gone differently in his life. If fewer people had died.

"Sebastian. I know every terrible thing you think you have done." My voice was steady, even if I wasn't. "I know that Captain Goode and Dr. Beck and some horrible people have twisted your powers into something monstrous. I know how much you loved your parents. How much you loved the Lodges. How much you love helping people. I have seen you when you have hope that your powers can do good, and it is a beautiful thing. The best part is that it's not impossible. I have seen what you are capable of, and it's so much more than you realize. You help Rose every day by showing her how you work around your powers. And I know, years from now, when your power goes to the next person, your words, your guide, your life will save theirs."

"Evelyn, that is, you . . . I am not . . ." He seemed so frustrated with me, with the world, but this was not the way to solve anything.

"You can't turn yourself in. I told you on the bridge." I felt him stiffen at the word. "I told you I wouldn't let you go. And you didn't leave me. You didn't leave then. You can't do it now."

"But, I—"

"I clearly do not have all the answers. But this is not it. I know that. I know it as surely and deeply as I know your power."

He was brimming with something, and I tried to look ready to hear it, whatever it was he needed to unburden. He tried a few times and finally stopped, his head bowed. He had been about to say something else, but all that came out was a frustrated, "I don't know how to say it."

I frowned at him. "It's very simple. You open your mouth, think of what you wish to say, and—"

He kissed me.

One moment I was ready to bring down the house if it meant keeping him here, the next I was pulled down against him in a rather expert embrace. His lips were so warm beneath mine, and only when a series of shudders ran through me did I realize how cold I had been. Or maybe I had been lacking him for too long—I couldn't really think, too consumed with this kiss that filled my head with stars. Frissons of Sebastian rippled through me in every place our bodies met as he pulled me tighter. I could feel his heart pounding against my chest, and I wanted to take it and heal it and hide it away with mine.

Both his hands gently settled on my cheeks as we broke apart for a breath. In the dim moonlight, I could see his eyes darting across my face, trying to take it all in at once. "Thank you . . . for everything."

I blinked a few times, my lips positively tingling, as though doused in peppermint oil. I tried to force my mind back to order, but his sentence still did not make sense and I was so aware of every part of him, of every part of me, that I really was not able to come up with anything beyond, "Including dragging you to the floor? And sitting on you?" My voice managed to be too scratchy and too breathy together and I cleared it a few times.

He looked around as if realizing for the first time that we were still on the floor. An actual smile broke out on his face and it was all I could do not to kiss him until he had no facial expression besides smiling. Until he was nothing but happy.

"Yes. And for constantly rescuing me." His eyes glistened. "I do not deserve your trust."

"I trust approximately three and a half people, Sebastian. I do not give it lightly."

"That makes it all the more valuable. And I am sorry I am not worthy of it."

"You are," I said, finally releasing my hold on him and climbing to my feet. "So stop being so . . . you-know-what."

"After you," he said, taking my hand and standing.

I kept his hand in mine. "Promise me you won't just turn yourself in to Captain Goode."

He looked behind him at the door, longingly, then back at me, torn. "I won't. I promise."

I tugged at him, leading him back up the stairs, just to be certain. We walked up quietly and slowly, our fingers intertwining, the overwhelming sensation somehow serving as a comfort. At my bedroom door, he kissed my forehead, and the feeling stayed with me long enough to crawl into bed and reach against the wall to find him. It was faint, but it was there, that current.

And for a moment, it was stronger. I imagined him on the other side, hand to wall, matching mine. And then, somehow, I was finally able to sleep.

Chapter Seventeen

A HEAVY THUMP ON the ceiling interrupted my sound sleep, the most peaceful night since the ball. I opened my eyes to see early morning sun streaming in through the gauzy curtains. Another loud thump reverberated above me, and the more I thought about it, the more it sounded like someone dead on the floor.

I scrambled out of bed, yanking on a robe. Rose looked up sleepily, stirred awake by the noise, and I opened our door to find Miss Chen opening hers across the hallway.

"Whose room was that?" she asked.

"I don't know," I whispered.

My mind was full of horrible imaginings as we made it up the flight of stairs and to the end of the corridor, where I found one imagining come true. Tuffins emerged from his bedroom, his nightshirt bearing streaks of blood.

Oh God.

"Tuffins, are you all right?" I asked.

"Only a bit startled," he said, looking completely composed. "Your guest, Miss Rao, has climbed into my room."

A heavy breath left my body. He wasn't hurt.

"Miss Rao?" I asked, as he opened the door and ushered us inside.

It was her. She had collapsed in a corner chair, her head lolled back, her clothes covered in blood, a bag of her belongings strewn on the floor. Her eyes slid over to me. She was still conscious.

"I need to be healed," she rasped, as if that wasn't apparent.

"Someone help me," I said.

With Tuffins's and Miss Chen's help, I carried her out of his room and to the last empty bedchamber, setting her down gently on a clean coverlet. Tuffins hastened downstairs to get supplies, employing Rose's and Catherine's assistance, while I took a chair next to Miss Rao and held her hand. Miss Chen yawned and leaned on the wall by the window.

"What happened?" I asked.

Miss Rao gritted her teeth. "I was ambushed. The night before last."

"How?"

"The power remover. He filled the India Secretary position with someone from your Society," Miss Rao said. "They were with two others, waiting for my attack."

"He's . . . taking over the government now," I said in disbelief.

"He must have used Miss Fahlstrom to predict the attack," Miss Chen said. "And you still escaped from them."

"I used my fog. But he took my power from me." Miss Rao looked away from me, her face stricken, then flushed with anger. "Again."

A chill ran through me. When she was in the Society prison, I hadn't been able to fully understand what it was like to lose such an essential part of ourselves. Now I knew. "I'm sorry."

"How did you get in here?" Miss Chen was looking doubtfully out the third-story window.

"I did not have strength enough to find my way here until this morning. Then I climbed through the window."

"Of course, that's something most people can do with extensive injuries." The look Miss Chen gave Miss Rao was somewhere between fear and worship.

"You're welcome to rest here for however long you need," I said. "Your powers should return in a day and a half."

Miss Rao turned from me, her lips thinned, looking unhappy about the time frame.

"Is there a chance that you might have been followed?" Miss Chen asked.

"I do not think so, destroyer," Miss Rao answered. "But I am not certain."

"Destroyer. . . . I should put that on my cards," Miss Chen muttered to herself, heading for the door. "I'll wake Mr. Adeoti. We need him to take a walk around the house to check and make sure she wasn't."

Miss Chen left the room as Tuffins brought in a basin of water and Miss Rao's bag.

"Thank you, Tuffins," I said.

He nodded and left us.

"I like that man, Tuffins," Miss Rao said. "If all Englishmen were like him, this country would be better off."

"I can't argue with that," I said.

As the healing ran its course, I took one more survey of Miss Rao's injuries. It was hard to tell through the crusted blood, but the wounds that were once visible to me seemed to have closed.

"Do you still feel pain anywhere?" I asked.

"No," she said, testing her cuts. "Though I find I am still tired."

"My healing doesn't usually fix that," I said. "You must not have eaten for some time. Breakfast will be downstairs when you're ready."

I rose up and slid out the door, giving her the privacy to clean up.

As I made my way down the stairs, I wondered if it were at all possible to persuade Miss Rao to join us. Despite our common enemy, despite the healing I'd done for her, she still didn't seem to trust me. She'd called me selfish the last time she was here, and she had been right. I was still a risk.

When I entered the dining room, a sudden silence greeted me, hushed whispers abruptly cut short. Rose and Catherine stood at the table, hiding something behind their backs, both looking pale. Laura had Soot settled on her lap, and she was busy petting him repeatedly, as though only he could make everything better. Emily started digging into a plate of fresh eggs and slices of bread. I took the seat across from her.

"Ev, I—" Catherine started.

"Good morning, Miss Wyndham!" Mrs. Tuffins emerged from the kitchen with a plate of pastries and cakes and set it down on the table in front of me.

"Oh, I—thank you. Good morning," I replied, overwhelmed with the food.

Catherine waited for Mrs. Tuffins to return to the kitchen before she pulled out a newspaper and set it on the table in front of me. "I'm so sorry. I went to take a walk and . . . everyone is talking about it. Mr. Braddock turned himself in to the police."

My entire body tensed as my vision went a little fuzzy.

"How . . . no . . . no, Sebastian's here. I stopped him from doing that last night." I glanced down and tried to make sense of the flagrantly inaccurate news story.

"There isn't much information there since it happened early this morning," Catherine said. "All that we know is there's going to be a trial at noon at Lincoln's Inn Fields."

My mind went blank, and I stopped understanding what words were. I came to a few moments later, at the door to Sebastian's room. I looked down to see my hand on the door handle, not knowing how I had gotten here. But Catherine's arm was around my waist, and she seemed to be holding me up. She was talking at me, but I still wasn't able to make out the words. Just her concerned eyes and slightly confused expression.

"Evelyn. Are you listening? Rose, I think . . ." Her words faded in and out as my body drifted into Sebastian's room. It was extremely tidy, which was unsurprising. Everything was in order, except a sheet of paper folded on the pillow. I found I had been expecting that, without knowing it. My given name was on the front in small, neat script. Inside were two words.

Trust me.

That was it.

That was all he had to say for himself.

The lying, impossible, infuriating, selfishly self-sacrificing fool.

I sat down heavily on the bedspread, and Rose's face swam in front of me, her mouth set severely.

"Ev. Pay attention to me."

"I am," I said as the sound rushed away from my ears and I focused on the present.

"He could very well have some plan," my sister said. "I think we need to assume he has this under control."

I leaped up. "He turned himself in! After he promised me, *promised* he would do no such thing!"

"Maybe there's something he couldn't risk telling you," Catherine argued. "Your desire to kill Captain Goode would compromise it."

"Well, I only plan on murdering Sebastian now, how about that?" I was snapping, and I knew I was snapping; I could not reconcile any of this. How could Sebastian make such a terrible, foolhardy choice?

A door slammed downstairs and hurried footsteps headed up. Mr. Adeoti and Miss Chen appeared in the doorway. She looked between us, saw the note lying limply in my lap. "The fool."

I threw my hands into the air. "Finally, someone agrees!"

"He left early this morning," Mr. Adeoti said, sounding as mournful as if Sebastian were already dead.

"You tracked him?" Rose asked.

"Only a little. I saw he left and was planning to turn himself in to the police. Perhaps that will help him get a fair trial," Mr. Adeoti said, stretching his optimism to its limits.

"I should wake Mr. Kent," Catherine said, heading out of the room. "He will want to know."

"He wasn't there when I woke up," Mr. Adeoti called after her. "I don't know if he's had a very late night or an early morning."

"Impossible to tell with him," Catherine grumbled.

The others stared around the room helplessly. My heart was beating dully beneath my wrapper, the thumping sounding a little off, as if it had lost its natural rhythm.

"I need my boots," I murmured, heading to my room.

Rose sighed, sending me a doubtful look, but followed me to change into our day dresses.

"I truly believe he will be all right," she said.

"I wish I had your confidence," I said, shrugging on my traveling coat.

I strode downstairs, finding Miss Rao glaring up at me. She was wrapped in a cloak as if she couldn't stand to spend another minute in the house with us. I could feel another chastisement coming. That I was unable to control myself. That I was going to get all my friends killed. When all I wanted to do was to see Sebastian once more and help him in any way I could.

"You are going to this trial?" she asked.

"I am," I said firmly. "You don't have to stay if you're worried I'm going to get us all killed."

She cocked her head at me, her long braid slipping over her shoulder. "You won't. I'll be making certain you do nothing foolish."

"Oh," I said, finding myself prepared for everything but that. "You . . . you're helping us, then?"

"I'm finding you useful, healer," she said. "That's all."

That was a start, at least.

I turned around to find everyone ready in the cramped vestibule. Rose and Catherine following down the stairs, Miss Chen and Mr. Adeoti watching from the top, Laura and Emily putting their coats on, and Mrs. Tuffins making them promise to be careful.

"Do take care, dears. The streets are quite lively today," she fussed.

I opened the door and found that to be rather an understatement.

Outside was chaos. Groups of neighbors congregated outside of market stalls, storefronts, and homes, gossiping about the news. Vendors with their stocked wagons clogged the road, all headed in the same direction. Newspaper boys ran through the streets, shouting the news too fresh to be in their papers.

"The trial starts at noon! Lincoln's Inn Fields! The Cap'n seeks justice for Braddock's crimes!"

I stepped outside, across the threshold where I thought I'd convinced Sebastian to keep fighting. My lips burned as I pressed my hand to the door, wishing I had Mr. Adeoti's power so I could sink back into that moment mere hours ago, when Sebastian's kiss seemed to be a promise to stay.

Before it became a kiss good-bye.

Chapter Eighteen

F ROM THE MOMENT we entered Lincoln's Inn Fields, one thing was apparent: This wasn't a trial. This was a blasted festival.

All of London seemed to have descended upon the square, and where there was money to be made, there were vendors to make it. Their stalls lined the footpaths, displaying every sort of Sebastian Braddock–related souvenir one could imagine. Veils and gloves to protect oneself from his deadly powers. Captain Goode charms that warded Sebastian off. Even Braddock Be Gone was for sale, a restorative tonic to counteract any prolonged exposure.

Our group managed to resist such temptations and make our way to the center, where crowds converged on the latest addition to the square: an amphitheater, carved into the ground, resembling an ancient Greek excavation site. The trees and plants had been cleared out to fit the thousands of spectators, tiers had been sculpted out of rock to give everyone a view of the stage, and a metal shell had been formed around the stage to ensure everyone heard the proceedings. Captain Goode had used all the powers at the Society's disposal to make this as public as possible.

"A bit of a change from the Old Bailey. . . ." Catherine said.

She and Miss Rao were on both sides of me, one propping me up and the other keeping me from rushing down to the stage.

Rose, Emily, Laura, Miss Chen, and Mr. Adeoti followed us as we slipped into a row near the back. I could feel their worried eyes on me. I didn't know if that was better or worse than the delighted exclaims and gleeful grins surrounding us, waiting for the main attraction. There hadn't been a public hanging in London since I was a child, but I had the sinking feeling that if you added a noose and an executioner, this would feel rather like one.

The stage below, however, had been set up like any other criminal court, as if to give the impression justice would somehow be served here. On the left side was the judge, sitting at a raised bench above tables of clerks and writers. At the back of the stage, a box of jurors looked angry and ready to condemn Sebastian already. And in the center of the stage were tables for the prosecution, which consisted of Miss Fahlstrom and several men organizing their notes. Captain Goode stood out among them, the sun catching on his excessive number of medals. From what I could tell, there was not a single defense lawyer for Sebastian.

Boos and jeers spread through the crowd from front to back, which could only mean one thing. Sebastian was escorted in by Mr. Seward, the man who controlled water, and the ice guard, Miss Quinn, to the right side of the stage, where he was placed, handcuffed, in a raised and enclosed box.

"Murderer!"

"'Bastian Braddock the Bloody!"

"The noose is too good for him!"

"Hang! Hang! Hang!"

The air was positively flammable. One match and this could turn to riot. The wall of policemen standing at the bottom of the stage were mumbling and shuffling, unsure about whether to be more afraid of Sebastian on one side or the unruly mob on the other. But some of Captain Goode's society members and bodyguards were interspersed among the police, and they looked rather confident they could handle anything and preserve the peace. To be fair, they probably could.

In fact, the cannibal girl who attacked me the other night lifted her hand up, crackling sparks of electricity into the air. The display silenced the crowd and earned a scornful "pah" from Miss Rao.

With everyone in place, a clerk rose from a desk below the judge's bench and stepped to the center of the stage. He addressed both the crowd and the jury, his voice echoing off the walls. "Sebastian Braddock stands charged with one hundred and thirty-eight counts of murder, treason, attempted assassination on the Queen, setting fire to the British Museum and the colonial office, and the destruction of a home at 34 Lowndes Square and two trains at Paddington Station. How say you, Mr. Braddock? Are you guilty or not guilty of these offenses?"

Sebastian cleared his throat. "Not guilty."

More jeers and hisses erupted around the court. Sebastian didn't acknowledge them. He seemed for all the world to be perfectly at ease. His ink-dark hair was ruffled but only enough to appear dashing, his eyes were cast up to the sky, and his arms were comfortably rested on the bar. He looked like a young lord who figured his good wealth and privilege could get him out of anything. Only those who knew him well—my heart skipped for a horrible second as I realized I might be the only person left alive who could claim to truly know him—could see that it wasn't arrogance. That shell was no thicker than an egg's and cracked with less pressure applied. I had been mistaken at first, thinking Sebastian masqueraded as a melodramatic, prideful fool. But he was not any of those things.

Perhaps a fool, actually.

But seeing him up there, exposed and vulnerable, I desperately wanted to save him. I knew that this was no play at melodrama, but his deep, grounding wish to do something right. Only he was wrong, of course. This solved nothing except likely getting him killed.

And all we could do was watch as the clerk took his seat and the judge motioned for the prosecution to begin.

Captain Goode rose to his feet and put his hand to his heart as he addressed the jury and the crowd. "Ladies and gentlemen, you are very brave to be here! Let no man say that England is not full of brave men and women!"

The crowd around us ate up his pandering remarks.

Captain Goode crossed the stage toward Sebastian. "No doubt you've read the newspaper reports of Mr. Braddock's power, and some of you may be understandably nervous about being in the presence of such danger. Allow me to reassure you that you are in safe hands." He reached over the bar and clapped his hand on Sebastian's arm like he was reaching into the lion's cage of the zoo.

Captain Goode didn't fall over and die choking on his breath like I hoped. He gave us all a reassuring smile. "As you can see, I've turned off his power, so there's no need to worry about his deadly touch or his so-called 'death blast' that affects everyone around him. But that doesn't mean he isn't a threat. I intend to prove Mr. Braddock used this power in a willful and malicious manner, I intend to bring him to justice for his many crimes, and I intend to bring peace to our city again. I won't let him take a single innocent life more!"

A laugh escaped my mouth when he finished. Or a sob. I couldn't quite tell. This whole trial was already absurd.

Of course, appreciative murmurs rumbled through the crowd. They had all heard of Captain Goode's power, but it was another matter to see their new hero render the most feared man in London completely powerless. A man with such confidence that death did not bother him.

Captain Goode confidently returned to his table and took the seat beside an impassive Miss Fahlstrom. My stomach twisted as I wondered what death she saw for Sebastian. Did she already know how this trial would end?

"Prosecution, you may call your first witness," the judge said.

"I'd like to call Mr. William Shaw," Captain Goode announced.

"What? Doesn't Sebastian get to make a statement?" I asked Catherine.

"Only near the end," she whispered back.

Wonderful. After everyone's made up their minds. If they hadn't already.

From a box of witnesses near the front of the stage, a familiar, slim man—compact enough to resemble a young boy but bald enough to prove he was not—emerged and stepped into the witness-box in front of the jury. The smoke man who attacked us on the train. The completely impartial witness swore to tell the truth as Captain Goode stepped back on stage to begin his questioning.

"Mr. Shaw, will you tell the court what your profession is?"

"Yes, I have been a member of the Society of Aberrations for a month and a half," the man said, his limbs loose and easy. They all seemed so sure of today's outcome.

"And what is your unique power?" Captain Goode asked.

"I can create a thick smoke," Mr. Shaw answered. "If my target is caught within it, they will find it difficult to see and breathe."

"Would you demonstrate this power, safely, for the court?"

"Of course," Mr. Shaw said. He lifted his hand straight up in the air and a black plume of smoke flowed upward from his palm. The crowd tittered in excitement, watching it join the smog of the city. Mr. Shaw's face was not one made for smiling, but he seemed pleased.

"Thank you," Captain Goode said. "Now, what is your relationship with the prisoner?"

"I didn't know the prisoner personally, but we were both members of the Society for a time before he turned against us," Mr. Shaw said. "My only encounter with him was about ten days ago, when I was ordered to capture him."

"And why were you ordered to capture Sebastian Braddock?"

"He was suspected to be involved in the Belgrave Ball, which had occurred three days earlier."

They were so rehearsed, so efficient in their questions and answers. How could no one see that this was all an elaborate, fabricated farce? My face was burning.

"And what happened during this encounter?"

"I, along with four other members of the Society, tracked Mr. Braddock and his followers to Victoria Station and onto a train. They attempted to flee at the first sight of us, but we managed to corner them in one of the carriages. Rather than come peacefully, they attacked us with a complete disregard for the safety of the other passengers." Mr. Shaw was actually idly looking at his fingernails, picking something out from under one.

"What happened to you in this attack?"

"I attempted to minimize the damage by blocking them with my smoke," Mr. Shaw said. "But Mr. Braddock managed to seize me and use his power on me."

"And what were the effects of his power?" Captain Goode asked.

"It became very difficult for me to breathe," Mr. Shaw said. "I felt feverish in seconds. It felt like my energy, my life was being drained from me. I don't remember anything except fear. And then I fell unconscious."

"When did you wake up?"

"The next day. I had been brought to the Society of Aberrations medical ward, but I was still very sick."

"What was the sickness like?"

"The same as I had on the train. Fever, coughing, difficulty breathing. There were blue markings all over my body. It took me almost a week to recover."

"And we are all very glad of that," Captain Goode said. "Thank you, Mr. Shaw."

The judge turned his attention upon Sebastian as Captain Goode returned to his table. "Defense may cross-examine the witness."

Sebastian and Mr. Shaw stared at each other for a moment, Mr. Shaw entirely unconcerned, holding back a yawn, even. And then Sebastian shook his head. "No questions."

The crowd murmured at that, taking it to be obvious proof that Sebastian was guilty of it all.

"Oh, for God's sake," I said, dropping my head into my hands. "He's not even going to try?"

I felt Rose put a comforting hand on my back, but she had no words of encouragement. Catherine opened her mouth and closed it a few times, finding no possible explanation of a secret clever strategy Sebastian could be employing. But he said to trust him.

So I clutched his note tightly in my fist and tried to trust him as Captain Goode called his next witnesses. A coroner who determined the cause of death for victims at the Belgrave Ball. The first policeman to find the bodies. A doctor from the Royal Hospital Chelsea who saw a number of patients with similar symptoms that night. Two occupants of other houses in Belgrave Square who briefly suffered the effects of Sebastian's power. A driver who fell unconscious on the street after seeing Sebastian fleeing the scene. A neighbor who saw him climbing into the window of the home of John Bell the night of his murder. A maid who encountered him entering her employer's home before his murder. A soldier who saw him attack the Queen. A hotel guest who saw him holding a

gun. A conductor who saw him running from a train in Paddington before it erupted in flames.

And, of course, Sebastian stayed nobly silent the whole time, doing nothing to exonerate himself, asking no cross-examination questions of his own.

As the hours passed into late afternoon and Captain Goode finished calling all his witnesses, the air grew even more charged. The evidence against Sebastian had piled up to the sky, and the crowd was restless. They no longer needed to be convinced of his guilt. They needed to see him punished for it.

"Defense, you may call your first witness," the judge declared.

Well, they were going to see it very soon. Who did Sebastian have for witnesses if he wanted to protect us all? Couldn't I go down and be a witness? It wasn't as if Captain Goode could do anything to me there in front of all these people.

No. Deep breath. Trust him.

"I wish to call Mr. Charles Warren," Sebastian said.

I blinked. The name didn't register for a moment. Then I saw him emerge from the table for reporters, step up into the witness-box, and swear on the Bible. The editor from the *Daily Telegraph* whom we had tried to blackmail. This was the best character witness he could find? My trust in Sebastian was reaching its limits.

"Mr. Warren, would you please tell the court what you do?" Sebastian asked.

"I've been an editor at the *Daily Telegraph* for ten years," he answered.

Sebastian leaned closer, still restrained by the railing. "Would you please describe the last time we met?"

"Very well," Mr. Warren said, turning to the jury. "It was one week ago. Mr. Braddock barged into my office with a male and female accomplice of the same age with the intention of correcting my story about the murder of Sir Thomas Cox. They claimed to have the true story. That it was not Mr. Braddock who committed the murder."

"How did we attempt to prove it to you?"

"The male accomplice revealed a special power of his own. Any question he asked forced the listener to give an honest answer. It was then Mr. Braddock revealed who he was and answered the accomplice's questions." Mr. Warren was as neat and confident and blastedly accurate as he had seemed when we visited him days before.

"Was this truth power used on you at any point in this conversation?"

"Yes, the accomplice attempted to learn of any secrets I had, so he could blackmail me into writing a new article."

How courteous of Sebastian to add more crimes to the list.

But Sebastian didn't seem at all bothered about this. "Please describe how his power forced you to speak the truth."

What on earth was he doing?

Mr. Warren thought about it for a moment. "I . . . I couldn't keep my mouth closed. And my immediate response could not be controlled. The truth simply came out. Only after my truthful answer was given was I able to speak freely. Unfortunately for them, I have no damaging secrets, so their attempt failed, and I called for the police, while they fled."

"Thank you, Mr. Warren," Sebastian said, then looked to the judge. "I have no further questions for this witness."

"Prosecution may cross-examine the witness," the judge said.

Captain Goode rose from his seat and looked between Mr. Warren and Sebastian, a faint expression of amusement on his face. He shook his head and sat back down. "I don't believe we need to."

"Thank you, Mr. Warren, you may be seated," the judge said. "Does the defense have another witness?"

The crowd grumbled audibly now, and I heard someone call for a hanging already. I didn't know whether to hope Sebastian still had some miraculous plan or that he'd simply stop digging himself into a deeper hole. Trust him. Trust him. Trust hi—

"I wish to call Captain Simon Goode as a witness."

He'd gone absolutely mad.

Upon my first movement toward the stairs, Miss Rao's grip tightened around my arm and her glare pinned me to the ground. She wasn't going to let me go without a fight.

"Please tell me I am seeing an absurd illusion," I whispered to Catherine.

"Unfortunately, I don't think we are," Catherine said. "But we are trying our best to trust him, too."

I stayed in place, feeling sick and quite sure I would cast up the little water I'd had this morning. Captain Goode stepped into the witness-box, swore on the Bible, and then waited patiently for the questions, ready to lie.

Sebastian said nothing. He stood silently and glanced up at the sky, waiting as well.

The judge cleared his throat. "Mr. Braddock . . . you must begin your questioning."

"My defense counsel will be questioning him," Sebastian said.

"You have no defense counsel," the judge said. "So if you have no questions for Captain Goode, then—"

"Apologies for being late," a voice rang out from above. "But I really didn't want to be here on time."

My head craned up, along with everyone else in the court, to be greeted by the oddest sight of my life.

Floating high over the square was a hot-air balloon.

Poking out of the balloon's basket was a speaking trumpet.

And booming out of the speaking trumpet was Mr. Kent's voice.

My mouth dropped open. My stomach dropped down. I was surprised I managed to stay conscious.

"Nicky!" Laura squealed, clapping her hands together.

"Captain Goode!" Mr. Kent shouted into the horn, the sound rising over the square. He had to speak slower to be understood, but his voice still boomed over the confused chatter of the crowd. "Tell the good people here, were you the true cause of the massacre at the Belgrave Ball?"

"Yes," the answer came out, clear as day.

"And the train crash at Paddington?"

"Yes."

"And the assassination attempt on the Queen?"

"Yes." Capitan Goode's shock turned to fury, and he tried to correct himself. "No! I was not; these are all l—"

"Remind everyone, what is my power?" Mr. Kent cut him off.

"The ability to ask a question and receive the truth in response."

Captain Goode was ash-gray now, concentrating hard on Mr. Kent's balloon. I laughed among the baffled crowd as I realized that he couldn't do anything to turn this power off as long as Mr. Kent remained out of sight.

"Please tell me this isn't an absurd illusion," I said.

"Dear Lord, this might actually work," Catherine said. "If he gets everyone to turn against him."

"How did you get Mr. Braddock blamed for these crimes?" Mr. Kent asked.

Captain Goode leaped out of the witness-box, but his answer still came. "I raised his power to a deadly level at the Belgrave Ball to kill everyone in the room. I sent members of the Society of Aberrations to Paddington Station to destroy the train. And I ordered a member to create illusions of Mr. Braddock fleeing Paddington and attacking the Queen." He shook his head wildly and turned to the crowd. "No, these are lies, I did not—"

"Are you blackmailing some members of the Society of Aberrations into working for you?"

Captain Goode tried to block his ears, but the question was loud enough to get through. "Yes! N—"

"How?"

"Threatening their families and friends. Imprisoning them. Hurting them." Captain Goode waved to his guards below the stage. "No! He is lying and manipulating my mind. Stop him!"

"Arrest that man!" Mr. Kent fired back.

Most of the Society members and the police stood frozen, unsure what to do. Even Miss Fahlstrom rose from her seat, looking rather disturbed.

But there were enough who were still loyal to Captain Goode. One extremely large man leaped from the bottom of the stage straight into the middle of the crowd and out of the stadium with a few swift bounces like a spring-heeled jack, a sight made even odder given the man's height and breadth. A worn, worried-looking, almost motherly woman fired needles from her hand, puncturing holes in the balloon. And a loud crack rent the air as the electric woman fired a massive bolt at the basket of Mr. Kent's balloon, setting it ablaze.

"No!" Laura screamed. The crowd erupted, but not in the direction Mr. Kent had hoped. The tension from the trial, the strangeness of the balloon, Captain Goode's sudden revelations, the startling display of powers—it was too much. Everyone rushed up the stairs, climbing up the court steps, a massive tide of bodies that pushed us in the wrong direction.

"I appear to be on fire." Mr. Kent's voice wavered nervously through the speaking trumpet as his balloon descended. "Miss

Wyndham, if you're out there, this was entirely Mr. Braddock's fault. He used flattery, and I was powerless to resist."

I looked around frantically, catching a glimpse of Sebastian being dragged up the stairs by Captain Goode on the other side of the court. The rest of the Society members followed in the direction of Mr. Kent's balloon, which drifted toward the end of the fields. Smoke started to fill the court, courtesy of Mr. Shaw.

"We have to help him!" Laura cried, pulling desperately out of Emily's hold. She forced her way upstairs and into the sea of bodies, trying to get around the court the long way, to get to Mr. Kent's balloon.

"Laura! Laura!" I shouted, struggling forward. "Dammit, stop her!" I tried to keep my eyes on her, Sebastian, and Mr. Kent all at once, fear for them rising.

Emily was already chasing after Laura, climbing up the steps, telekinetically stopping the people in her way, creating a narrow path through the crowd.

We stumbled through the screaming masses in her wake. People knocked into us from the side, but I kept Emily in my sight and pushed and elbowed everyone else out of the way without much restraint. My touch would heal them anyway.

We finally got to the other side of the court, where there was actually room to breathe, and joined the spectators confused enough to run in the direction of the chaos. I lost track of Captain Goode, Sebastian, and even Mr. Kent's balloon as the smoke blocked our view, but we pressed on behind Emily, coughing our way through.

And suddenly the balloon was in front of us, deflated on the grass, the empty basket still burning away, the source of the smoke. No one from the Society was there. Only a few gawking spectators, policemen, and Laura, her feet locked to the ground, struggling against Emily's telekinetic hold and then her real hold.

"No, no, no, no," Laura whispered, every bit of her small and helpless. She sank back into Emily's arms. "He's going to kill Nicky!"

I put my hands on Laura's shoulders, trying to keep her still, trying to calm myself at the same time. My body was vibrating with tension, every nerve on alert, every bit of me stretched to the limit. "Laura. Look at me. Captain Goode won't. He told me himself. The powers are valuable. He'll keep them alive. And we'll get them back. Say it."

Laura repeated me, sniffles between each word. "We'll—get—them—back."

I took a deep breath. She took one herself. And another. Calming herself enough that Emily and I could loosen our holds.

Miss Chen's frown cut between us. "I know he wants them alive, but that's exactly why we should be back to panicking and running."

"What . . . what do you mean?" I asked.

"He can enhance Mr. Kent and ask Mr. Braddock anything," she said. "What do you think will be his first question?"

Chapter Nineteen

"MRS. TUFFINS!" I burst through the door after Miss Chen, the others close behind us. "Are you here? Mrs. Tuffins!"

My panic was in full force. With Mr. Kent and Sebastian captive, there was no doubt Captain Goode knew our hiding place. And with so many Society of Aberrations members already gathered with him, an attack was likely minutes away. It was one thing to put ourselves in danger, but now we'd put the lives of Mrs. Tuffins and her people at risk. More innocents with the unfortunate luck of simply knowing us.

"Dears?" She shuffled out of the parlor, her face wreathed in concern. "What's happened? Is something the matter? Let me get you some tea—"

"No! No time! I am so sorry, this is very, ah . . ."

I looked at the others, suddenly realizing this was going to be impossible to explain quickly. Miss Chen's wide eyes and swift head shake made it clear she did not want the responsibility. Catherine opened her mouth a few times and shrugged.

"We all possess strange powers. Except Miss Harding and Miss Kent," Emily announced, floating a ribbon in the air as proof. "And Captain Goode is an evil man who very much wants to kill us."

She gave a nod, as if the matter was very much settled. I stared between her and Mrs. Tuffins's puzzled face. This was rather a lot to take in. There was a part of me that hoped she might faint.

But Mrs. Tuffins seemed to be puzzled for an entirely different reason. "Why I know that, my dears. Was that a secret?"

"Oh, um, a little?" I said.

"Well, goodness me, I don't believe I have told anyone—I always keep my guests' affairs private—but it would be a little hard not to have noticed!"

A very good point.

"Thank you, you are such a wonderful, understanding hostess," I said, taking her hand. "But I am afraid everyone here needs to leave. At once."

This time she took in Laura's tear-stained face and looked completely bewildered. "Leave? The house? Oh heavens, did Mr. Braddock's trial not go well?"

She paid much more attention than I thought. I really should have expected that from a Tuffins.

"It did not. And Captain Goode and other members of the Society will be here any moment, and I do not think they would hesitate to kill everyone in the house," I said, adopting Emily's blunt manner. I gestured for the others to go and pack up their things. "Is there somewhere you can stay for some time?"

"Well, my sister's, but . . ." Mrs. Tuffins looked terribly distressed, and I felt like the worst possible person.

"I am so very sorry for this. We will find a way to make it up to you," I said. "But we need to get everyone out of here. Our lives depend on it."

I gave her hand one more squeeze and ran upstairs to grab whatever I could stuff into a small bag. Rose was in our room, lips white as she hurriedly packed up her borrowed medical supplies.

"We will find a way through—"

"It will be all ri—"

We both spoke at once, and I threw her a rueful smile. It was not all right, and both of us knew it. But thinking that helped nothing. We had to make do with what we had. Which at least helped with the packing. It took our group no more than a minute to finish—one of the few advantages to already losing everything we had.

Back downstairs, the house was full of commotion. The cook was running out the front door, her face full of terror. In the middle of it all stood Tuffins, directing the chaos with the efficiency and grace of a general in battle.

"Everyone else is out front," he said, picking up a small suitcase. "The carriages are ready."

"Carriages?"

"I know a coachman nearby, and he is lending us his. We will not all fit in one."

"You are extraordinary. I think you should run England."

"I will consider it."

Outside, the sun was setting, a wound bleeding across the sky. Gas lamps were being lit and the streets were crowded with people headed home, eagerly discussing the latest news of Captain Goode and Sebastian. Miss Chen and Miss Rao waited in the first carriage, while Rose and Catherine climbed up. Laura and Emily hurried down the stairs to the other with Mr. Adeoti behind, clutching his notebooks tightly to his chest.

Finally Tuffins and his mother exited, descending the stairs behind me. She looked troubled but composed, and Tuffins simply looked like he always did. He handed his mother and me up and climbed up to the driver's seat in front. The borrowed carriage took off and we were about to follow when Laura banged the roof.

"Oh no! Soot!" she yelped.

"Oh dear." Mrs. Tuffins looked truly panicked for the first time since I had met her.

Laura scrambled for the door. "I have to get him!"

Emily stayed her with her hand, already peering out the window. "He's coming," she said calmly.

She pointed up to the rooftops, where she held the black cat floating in the air. Gently, he drifted across the street, curled up and unbothered, looking like an errant plume of smoke from a chimney. As Soot made his descent, Tuffins opened the carriage door for him and Emily safely landed him in Mrs. Tuffins's lap. She clutched him to her bosom, while Laura burst into tears again and the carriage rumbled forward.

Thank goodness. We were all out. Everything was all right, for the time being.

But as we reached the main thoroughfare, a loud crackling and a boom erupted from behind us. Our carriage turned to join the traffic and our heads turned with it, out the right side window, upon the street we'd left.

The boarding house was on fire.

The street glowed and flickered as lightning struck it repeatedly. But it didn't come from the clear, twilight sky. It came from below, from the electric woman in front of the house. Sparks leaped from her fingers and ignited the house, the fire spreading so quickly, I would have thought the roof was doused in spirits.

"Oh heavens!"

Mrs. Tuffins was clutching the drapery of the carriage, knuckles white as she stared, even when we rolled along and the house was no longer in sight. Black smoke billowed up from the roof. I tried to find some words, but they all died by the time they reached my lips, a heavy guilt crushing them down.

"I will find you another house," Emily said into the shocked silence. "I will move Buckingham Palace wherever you want it. We'll help you decorate it exactly like yours. This isn't fair."

Mrs. Tuffins shook her head and held Laura to her. "It will be all right, dears. It will be all right."

This was our fault. We should have never come here to bring this chaos to good people's lives. Mrs. Tuffins had saved wages her entire life for that boarding house and only ever wanted to help us, far past the point of kindness.

As the carriage rolled to a stop at her sister's home and we said our good-byes, I silently promised myself to make this up to her. I would heal her every day. I would ask George to grow her the most beautiful garden. I had no idea how, but we would find a way to un-ruin this charitable woman's entire life and give her back a home.

The driver's hatch opened, and Tuffins's voice floated down. "Where to now, Miss Wyndham?"

I gave him the directions and instructed everyone to stay in the carriage once we reached our destination until I gave the word. We were off again, the horses trotting swiftly through the evening traffic that Tuffins navigated with ease. When we arrived, I opened the carriage door but did not get out. Instead, I spoke softly through the crack.

"Arthur? It's Miss Wyndham. If you can hear me, please, we need your help."

I opened the curtain on the window and gave a wave up to the dark roof where I'd last met them—in case William was looking out and on duty. Emily and Laura gave me curious looks but said nothing. Only Mr. Adeoti's eyes went wide. He would have heard of my friends before—fringe Society members who ran a gambling hall.

The minutes stretched on, my mind spinning through the other places we could hide, acquaintances we could call on. Nothing seemed safe. Sebastian and Mr. Kent knew me too well. Every idea I could think of was an idea they would have and tell Captain Goode. I knew Arthur and William would probably be on that list, too, but maybe they knew a place that Sebastian and Mr. Kent didn't. Our best hope was to catch them first. But it seemed we were too late.

I was ready to tap the roof to send us to an inn when a rough voice sounded outside the carriage, speaking to Tuffins.

"'Round through 'ere."

Arthur. He'd heard me.

We slowly rolled around the corner, pulling into a dead-end alleyway. I cautiously opened the door to see Arthur's wide, bearded face. He smiled and helped me down.

"Why, Miss Wyndham. Nice to see you're still safe."

"You too, Arthur. Is William here, too?"

"I am!" William peered around a door cunningly hidden in the wall of the gambling house. "You brought friends." His keen eyes took in the two carriages.

"I hate to bother you, but I am afraid we have nowhere else to go. Captain Goode has Sebastian." I didn't try to disguise the heartbreak I felt at the thought. They would hear it in my voice and see it on my face.

Instantly their mood changed at the mention of the man who had saved them from Dr. Beck years before. "Aye, we've been followin' the news. Come on, inside, all of youse."

"He has Mr. Kent, too," I said. "Which means they could be on their way here next."

Arthur cocked an eyebrow at me. "Don't worry, we'd 'ear them long before they get 'ere."

"And we're a gamblin' hall," William added. "We 'ave more secret exits than regular ones."

I turned back to the carriages and nodded, finding it strange that brothels and gambling halls filled me with more confidence than the police and courts. "We can trust them, I promise," I said to the others.

My friends all filed out reluctantly, belongings in hand. Arthur and William ushered them inside, making introductions.

Laura gave Tuffins an extremely long hug. "Tuffins, please be safe. Don't do anything dangerous."

"I'll try to resist the temptation," Tuffins said, hugging her back, "as long as you're safe as well."

She finally let go with a watery sob, and Emily took her inside.

"Thank you, Tuffins, for today and every other day," I told him. "You are remarkable, and I am sorry to have put you through so much. Please be assured that we will find another house, something to repay you and your mother."

I thought it a testament to him that he did not protest, just nodded solemnly.

"You will find them," Tuffins said with a simple certainty. "Please call on me at my aunt's when you do."

"I will," I said and gave the best steward in possibly the whole world a small wave as he hopped back up on the carriage and led his neighbor off. The steady clacking of hooves faded away down the street.

Arthur and William waited patiently for me by the small side door.

"Thank you for taking us in," I told them as we ducked inside. "I know it's a risk since you're still part of the Society."

William led us through the winding and cramped back halls

and stairs. "We'd been 'oping you'd stop by since Braddock's been in the papers."

"Wanted to 'elp, but didn't know where to find ya," Arthur said.

"Arthur wanted to walk down every street listening for you," William put in.

"Still better than your balloon idea."

"Hey, that Kent fellow's balloon worked, I heard," William argued, looking to me for confirmation.

"Yes, it was brilliant and foolish," I said. "Like most things Mr. Kent does."

"Well, it's confused a lot of people, from the chatter I hear," Arthur said. "Some think Goode's been lying; others think Braddock's even more of a villain; some think they're working together."

"I hope everyone comes to their senses soon," I said.

They let us into their office and stopped at a seemingly ordinary bookshelf.

"You lot can hide in here tonight. Best stay out of the way of the customers."

With that ominous pronouncement, William pulled out a book and the wall creaked open.

"Oh my!" Emily said. "A secret room!"

"Not only that," Arthur ducked in and motioned for the rest of us to follow.

The room was barely large enough for all of us to stand in, and I wondered how we could stay the night.

"Through here." He was suddenly opening up yet another wall with a lever I couldn't see.

"A secret room inside a secret room!" Emily said, nudging her friend. Laura wiped her tears and looked up, curious.

Miss Rao pinned me with a look. "This is a proper shelter," she said, as if England and I had failed her to this point.

This room was larger than the last and filled with threadbare couches and a couple of camp beds covered with fraying fabric. It wasn't the coziest room, but it also wasn't on fire, which was our main criterion at the moment.

"Sorry there ain't much," William said. "We'll have more for you in the morning."

"'Til then, try to get rest," Arthur said. "If you need anything, tap this wall. I'll 'ear you."

"But don't tap this wall," William said, pointing to one displaying several seascape prints. "That drops you into the sewers."

With that, the two men left, the wall clicking shut behind them.

Our ragtag group ambled around the space, looking lost and uncomfortable. Rose and Catherine settled onto one couch, taking up the old newspapers on the side tables for some distraction. Laura curled up with a pillow on another couch, while Emily squeezed in next to her and floated a blanket onto the both of them. Mr. Adeoti wandered around the room, pausing at some of the objects, reading their pasts. Miss Rao took a seat in front of a chess board, and Miss Chen took the opposite place.

"I hope those two remembered to tell us all the secret traps." Miss Chen said, warily glancing at her chair.

"It should please you to know that no one has died in here," Mr. Adeoti declared. "In the past week, at least."

"Oh, good," Miss Chen replied. "Now I'm going to worry about every room where you don't tell me that."

I took a place on the couch, feeling as helpless as I did that awful night in the church. As tired as I was, it was impossible to sleep a wink, even as the candles around the room went out one by one, and everyone else dozed off. My mind whirled with fretful thoughts, and after sitting wide awake for hours, coming up with fourteen more painful ways to kill Captain Goode, I gave up on that list.

Instead, I thought about all the ways I might help Sebastian. And soon, I was dreaming of them.

Chapter Twenty

ARLY THE NEXT MORNING, Arthur and William led us into the main gambling hall, the sunlight pouring into the room through the high windows. There was something strange about seeing such a rowdy, chaotic place so vacant and lifeless. The sound of our footsteps bounced across the room. The absence was almost palpable with the pungent stench of cigars, alcohol, and sweat lingering in the air.

"This is, ah . . . pleasant," Miss Chen said.

"It smells like a dragon that got very sad and lonely," Emily put in.

"That . . . actually describes it rather well," I admitted, glad I didn't have an enhanced power of smell.

Fortunately, our hosts had ways of countering the scent: freshly baked bread and fragrant tea waited for us on the bar. Starving, I practically inhaled the food. But the momentary pleasure gave way to suspicion. Mrs. Tuffins had a habit of bringing us delicious pastries on the worst of mornings.

"What's happened?" I asked.

Arthur and William looked sheepish.

"Did someone from the Society come by last night?" I asked.

"No one, surprisingly," William replied. "It was like any other night."

"'Cept the conversation," Arthur said. "Everyone going on about the trial, about the balloon, about where Captain Goode's gone. Some of 'em wanted to make bets about the verdict."

"There's a verdict?" I asked.

"It's not good." William sighed and reached behind the bar. He pulled out an assortment of morning newspapers, all with the same bold word in the headlines.

EXECUTION.

My heart twisted upon itself. The bread tasted like sawdust, impossible to swallow. My sight blurred.

"The jury reconvened last evening after the interruption," Catherine read. "They found him guilty. The execution is set for tomorrow morning in public at Tower Hill. What utter nonsense! How is this allowed?"

"Evelyn," Rose said, holding me from behind. She gently took the bread from me and set it on a plate. "We will get him back."

"Captain Goode's scared. That's why he's doing this," Miss Chen added, skimming the newspapers. "Some of these columnists aren't happy about his confessions."

"It'll be an illusion," Catherine insisted. "He wouldn't kill Mr. Braddock. It doesn't make sense otherwise. Captain Goode wanted all the powers."

I shook my head, which felt light as air. "He doesn't need Sebastian's power. He has plenty of other ways of hurting people. This is to bring an end to any doubts the trial stirred up."

"Mr. Adeoti, do you have any more ideas for where they are?" Laura asked, her eyes red-rimmed from the difficult night. "Maybe you can find out where Captain Goode bought his clothing, and you can go touch the tailor's suit and find out something bad he did and make him bring Captain Goode in for a fitting, and we catch him."

"I'm sorry. I don't have the tailor information," Mr. Adeoti said and gave an uncomfortable laugh. "I also don't believe I have the constitution for blackmail."

"I'll do it," Emily said. "I'll blackmail everyone."

"Wait a moment." Arthur froze, tilting his head up. The room fell silent. "I 'ear something. Willy, check the roof, to the north."

William was already bounding up the stairs. He disappeared into the hidden door in the wall while the rest of us watched Arthur's face for clues and waited with bated breath for things to somehow get even worse.

"How many do you hear?" I whispered.

"Only one so far," he said. "Flying girl."

"Which? The young lady who can grow wings, or the one who flies without?" Mr. Adeoti asked.

"Don't hear wings."

My heart leaped at that. Then it had to be her. . . .

William shouted something muffled from the roof.

"'E sees 'er," Arthur translated. He started leading the way upstairs. "It's 'er alone. She usually delivers orders, but we best get you in the secret-secret room in case."

"A girl about fifteen or sixteen, yes?" I asked, climbing up to the second floor behind him. "Her name, what is it?"

"Miss Lewis," William said, opening the secret door from the other side and ushering us through. "Eliza Lewis."

"Yes! That's her," I said. The girl from that day I healed Oliver at the Society. I couldn't forget the way he looked at her with concern. "I need to speak to her."

The two men exchanged doubtful glances. "Not a good idea. You see, she works for 'im."

"I know that," I said. "But I don't think she wishes to work for the Captain. She might help. Especially after the confession at the trial. He admitted to killing a friend of ours."

They stared at me, hard. "If she tells 'im you lot are here . . ."

"It's already a risk being here," I said. "And we're going to need their help against Captain Goode."

I could feel the doubts on the tips of everyone's tongues, but Arthur and William finally conceded with sighs. "All right. If you're sure, miss. . . ."

"I am not. But we have to know more."

As our group made its way up into Arthur's and William's office, Catherine held me back. "Evelyn." She was beginning to issue a dire warning, I was sure.

"He's going to die." I turned to her, holding her with my gaze. "I have to find a way to help him."

"I was just going to say, I agree." She smiled a little. "It's worth the try."

"Oh," I said, a pang of guilt in my chest. "Well I—thank you for constantly being sensible and . . . you. Even though that's meant all these arguments."

"It makes it all that much better when we finally agree," she said. "Then I know we truly have a good idea."

We followed everyone else up and found empty seats around the cozy room. Arthur opened the window, and seconds later, Eliza veered to a controlled stop outside. She carefully floated inside, blinking as her eyes adjusted to the dim office.

"No!" She caught sight of us and turned to flee, but William closed the window and tried to calm her.

"They just want your help," he said.

"You can't be here!" She looked trapped and hovered near the ceiling, buzzing with fear and irritation.

"Eliza, do you know me? I saw you training with Oliver; he mentioned you as a friend." She looked pained, and I pressed on.

"Captain Goode killed Oliver, using Mr. Braddock. All I want is to save him, Mr. Kent, and anyone else who doesn't want to be in the Society. Do you think you can help us? We would never harm you; we want to help. I know George doesn't want to be there. He's another friend of yours, right?" I tried to speak as calmly as possible, though it was probably still a nervous jumble.

Slowly Eliza lowered herself to the ground, her eyes still darting anxiously between us. "He'll hurt my pa and sister if I try to leave."

"He made the same threats to us when we were part of the Society," I tried to say soothingly. "I refused to do something for him, and my sister would have died had it not been for Miss Chen here refusing her order as well. Just know that if enough people refuse him, he can't carry out his threats."

"But if the Captain finds out I talked to you—"

"Is he still looking for us?"

"We won't tell 'im nuffin'." Arthur smiled gently, his cheek dimpling as his face relaxed. The two men might have menacing disguises from Camille, but they barely covered up their gentle natures.

She bit her lip and nodded, seeming more reassured by him than me, and spoke to Arthur directly. "I heard he questioned the prisoners all night."

Hmm. If he was asking them about where I and the others would go, Mr. Kent and Sebastian must have come up with a long list of places to search for us.

Or he was learning more about our weaknesses to keep us from stopping the execution.

"Is Captain Goode really planning an execution for tomorrow?" I asked.

"Yes, we all have to be ready at nine o'clock. He wants all Society members, including you two." Eliza tilted her head toward

Arthur and William. "Those are the orders I'm delivering to everyone right now."

"That's very helpful," I smiled even as I wanted to be violently sick. He was using the execution as a trap to capture us. I paused, choosing my next questions carefully in case Captain Goode decided to question her. "Do the orders explain what's going to happen?"

She pulled out a few rolled-up sheets of paper and set it on the desk. Arthur unfurled them, revealing written instructions and diagrams of Tower Hill.

"Do you have a map of London with this area?" I asked.

William found one on their bookshelf and opened it up on a large table in the middle of the room that we all gathered around. Using the diagram as a reference, he pointed to the gardens on the map. "The scaffold seems to be set up 'ere in the center. And looks like Society members surround it on the south, west and east. 'E wants Arthur and me to be watching the south."

Trying to keep my hand from shaking, I pointed to the map, south of the gardens, where the Tower of London sat. "Where is he going to bring the prisoners from? Is he staying with them?"

Eliza nodded and traced a route on the map. "In the White Tower. They're going to walk them down this way, over the moat, and up here."

"And where is the rest of the Society coming from?" I asked.

"We're staying in these houses here," Eliza pointed.

"And do you know how many people there are?"

"Maybe twenty or thirty? I don't know them all."

"That's all right," I said. "Do you know if anyone else is unhappy with the Society?"

"Well, Georgie is. And my friend Shirin."

"Can you tell me about Shirin?"

Eliza smiled a little, obviously adoring of her friend. "Shirin can control rocks. Makes them fly or shift or create neat sculptures. She's really clever with them. She built the court at Lincoln's Inn fields all by herself."

"That's remarkable," I said, remembering that girl from their training with Oliver. "Is there anyone else?"

"I don't . . . I don't know," she said. "Sometimes others seem to hate it, but no one says anything. It's hard to trust anyone."

"Don't worry. I understand. That's all we wanted to know." My heart sank a little. Only three young people would maybe—*maybe*—be on our side.

"Eliza, you best be getting back to your duties," Arthur said. "Are there any other questions?"

Our group was silent, not wanting to push Eliza any further. I answered for everyone. "Thank you, Eliza."

She pursed her lips and gave a quick nod before William opened the window to let her out.

"I take it this is our plan then," Catherine said, pointing to the map.

"So we attack from the north at the execution?" Miss Chen asked.

"Willy and I won't warn anyone 'til it's too late," Arthur said.

"I will sweep up the power remover with my winds," Miss Rao offered.

"No, we're not attacking during the execution," I said.

The group stared at me as though I had gone mad.

"But I . . . I thought you wanted to save them," Laura's voice was thin and high, and Emily took her hand.

"I do," I said. "But Captain Goode wants us to as well. I think that's why he's making it so public and obvious. It's another trap. To get us to attack him when he's fully prepared and expecting it."

"But what's the alternative?" Catherine asked.

"We attack the Tower of London tonight," I answered. "Captain

Goode will be preparing for tomorrow and won't be expecting us at all. It'll be dark, Miss Chen can extinguish any lights, and we'll stay behind the walls so he can't see us and turn our power off from the White Tower. We'll sneak over to where the Society members are staying and ask for their help. I know everyone won't turn, but between our powers and the plants and rocks, we'll be able to restrain the others without harming them."

"But you saw how nervous this girl was," Miss Chen said, gesturing out the window. "No one helped Mr. Braddock and Mr. Kent when they tried to expose Captain Goode. How will this be any different?"

"That was very sudden," I said. "They barely had time to consider it."

"And this time I'll ask them," Rose said.

She had such a quiet, low voice. And yet instantly everyone froze, acutely focused on my sister and her calm, monumental declaration.

"No," Catherine said firmly.

"It has to be me. If they are reluctant, it's the only way to persuade them to join us." Rose spoke as though she had decided this ages ago. But because it was Rose, and because everyone wanted to protect her, voices rang out in protest across the room.

"Too dangerous."

"You can't be harmed!"

"We will find another way."

Even Miss Rao was shaking her head in disapproval.

I was torn clean in two. It would help, of course, to have Rose there, but the desire to wrap her in blankets and keep her safe forever was overwhelming.

But my glorious sister, who was secretly at least as stubborn as I was, calmly insisted. "I know you want me safe, but this is what I want. I couldn't live with myself if you were all captured or killed, or if everyone in the Society was trapped there for the rest of their lives. I want to go."

Whether or not Rose ever went to medical school and became a doctor, she would always want to help people. It made the decision easier for me.

For Catherine as well, it seemed. "Then if it's what you want to do, you should do it." Catherine's clear, firm voice cut through the grumblings.

And as my sister's jaw dropped a little, I realized something about Rose's power. It wasn't just the amount of exposure that affected how we treated her. Part of it was who we were. It was why Mr. Hale's and Camille's love manifested itself as selfish and possessive. Why the murderous Mr. Jarsdel was quite eager to kill for her. Why our protective mother was so strict with us. And why Catherine and I agreed to put her at risk if it's what she wanted.

Though my sister said nothing, I had the feeling she realized this, too. Her eyes looked different, hope brightening the blues. I could swear I watched Rose fall further in love at that moment.

"Really?" she asked.

"Of course." Catherine looked almost puzzled. "I want you to be happy." Her voice trailed off and she blushed as she realized the others were looking on, bewildered.

"I am going," Rose announced again, more firmly, still smiling at Catherine.

"She is going," Catherine repeated, before dropping her smile and fixing the rest of us with very stern stares. "So we better come up with a plan that keeps her safe."

Chapter Twenty-One

―――――――

THE TEN OF us stood gathered on a rooftop, staring at the Tower of London, the Thames resting between us. The city lay shrouded in shadows at three in the morning. The sky sat starless, and silence blanketed the river. It felt like the world was closing its eyes and taking a deep breath.

With my opera glasses, I swept my gaze over our target. The White Tower was the one brightly lit building, standing tall in the center of the inner ward, taunting us. It was surrounded by smaller buildings and houses and then an inner wall and an outer one. I could barely make out anything else beyond the general shapes of the battlements and towers, but Arthur and William could apparently hear and see straight to the heart of the castle.

"It's as Miss Lewis said, 'e's in the White Tower," Arthur said, pointing to the tall keep. "Sleeping."

"And 'e's got Braddock and Kent a floor below, chained up," William said with a cringe. "A couple guards watching them, I see."

"But only a few along the outer wall. No one watchin' the Traitors' Gate," Arthur added, pointing to the half-hidden boat entrance.

"Get through there, break a small hole in the inner wall, and you'll find the rest sleeping in those houses," William said, making it sound like a simple trip to the market.

"Could Mr. Pratt be creating an illusion?" I asked.

"He's not good enough to hide all those people, even enhanced," Miss Chen said. "Too much movement to keep track of everything."

"And we can see through them," William said.

"Good."

"That doesn't mean I don't think there's a trap," Miss Chen clarified. "I would like it on the record that there will probably be one."

"As long as we can sneak Rose inside," I said, watching Miss Rao's thick fog over the Thames grow even thicker. The black river was much more daunting in person than on a map, but I had to keep reminding myself that it was better to approach from the dark river than the well-lit streets north of the tower. Rose just needed a moment to speak to the Society peacefully, to sway them before they were ordered to kill us.

"Is everyone ready?" I asked.

Our group slowly came together on the corner of the rooftop. Miss Rao and Miss Chen nodded to me. Emily gave Laura a big hug and promised to bring her brother back. Mr. Adeoti gave me an encouraging smile and wrapped a ribbon around my wrist so he could record the adventure in case I died, which he assured me I definitely wouldn't. Rose handed her medical bag to Catherine, and they spoke softly in shadows at the far corner. Before Rose turned to join us, Catherine pulled her back and gave her a gentle kiss, and my heart leaped. I bit my lip against a smile, praying that we could keep Rose safe so this would be their first of many.

In pairs, Emily floated Miss Rao, Miss Chen, Rose, and myself down to the ground before following herself. Silently, we made our way to the embankment. Clouds covered the moon, their outlines glowing gray and blue in the sky. The water was a mirror image with patches of fog floating along the surface. Silhouettes of masts and docks matched the spires and towers along the skyline.

We found a skiff nearby, locked to a dock, rolling with the steady tide. Miss Chen broke it free, Emily adjusted the sail with a wave of her hand, and Miss Rao's gentle wind came in from behind. We crossed the quiet river, not a word passing between us. The sound of a distant ship horn echoed. The water kept time with its gentle, rhythmic splashes. Thunder rumbled across the Thames as Miss Rao eyed the sky, setting dark clouds in place over the tower in preparation for her lightning strikes. Emily stood at the bow, ready to maneuver around any obstacle that might suddenly appear in the thick fog. Miss Chen closed her eyes, deep in meditation as she tried to raise her powers as much as she possibly could.

About halfway across, we veered rather close to a small boat. Drunken men who had decided to end their night with a trip down the river. Even through the haze, their eyes slowly settled on Rose. "'Ey, girlie," one managed before his jaw snapped shut, courtesy of Emily.

Another tried to charm us, and she quieted him, too. I held a finger to my lips, a message that the third sailor apparently could not comprehend.

"Now listen here—"

And Emily flung him overboard, which quieted the rest of them.

As they faded into the fog, trying to pull their friend out of the water, I breathed a sigh of relief. Only a little farther and—

A blast of water surged out of the river, coiling around my arm like a tentacle. It wrenched me halfway out of the boat, but

Emily reacted quickly, seizing me telekinetically by my other arm, pulling me back in. More tentacles of water slithered out, wrapping around our boat, hugging it like an affectionate octopus. Before they could crush the wood to pieces, the tentacles burst apart into harmless splashes of water, thanks to Miss Chen's gaze. Miss Rao's winds increased, pushing us faster toward the tower.

Unfortunately, there was plenty more water between our destination and us. A giant wave emerged, slowly blocking our view of the tower. Behind it, Mr. Seward rose up atop a spire of water, looking entirely drenched and grumpy, like I imagined Poseidon might.

"Was he sleeping down there?" Emily asked.

"We'll see soon enough," Miss Chen said. "I can't break that wave. It's absurd."

"Then we'll use it against him," I said. "Miss Rao, can you—"

"I can," she said, already shifting the clouds. "Turn right, mover."

Her winds changed direction, pushing in from the port side, as Emily turned the sail to veer us east around the massive wall of water approaching. We bounced along the rising waves, the winds blowing my hair loose. The wave grew horizontally with us, looming closer like the great hand of a god, ready to swat us down.

Thunder reverberated in the sky. Mr. Seward heard it, leaping back right before the bolt of lightning streaked down. He lost control of his wave, but its momentum carried it. We still weren't going fast enough. I didn't know how Miss Rao was planning to outrun it.

Until we veered behind a massive ship that shielded us from the attack. She'd steered us into St. Katharine Docks. Emily threw us off the skiff and up onto the soaked deck. I mouthed an apology to a shocked sailor and peered past him at our destination. We'd gone a bit off course, but we weren't too far. I could see a path along the crowd of boats.

"This way!" I shouted, grabbing Rose's hand.

Emily pulled the three of us up into the air and over the five-foot gap down to the barge below. Behind us, Miss Rao and Miss Chen made the leap, propelled by a heavy gust of wind.

Mr. Seward, however, followed as well. More tendrils of water rose up around the barges, some battering our bodies like quick punches and others attempting to drag us into the water. Miss Chen and Emily did their best to divert the attacks as we hopped from boat to boat, heading ever closer to Traitors' Gate. Crates toppled around us, leaks sprang up and swung at us, and suddenly the air was full of fire. We coughed through the smoke and dodged the growing flames, desperately looking for the source.

On the next barge, Mr. Jarsdel was waiting for us.

Rose waved to him for help. "Mr. Jarsdel, please—"

"You won't manipulate me again!" he cut her off.

A blast of fire erupted from his palms, giving us the choice of staying put and burning or jumping into the water and drowning. The former seemed slightly more manageable, so I pushed Rose behind me, but before the flames hit, a third option presented itself. From an adjacent barge, Emily redirected Mr. Seward's water attacks in front of us, blocking the blast of fire, the steam hissing inches from my face.

Before Mr. Jarsdel could attack again, Miss Chen broke a mast above him. Using his hands like twin rockets, he thrust himself off the barge and retreated onto the roof of a low dock-side warehouse.

Rose and I hopped across two more barges and a rowboat and rejoined the others at the end of the wharf. Traitors' Gate loomed ahead like a beacon.

"Ev! Mr. Jarsdel hates me! He wants to kill me!" Rose gasped. She had a giddy grin on her face. "My power must wear off!"

"Rose, I'm happy for you," I said, feeling a blast of heat come far too close to my head. I pulled her forward. "But we might want to survive this to tell Catherine."

"Yes, that," Rose said.

"Keep running, charmer," Miss Rao said.

That's when I noticed how windy it had gotten. The smoke from the burning boats swirled around us at Miss Rao's command, giving us the perfect cover to escape. We pounded toward the tower, wayward shots of fire and desperate tendrils of water flying into our path, but we pushed forward, refusing to let the plan go even more astray. We had to sneak in and address the rest of the Society before they attack—

A blast of electricity struck me before we could reach the entrance. It burned my chest and knocked me flat on my back on the stone wharf. Miss Rao was on her knees next to me, blood dripping from two spikes embedded in her chest. Lanterns and dimly lit faces dotted the top of the tower's outer walls. I made out the face of our electricity-producing friend. The other Society members were already awake and ready. And they weren't going to give us a chance to sway them.

Acid and electricity assaulted us from the front while smoke and needles came from behind. But Miss Rao's winds were stronger and more concentrated now, encircling us like a protective shield.

I set my hands on her shoulder and took deep breaths, attempting to heal both our wounds as quickly as possible. She wrenched out the spikes and climbed to her feet, the winds growing stronger, sweeping up the renewed fire attacks from Mr. Jarsdel and the surges of water from Mr. Seward. Miss Chen, Emily, Rose, and I were trying to catch our breaths in the safety of the hurricane's eye, but its sheer power kept stealing them away.

"Do you still plan to sneak in and talk to them?" Miss Rao asked.

Her face showed no smile, but I could sense the sarcasm.

"Sneak? No. Are we still breaking in? Yes. If you can move this to the west, we are going to link arms and move with it." Everyone did so, forming a circle. The wind was roaring around us, and I shouted to be heard. "Miss Chen, break the gate when you can see it, and we will get inside as planned. Go!"

Miss Rao nodded tightly, and I held her arm, hoping my healing was at full capacity. We began to move, step by step, to the lip of the wharf, while the attacks rained down above us. Miss Rao gritted her teeth as fire and acid joined the storm, and Miss Chen grunted as stray drops fell on her shoulder. Without a free hand, I pressed my back into hers, healing the burning wound quickly and pushing her into view of the wooden gate.

"And what about when we get inside?" Rose yelled. "How will I get them to listen to me long enough to stop them from killing us. We have certainly lost the element of surprise."

Below us, the great gate splintered and cracked apart to form a small hole. Miss Chen concentrated hard on the wooden columns and iron bars in the center, ignoring the fire licking at us through Miss Rao's winds.

"I know how," I said, following the streaks of fire up to its source. "Emily, the moment Miss Chen is through, can you grab Mr. Jarsdel and keep him pinned him to the ground?"

She strained to see through the congested whirlwind and the darkness along the wall, but his flames made him easy to find. "Yes, there he is!"

"Good," I said. "He will use his blinding powers to break free. Everyone else, be ready to shut your eyes!"

Miss Chen pushed harder now, the metal cracking and exploding like dry twigs. We inched closer to the edge.

"Now, Emily!" Miss Chen shouted.

Mr. Jarsdel's fire blasts disappeared and his body crashed to the ground next to our circle. I shut my eyes, trusting in Emily. She huffed out a heavy breath and groaned with effort as she held him in place. Even through the roar of the winds and attacks, I could hear Mr. Jarsdel screaming and straining on the other side to be freed.

A few seconds later, a bright light flashed beyond my eyelids. I opened my eyes to peer through the whirlwind, finding the assault had stopped. Mr. Jarsdel had blinded everyone attacking us.

Emily yelped in shock. "Evelyn? Where are you?"

"I'm here," I said, taking her hand. "Your sight will heal in a minute or two. You did it perfectly. Just hold on; we're going to jump."

The arched entrance sat a few feet below the tower wharf. Miss Rao kept her fierce winds shielding us, while we hopped down over the edge, landing gently in the cold, dark water. I tugged at Emily's arm as we clambered over the broken remains of Traitors' Gate and up a set of stairs.

At last, we were in the Tower of London, huddled in the outer ward, the street between the inner and outer walls. Miss Rao shrouded us in fog and Miss Chen glanced at a few lanterns above, shattering and extinguishing the only sources of light. The defenders panicked.

"Dammit, they're inside!"

"I still can't bloody see!"

"Find them!"

Cursing and shuffling echoed down from the battlements as the Society scrambled to turn their attention to the inside to find us. Which is when we decided to make their task a little easier.

"Rose, ready?" I asked.

She took a deep breath. "Yes."

I grasped her hand and held it tight.

"My name is Rosamund Wyndham!" she shouted. "We aren't here to hurt any of you, I promise."

The booming voice echoed off the walls as the defenders hushed one another and searched for the source. As a precaution, I prodded Miss Rao and Miss Chen forward and pulled Rose and Emily farther down the passage.

"Captain Goode admitted he is threatening some of you and your families, forcing you to stay under his command. But if we all work together and stop him tonight, there will be no one to enforce those punishments."

We continued farther down the street. The sounds of footsteps above us followed. "Those of you voluntarily helping him for more power, you are only giving him more control over your life. There will be a day when you'll receive an order that hurts someone you love, and you will be powerless to do anything about it."

I turned us back around toward where we started, right outside Traitors' Gate. The fog surrounding us slowly began to dissipate, and the clouds shifted as the moonlight revealed the tower walls, the battlements, and the faces of our Society of Aberrations allies or enemies. Some of them blinked rapidly, their sight restored, looking as if they were coming out of a dream. They stared down at us, deciding our fates. My nerves were on edge, and I felt naked when the fog cleared.

"Please help us against him. So we can all go home. So we can all be safe."

For a moment, no one moved on either side. We waited in complete silence, my gaze shifting between indecipherable faces and landing on Eliza, floating above us. I pleaded with my eyes, and she turned her gaze to her fellow members, judging their reactions to Rose's proposal.

"No!" Emily whispered suddenly, looking around in an absolute panic. "Evelyn, something's here!"

A pair of yellow eyes flickered in the darkness. I pulled Emily behind me with one hand and reached for my dagger fan with the other, ready to deal with the threat. But a winged woman was already in front of me, her warm breath on my face.

"I'm sorry," she said as her claws sank into my chest. "We have orders."

Chapter Twenty-Two

IT FELT HOT. As if five holes had burned right through me at once. I stumbled forward, swinging at her in desperation as I felt her other hand wrap around my throat. I didn't have the leverage to push her away, but fortunately, Emily didn't seem to have the same problem. With a scream, she flung the woman up over the stone wall and out of the castle.

As I coughed and tried to catch my breath, chaos broke out all around us.

Miss Chen and Rose spun around to give me support, leaving their backs open to a blast of fire. Miss Rao roused her heavy winds to shield us, but a man moving in bursts of speed slipped through and tackled her to the ground. And as Emily turned to help her, my animalistic attacker returned with her wings spread, swooping down like a bird of prey. All I could do was wheeze out a pitiful warning.

"Watch out—"

A miraculous blur knocked her out of the sky. She crashed to the ground with Eliza on top of her, keeping her pinned. The earth rumbled violently underneath us. A massive rock wall sprang up around us, shielding Miss Chen and Rose from Mr. Jarsdel's blast. Emily wrenched Miss Rao's attacker off and threw him at

Mr. Jarsdel. Vines slithered out of the ground like snakes, trapping all three attackers to the ground.

Oliver's friends. Thank God. I caught a glimpse of Eliza taking off toward a burning rooftop before a blast of electricity forced us to take cover under an archway.

"Rose, get in the center," I said. "Emily, up here with me. Miss Chen, Miss Rao, you watch the back. We need to help them."

"Can you even move?" Miss Chen asked.

Right, those stab wounds. I pressed my chest gently and felt a shock of pain course through me. Yes, very much still stabbed. But the fact that I'd forgotten about the injury for a moment had to be a good sign.

And there was no time to catch our breath. The rest of the Society members were picking sides. And there seemed to be plenty more still too scared to join us, judging from the fact that acid was melting through the archway. That was also on fire. And not at all suitable cover.

"Yes, it'll heal," I said, my eyes darting around, watching for movement on the battlements. "Remember the plan!"

I led the group forward out of the archway, toward the burning rooftop, hoping we'd find allies there. Beyond that, it was nearly impossible to know who was on our side, and no one was taking the time to hand us cards declaring their intentions. We marched down the outer ward street, keeping behind walls, staying out of sight of the White Tower, watching for attacks from the enemies above us.

A line of spikes flew at our heads first, and Emily flung them into a wall. Behind us, Miss Rao's winds did the same to acid, the stones sizzling. Another bolt of electricity lit up the passage, a streak headed straight for me, and Emily diverted it to the rooftop where the spikes had come from, earning an explosion and a yelp.

Sounds of other roof skirmishes echoed off the walls as we neared the burning rooftop. Rocks and vines and smoke spilled over the edges and then Shirin herself. The earth rose up to catch her, but the massive man with the powerful jumping ability pursued her, leaping off the roof, aiming his landing right where she lay.

And he hovered in midair helplessly. Emily floated him to the ground, and Shirin opened up the earth to swallow him up to his shoulders, leaving him stuck.

The street led us into a small square, where Shirin's friends were working together with other converts. Eliza plucked the metal-covered man from the battlements and dropped him over a pile of vines for George to ensnare. An older woman dressed in shawls and surrounded by ravens ordered the birds to swoop down at a long-haired man, whose hair moved to his every whim. He clutched a fistful that twined itself into a thick rope and swatted at the birds, but while he was distracted, an agile, strangely flexible man wrestled him to the ground and held him there until the ground opened up and trapped him there.

At the sight, I felt a little glimmer of hope. There were people fighting against Captain Goode. And we were winning. I couldn't help but imagine what was happening in the White Tower. Captain Goode did not want to leave the safety of it to join the fight. He was likely too scared of what we might do to him if he wasn't hiding behind his hostages. Stay safe, Sebastian. Hold on, Mr. Kent. Just a little while longer. We're coming.

"Miss Rao, catch," Miss Chen said as I heard something crumble behind us.

The winds picked up, rushing over our heads, throwing the acid woman into the square, where the vines restrained her.

"Well, that's a terrible power," Miss Chen said, glancing at the man's flailing hair. "Not jealous of that one."

I wasn't either until I realized where his hair was going.

"Miss Chen, the hair."

"Yes, I'll focus on the hairy man while there's an electric woman lurking in the shadows," she said, her back turned as she searched the rooftops. "There!"

Miss Chen exploded something behind me, and I felt the winds of Miss Rao throwing the electric woman into the square, where the hair crept through George's vines. The strands slipped into the metal man's hand, which rendered it into steel. Cords of steel that whipped up, cutting through the vines and rocks, freeing the prisoners, and wrapping around the raven woman's neck.

"*Miss Chen!*" Rose called.

Miss Chen finally turned around as a scream got her attention. "Oh."

Acid and lightning flew at us and veered into a tower as Emily and Miss Rao shielded us. The raven woman was lifted up high into the air, gasping for breath in the moonlight, her birds frantically fluttering around her. The steel cord snapped under Miss Chen's gaze, and Eliza swooped in to catch her.

And crashed on the ground in front of us.

Emily swept them behind us, and I knelt down to heal them. Bruised and bloody from the fall but nothing serious. Until Eliza stubbornly rose to her feet and tried to set off again. Nothing happened. She frowned in confusion and looked to the raven woman, who was watching her ravens abandon her. Then we both looked up to see Shirin, busy with shielding George, being caught by the leg from behind and flung over the wall into the inner ward.

"Remove the traitors' powers!" someone yelled.

Dammit. That's what they were doing. Putting them in view of the White Tower, where Captain Goode could see them and shut them off. Maybe he wasn't hiding. Maybe he knew the outcome, and it was in his favor.

"It appears they have a plan, too," I said.

And like that, the battle shifted. A group of five more emerged from the battlements to the north and strode down to the passageway to join the others. An ear-shattering scream came from one of them, tearing up the rocky street and knocking us back into the wall. In our daze, we found them raining everything they could down upon us. Electricity, acid, water, smoke, and steel.

Miss Rao responded by sending back the strongest winds she could. The air screamed, and I could barely hear my own thoughts as she and Emily pushed the Society's own attacks back on them. But nothing seemed to land. A man in the front had his hands out, encircling his group with a sort of shield blocking everything that came at them. They marched toward us, against Miss Rao's wind, as if they were taking a pleasant stroll through Hyde Park.

Some of their attacks, however, got through our defenses. I straightened up to guard my friends the best I could. I felt the sting of electricity hitting my cheek, the burn of the acid through my dress, even the lash of the steel hair cutting my arm.

"I'd rather have died at Captain Goode's house," Miss Chen yelled. "At least it wouldn't have been due to such a pathetic power!"

And that's when I noticed there was someone at the back of their group. Someone who hadn't used his power on us yet. Someone who had been up close to do it at Captain Goode's.

"Miss Chen, I have a terrible idea," I yelled. "Do you remember that man in the back?"

Miss Chen squinted through all the chaos, trying to place him. Her eyes widened in realization. "This is the least terrible of all your terrible ideas."

"Thank you."

"Miss Kane, as soon I remove that dark-haired man's shirt," Miss Chen yelled, "please throw him into his companions, one by one."

"All right," Emily said, as if that were a perfectly normal request.

I watched the metal man kneel down and shift the rocky street to steel, a path headed straight under us. As the electric girl took aim at the trail, I found it harder to swallow down my panic. "Miss Chen, they . . . are about to electrocute us."

Mr. Dunn's shirt ripped off, followed by the sleeves of the electric woman. They paused in shock, and Emily used the man like a billiard ball, tossing him against the others in turn. She knocked him into the electric woman first, and then Mr. Seward, Mr. Shaw, and the others as Miss Chen ripped their shirt sleeves and trouser legs open, revealing their limbs to be paralyzed by Mr. Dunn's touch. They had nowhere to run, the small shield their only sanctuary.

Not one minute later, as Miss Rao's wind died down, the bruised Mr. Dunn was the only one standing. Mainly because Emily was holding him up. A strange silence fell upon the castle. By instinct, my body braced itself for the next attack, but there wasn't one. They remained on the ground, unmoving.

"That should do it," Miss Chen said. "Keep a tight hold on him."

"How long will they stay that way?" Miss Rao asked.

"A day, I believe," Miss Chen said, adroitly stepping over them. She noticed Mr. Shaw's hand reaching out with faint clouds of smoke and seized it. "Oh, we missed this, Miss Kane."

Emily floated Mr. Dunn down to render Mr. Shaw's hand unusable. "What shall I do with him now?"

Miss Chen observed Shirin, waving from Beauchamp Tower. "I think they could use some protection."

We followed George and his depowered friends to the tower, where he sent up a vine for Shirin to climb down. He was the only one with a power left. While I healed Shirin, Emily floated

Mr. Dunn to George. He wrapped his vines around the man, holding him like a shield.

"Thank you for your help," I told them. "We're going to go get Captain Goode now. Make sure the other people you've restrained are no longer a danger. And stay out of sight of the White Tower."

"How are you going to get to him?" Shirin asked.

"We have a plan," I said.

Thunder rumbled as a storm churned overhead, and the clouds blocked the moonlight.

"Miss Rao, do you do those ominous rolls of thunder on purpose?" Miss Chen asked.

"Perhaps, destroyer," she replied.

Thunder rumbled again.

In pairs, Emily floated us up into Beauchamp Tower, which provided a clear view of the west side of the White Tower. We climbed to the top, staying low and hidden in the shadows as we peeked outside. Light flooded the entire tower green area. Trees had been cleared, and there was nowhere to hide. No one stood in any of the three floors of windows of the White Tower, but I could feel Captain Goode watching, waiting to catch us.

After a minute, Miss Chen explained why. "Bastard's put an illusion on the tower. I can't do anything."

"What do you mean?" Rose asked.

"He's covered up everything. I don't know where the lights really are," she said. "So I can't break them. And the windows only look empty so we can't attack them from here."

Thunder rumbled again, and we watched as Miss Rao's winds picked up within the inner ward. The stubborn lights seemed to be well protected. And if we tried to cross the lawn like this, our powers would be gone. We'd be helpless. And Sebastian wouldn't survive tomorrow.

"There is one alternative," I said slowly, feeling like I had said it before, like I had always known it would come to this.

Even in the dark, I knew they were all frowning at me.

"Ev, we didn't go through this whole plan so you'd charge after Captain Goode on your own again," Rose said.

"I won't be alone," I said. "All of you will help me from the outside."

"He'll still turn off your healing."

"But he wants me alive," I said. "He needs a healer. This is the best way I can think of."

Everyone sat in silence for a moment, thinking of something better. Nothing came.

"Are you sure?" Miss Chen finally asked.

I looked back at the path of destruction we'd carved across the Thames and through the tower to this spot. The path Rose, Emily, Miss Chen, and Miss Rao had made with amazing use of their powers. They had to keep them.

"I am."

As my friends spread out on the rooftops and battlements to find the right angles to watch the tower, I climbed down into Captain Goode's domain and stepped into the light. He could easily see me now. As I crossed the lawn, I tried futilely to raise my power, hoping my noble, self-sacrificing attitude or my Sebastian-focused mind might trigger something new. Of course, it did not.

There was no sensation, save for the chill that ran through me as he turned my powers off.

Chapter Twenty-Three

I FELT ANOTHER strange chill as I entered the White Tower and quickly received an explanation for it with a cold slash across my face. I pulled out my dagger fan and found myself facing that damn ice guard who refused to go away.

"Not so tough on your own?" Miss Quinn asked.

I swung at her, and she spat another ice shard at me, clipping my shoulder. She dodged my clumsy attack and kneed me in the gut. I lost my breath, and by the time I found it, she'd frozen my feet together into a block of ice and kicked me to the ground. I tried sliding away from her, chipping at the ice with my dagger and then resorting to banging the whole thing against the stone.

She smiled at the futility of the endeavor and then stared at me wide-eyed as the walls behind me started to crack and shatter, followed quickly by the ice around my feet.

I took the opportunity to kick her shins and scramble back up. I darted for the closest stairs I could find as more walls on the west side started to come down, exposing the inside of the White Tower and giving Miss Chin and the others a better view of my enemy.

I made it up to the second floor, where I found what I was looking for: the extensive armory. Figures in the shapes of past kings and their horses donning four-hundred-year-old armor. Glass cases of swords, pistols, and shields. I smashed one open with debris and pulled out the tallest shield I could find. It was heavy and unwieldy, but when Miss Quinn caught up to me and unleashed the full power of her freezing breath, I blocked the entire attack, beyond a slight chill in my feet.

She was getting frustrated, especially with the constant barrage from my friends. Every time Miss Chen broke open another section of the tower, Emily would grab Miss Quinn, dodging her attack and throwing her into the glass cases. In desperation, she fired shards at Beauchamp Tower and blew a mist into the air that gave her some cover, but that only helped her make it behind another wall that Miss Chen started cracking apart.

I maneuvered into the exposed areas, keeping my shield between Miss Quinn and me. Every wound stayed with me now, but it wasn't fear that made me defensive. It was trust in my friends' powers. That they were doing everything I couldn't do to help. I readied my shield, waiting for the last of the walls to fall away, when I discovered Miss Quinn had friends of her own. A knife sliced into my arm, and as I reflexively swung back at the attacker and found myself stumbling through a body, I knew exactly who it was.

"Fei, dear, this has gone far enough!" Mr. Pratt's illusion yelled out into the darkness.

Another slash tore across my chest, and I had to start swinging wildly, hitting air. He'd managed to render himself invisible. Emily tried to help by throwing debris, but nothing seemed to make contact with the invisible enemy. Blood dripped from my body onto the floor, and now I was certain my power had been shut off. My arm was a mass of hot pain and my skin stung where the shallower cut had sliced across my chest.

"I understand the need to preserve your feminine modesty by rejecting my first few proposals, but you need not destroy the Tower of London for it!"

Glass broke in a corner display case and a sword and shield quickly disappeared before Emily's rocks could make it there. I started to back away, though I didn't quite know where to back away from. I barely knew how to fight a visible enemy. How could I fight an invisible one?

Then I heard Miss Chen answer me with the crumbling of the ceiling. Dust sprinkled from above, disappearing wherever it fell upon Mr. Pratt. Holding my shield out, I backed away from him while keeping one eye on Miss Quinn, who seemed to be preparing an attack. Thunder growled in the sky with me.

"If it would make you feel better, your traitorous friend Miss Wyndham can attend our wedding!" Mr. Pratt's illusion offered from behind me. "We'd have to keep her in a box, of course, but we can make it look quite lovely!"

Three knives flew at me at once, two illusions making no sound as I blocked with my shield, and a real one leaving a burning slash in my leg.

I stumbled toward the edge of the building, where a patter of rain started to fall, and I felt the awful helplessness of slipping on ice. My legs spun out from under me, my dagger clattering out of my hand. I was completely open to attack, which, of course, is when Mr. Pratt charged.

A charge I could now see, with Miss Rao's barrage of rain droplets disappearing upon contact, forming an outline of a man swinging his sword down upon me.

I wrenched my shield up, blocking the attack from the ground, my shoulder screaming in pain. I kicked at his feet while Emily's stones struck his head. With a final push of my shield, I twisted it and slammed into Mr. Pratt's torso, knocking him off-balance and off the building with a scream.

A shard struck me in the shoulder. I spun around, putting my shield up to block, feeling the thumps of icicles lodging in the front. I rose up to my knees behind the cover as I felt shivers and heard Miss Quinn let loose another heavy freezing breath. Nothing touched me, but as I heard her footsteps come closer, I tried to move the shield and found it frozen to the ground. I pulled and pulled in desperation, waiting for Miss Chen to help. But the ice had been formed on the other side of the shield, out of her sight.

The footsteps came closer and closer. I reached out for my dagger on the ground, and another shard impaled my hand immediately. Which left me stuck on the edge with no weapon and one hand.

"I'm sure that will heal eventually," Miss Quinn said.

I turned with her voice and steps, trying to keep the shield between us as I tried to think of a plan. The rain had stopped, along with Emily's rocks, and it seemed my friends had also run out of ideas.

What was the most unexpected thing I could do? She knew I was cautious, afraid, searching for a way to survive without my healing. I wouldn't be reckless enough to charge straight at her.

So that's what I did. I steeled my nerves and leaped out from my cover, startling her into firing a shard straight into my foot. My terrible charge quickly came to an end as I hit the cold ground.

And slid on her ice. Right to her feet.

I slammed the shard of ice lodged in my hand straight into her leg, and as she toppled down over me, my palm turned up and caught her with it. She fell onto the shard and cried out in pain.

I shoved her aside and wrenched my numb hand free before clumsily scrambling to my feet. She remained on the ground, coughing up blood, unable to do the same. A scream left my mouth as I pulled the shard out. Bruised, bloody, and broken, I picked up my dagger and limped up the stairs to the third floor.

Time for the hard part.

I climbed the dark, narrow stairs slowly and loudly, every part of my body aching. No need for stealth at this point.

I reached under my skirts and pulled out Mr. Kent's pistol. I wasn't going to shoot Captain Goode, but I needed to be enough of a threat to distract him.

But before I even reached the top of the stairs, I heard his voice call to me. "Miss Wyndham, I want you to know that I have a gun pointed at Mr. Braddock's head."

I covered my mouth to swallow my cry. Of course it wasn't going to be quick and easy. I climbed the last stair and stopped at the doorway, my gun pointed at Captain Goode. The room was austere and unadorned. No displays of armor or weapons like the rest of the keep. Just three prisoners, wrists and legs tied to chairs. I winced when I saw the blood and cuts on Sebastian's face, the rag stuffed into Mr. Kent's mouth. But they were alive, this pair of brave, wonderful fools.

I didn't know what to make of Miss Fahlstrom being held as the third prisoner. Did our revelations about Captain Goode convince her to help us?

"Will you give the gun to Mr. Thorpe?" Captain Goode asked.

To my right, the torturer from the train cleared his throat, watching me closely with his uncovered eye. He was bandaged and leaning on a cane, but it didn't make him any less dangerous. Even if Miss Chen managed to break down the wall for Miss Rao and Emily to sweep everyone up, it would not be fast enough to keep Sebastian from getting hurt.

"No," my mouth answered, unbidden. He'd turned Mr. Kent's power up to make this a truthful conversation.

"I see," Captain Goode said. "Now, do you know what Miss Fahlstrom's power is?"

"Yes."

"What is it?"

"She can see the deaths of powered people."

"Good," he said. "Now, Miss Fahlstrom, how and when is Mr. Braddock going to die?"

"In forty-two seconds. When Captain Goode shoots him," Miss Fahlstrom answered.

I stared at her and Captain Goode, completely speechless.

"I don't think either of us likes that outcome," Captain Goode said. "But your prophecies can change, yes?"

"They can," Miss Fahlstrom replied.

"How?"

"When I tell another, it can change their behavior in such a way that they alter the future."

Dammit. I looked at Mr. Kent. "Has your power been raised this whole time?" I asked him.

He mumbled something unintelligible and nodded.

"Evelyn, don't give it to him," Sebastian said, shaking his head.

I took a deep breath and lowered the gun. And possibly us into a grave. But there had to be another way to save him.

The torturer limped over to me and took the pistol. He slipped it into his jacket pocket and kept his hand at my back. A familiar warmth filled my gut, that invigorating feeling of Captain Goode enhancing my power. My wounds practically knit themselves together by the time I glanced down. Only slight reddish hues were left to mark the spots.

Mr. Thorpe inhaled deeply as my healing fixed his remaining injuries. "Thank you," he said and stepped back into his corner.

My power left me again with a chill.

"There we are," Captain Goode said, his gun still on Sebastian. "Now Miss Fahlstrom, how and when am I going to die?"

"A Frenchman named Adrien Martin will poison you thirty days from today at a dinner party," she answered. "You will die in your bedroom the next morning."

"I will have to do something about him then. But for now, I'm satisfied," Captain Goode said, finally lowering his gun.

"When will Sebastian Braddock die?" I asked.

"At his execution tomorrow morning," she said.

The world shrank down to those five words.

That couldn't be. My follow-up question came out as a whimper. "W-what?"

"His execution is tomorrow morning," she repeated. "I'm sorry."

But then . . . that meant this plan would be a failure. My eyes flickered over to the window, where Beauchamp Tower sat quietly in the dark.

"If you're waiting for your friends to help you, it will be about twelve hours," Captain Goode said. "I asked my songbird, Miss Tolman, to wait for the fighting to come to an end before putting everyone to sleep. I believe you have met her. No one can resist her lullabies."

I tried to keep my body steady. The old woman who sang people to sleep. We'd met when Oliver was hurt, and I'd completely forgotten her. Which left me alone. Useless. Powerless. There was no other way to save Sebastian.

"Though I must admit, you did surprise me by coming here tonight," Captain Goode said. "Miss Fahlstrom told me I was going to die in fifty-seven years, in a prison. Which didn't provide much information about your plan. How did you do it?"

"By deciding not to kill you," I spat out.

Dammit. Do something. Do something. Do something.

"And here I was trying to give you more reasons to kill me at the execution," Captain Goode said, shaking his head in disappointment. "But you were more interested in saving him, weren't you?"

My eyes met Sebastian's heartrending gaze, and the answer came out as a growl. "Yes."

"That's quite useful information for Miss Fahlstrom's power," he said. "Thank you."

Do anything.

I turned to the torturer. "What is your power's weakness?"

"Only people in my sight can be hurt," Mr. Thorpe sputtered, trying to cover his mouth.

Captain Goode's flinty expression shifted to fury. "Remind her what you can do."

The torturer lifted the kerchief from his eye, and that awful pain seized me.

I cried out, as much as I didn't want to give Captain Goode the satisfaction. But the pain was worse than I remembered, constantly changing. It brought me to the ground and refused to let go. It was piercing, then suffocating, then burning. I hated my body for existing, for feeling pain. I just wanted it to stop, please.

Captain Goode's voice joined the agony. "This is the other reason I wanted to keep you alive." His footsteps came closer. I could hear muffled yells coming from Sebastian or Mr. Kent, but I could barely concentrate with the pain splitting my head into dust. His face seemed to be right next to mine. "So the rest of your life will serve as an example. As a deterrent for those who consider shirking the duty and responsibility their power demands. You're going to spend it in agony."

He sniffed and stood back up. "It is a necessity. And this isn't a pain healing fixes. This isn't even a pain you can get numb to. This is a pain you brought on yourself."

His footsteps faded away, returning to his prisoners. "Tie her up."

I moaned, managing a deep breath. He was right. The pain was excruciating. But I'd been choked, burned, stabbed, pummeled, electrocuted, frozen, and broken. I'd been knocked off a roof, thrown from a train, and forced to watch the people I love die. I wasn't going to let one man taking my power away and another glaring at me be the end of it.

My hand clicked the dagger fan tied to my wrist and I shot up through the pain with everything I had. My blade found the torturer's gut, and he doubled over, his gaze finally off me. I gasped in relief and pulled out the dagger, a lightness in my body. Captain Goode spun around and reached for his weapon, but I already had mine. I clutched the torturer's hair and aimed his evil eye right at my target.

Captain Goode got one shot off before he collapsed in pain. It hit the torturer in his chest and I felt him stumble, but I pushed him forward, one hand roughly pulling his eyelids up to keep his gaze locked on Captain Goode. The gun dropped out of Captain Goode's hand by Sebastian's feet, and he kicked it out of reach, while I snatched Mr. Kent's pistol back from Mr. Thorpe's jacket pocket. It took a few seconds for Captain Goode to find the strength to shut down Mr. Thorpe's power, but by that time, the torturer was falling to the ground, unconscious, and I was already taking aim. A shot in Captain Goode's stomach and another in his leg kept him down.

I trained my gun on Captain Goode and kept my distance, giving him a moment to feel the pain and realize the situation he was in. "If you don't want to die, you will turn my power on, turn over, and stay down."

He simply stayed still, stared at me, and breathed. No warmth of power came.

"You will bleed to death," I told him.

"No, I know how I am going to die," Captain Goode said with a disconcerting smile. "The same way as the rest of you." He turned his glassy gaze to Sebastian's foot and reached out. "I'll see you in fourteen years."

No.

His body went still in an instant. I fired futile shots at him, but it was too late. The effect was immediate, and it knocked the breath out of me. For the first time, I felt the full power of Sebastian Braddock.

One, two, three . . .

My legs went weak, my breath short. I struggled for air, choking, feeling energy leaving me, my coughs speckling the floor with blood. I spun around to find Mr. Kent and Miss Fahlstrom experiencing the same effects, patches of blue appearing on their skin. Captain Goode had turned Sebastian's power up so high that his presence was as deadly as his touch was. That meant twenty seconds until we would all fall unconscious. Thirty until death.

Four, five, six . . .

Tied up next to Captain Goode's corpse sat Sebastian, panic seizing his body. He struggled against his restraints with fervency and fury. Tears and sweat were streaking his face. "Evelyn!" he roared.

My legs trembled as my eyes met his.

Seven, eight, nine . . .

"Evelyn! Please! You must!" Sebastian pleaded.

I knew what he wanted me to do. What I had to do. I sucked in a desperate breath of air and took an agonizing step in his direction. And then another. It felt like I was wasting away as I lurched toward him. The life slowly chipping and flaking off of my body. I fell to my knees, wheezing, the world dimming and fading and disintegrating around me.

Twelve, thirteen, fourteen . . .

"Evelyn," Sebastian said, his voice close, encouraging. "Evelyn."

I kept going, kept crawling forward, following. Until he was suddenly there, in front of me, and there was nowhere to run.

"Sebastian," I gasped. "I don't—"

"Don't let this happen again," he said, he sobbed. "Please. Not to you. Never to you."

I gazed at him, not wanting this to be the last time, and not wanting this to be like last time. His long, wavering eyelashes, that stern brow, those lips searching for words. I wanted to kiss him. If there was a time for magic, then it would be now, and through some miracle of love my power would be enhanced and cancel his out and save all of our lives.

Fifteen, sixteen, seventeen . . .

My body remained cold and powerless. Our powers were not magic. A kiss would kill me. My brain was moving so slowly, searching for another way, there had to be something. Please, anything. Deep breath. Raise your power. You useless, useless girl.

His jaw tightened, and he gave me the poorest excuse for a smile. "Find the successor. Help them control it better than I could."

I took up my dagger and gripped it tightly. I felt weak. I felt powerless. I shook my head. "I'm sorry," I whispered. "I'm so sorry, Sebastian."

Eighteen, nineteen, twenty.

Before he could say anything else, the blade slid into him.

Chapter Twenty-Four

H E SOBBED OUT a high-pitched whimper as the dagger lodged above his hip and I prayed that I'd missed his vital organs. I felt a weight lifted, the thick smog of his power dissipating, and my breath came easier, even as I cried at his horrible groans of pain.

"I'm sorry," I choked out. "I'm so sorry, my love, but you're right. No one else can die, especially not you. I need you to fight. Please, Sebastian. Fight."

Blood poured out of his wound, and I staggered over to rip off Captain Goode's jacket to temper the bleeding.

I gently draped the thick fabric over his stomach, the proximity making my head spin. "Hold this firmly. Just for a little while. Please."

His hand shifted weakly onto the bloody jacket and he moaned. My heart twisted at the sound, tightening my chest so it was hard to breathe.

Though that was likely his power still.

I climbed to my feet, my bones aching, my head stuffy, shivers racking my frame. The effects of his power still wore on me without my healing to reverse them. I'd infected myself to the very edge. The next bit of exposure I had to him could knock me unconscious.

The same was true with Mr. Kent and Miss Fahlstrom. They looked about as bad as I felt, but they were still conscious and desperate to help. I set to work untying their restraints.

"Miss Wyndham, what did you do?" Mr. Kent asked.

"I weakened his power by hurt-hurting him." I said. "But I-I don't know how long he'll last or how long we will or—"

Mr. Kent grabbed my shoulders to stop me from shaking. Though he looked as pale and sick as ever, his brown eyes still glowed with urgency. "I am going for help," he reassured me. He knelt down to take his pistol and removed a handkerchief from his pocket. "I will bring them and keep them from running into that singing woman. Miss Fahlstrom, find something to help us carry Mr. Braddock out of here."

She nodded and stumbled down the stairs to the armory, while Mr. Kent followed, tearing the handkerchief in two and blocking his ears. Before he left, he turned and hesitated, eyes on Sebastian. "Don't let him die." And he was gone.

I made my way to a window facing the Thames and pushed it open. "If you can hear me, see me, Arthur, William, please hurry." Night still lingered, and it was impossible to see anything across the river. I received no response, but I had to trust they heard me. I had to trust they were coming.

"Sebastian?" I called out, my voice echoing across the room. "Are you still awake?"

He groaned, and I watched him readjust slowly and painfully. His hands and torso were drenched in blood. "Yes."

"Good. You have to stay that way," I said, limping over to the opposite end of the room from him.

I wanted nothing more than to fling myself onto him, heal the damage I had inflicted. Another cough and sob escaped me, and I turned away miserably. I could not go to him; I had no idea what level his power was at. I suspected I'd brought him down to near his normal level, but I didn't quite have stabbing down to a science yet. I didn't know whether his range would be ten feet or thirty, and I didn't know how many more seconds I could remain conscious in either case. My body had already been running on sheer panic for the past twenty minutes, and that had to run out sometime.

I collapsed against the wall and slid ungracefully to the ground. "Sebastian? How . . . how are you?" I asked.

"It's . . . a little uncomfortable."

"We are in a life-or-death situation; you don't have to spare my feelings."

"It's exceedingly uncomfortable. And exhausting."

"Help is coming. Don't fall asleep. Fight it," I said, trying to calm both of us. "Keep your eyes open and keep talking."

There was a long pause. "I . . . can't think of anything to talk about," he said.

"Understandable. We live such boring lives," I said, immediately regretting sarcasm for what could easily be my last words to him.

If Sebastian died . . .

"You . . . tell me . . . about tonight."

"Well, we had help from Arthur and William. And Miss Rao, even."

"Huh," Sebastian's voice was fainter, and I spoke louder in response, hoping to rouse him.

"Oh! Miss Chen received a proposal today," I said. "From Mr. Pratt."

Sebastian's head lolled forward. "What did she say?"

"She politely declined."

"And you . . . beat him?"

"Yes," I said numbly. None of the night felt real. "We used his power against him. Did that to a number of people on their side, actually."

"You are remarkable, Evelyn Wyndham."

"I . . . it was mostly the others. Rose, Emily, Miss Rao, and Miss Chen."

"They are remarkable, too," Sebastian said. "But you found a way to storm head-on through the entire Society to get here—"

"Half," I corrected.

"And if"—he coughed—"that doesn't sound like an Evelyn plan . . . I don't know what does."

"And if nobly sacrificing and turning yourself in to the enemy isn't a Sebastian plan, I don't know what is," I replied. "Honestly, when you are back to your old self, I will murder you for being so insufferably, horribly noble."

"Mm." The faint murmur from him barely made it across the room.

"Sebastian! Wake up!" I half yelled, half coughed.

His head shook and slumped back. "I am. I am."

"You need to talk."

"I was," he said. "I don't . . . my head . . . it's hard to think."

"Anything," I pleaded, hoping I didn't sound like I thought he was dying. "You can say anything at all, whatever is in your head. Just a little while longer."

Please. Please let help come.

Another silence.

"Sebastian!"

"She . . . she walks in beauty, like the night," he recited, his voice thin and terribly weak.

"Oh no," I moaned, tasting tears as my lips cracked into a watery smile. "Not that."

He ignored me, of course. "Of cloudless climes and starry skies. And all that's best of dark and bright; Meet in her aspect and her eyes; Thus mellowed to that tender light; Which heaven to gaudy day . . ."

"Rhymes with eyes," I encouraged him. "It's what you do when I accuse you of a Lord Byron obsession."

Silence.

"Sebastian!"

No response. I pushed myself back to my feet and crossed the room to him. I gritted my teeth and tensed every muscle, hoping to withstand a couple more seconds trying to wake him back up. "Sebastian, love, can you hear me?"

He wasn't moving. I tapped the hilt of my dagger, which was still lodged in his abdomen. It did nothing. I couldn't tell if his breathing had gotten too shallow, or he wasn't breathing at all and my useless, blurry eyes weren't helping.

And then I was sobbing, begging every god and demon I could imagine, praying feverishly to let him live, to let me stay conscious and find some way to heal him.

I took my fingers—they were freckled with terrifying blue splotches—and pressed them to his neck and closed my eyes.

There was a pounding in my head that sounded like footsteps.

Beneath my fingers, I felt nothing.

A voice rang out from the stairs.

And then I felt like nothing.

Come back, Sebastian.

Come back.

"Come back to me, Evelyn! Please!"

I opened my eyes at my sister's voice. I was so near Sebastian and still alive. It must have been seconds only that I lay next to him.

"Come to me, darling, please, I will heal him but you must

come to me." Rose was begging, her voice low and sweet, and I had to heed her, dragging myself to her with fingertips and great lurches of movement that exhausted me. But I fought the swirling darkness that wanted to claim me, pushing myself forward as she continued to promise me that it would be all right.

"Here, Emily, carefully."

The heaviness that had settled inside my head lifted as I dragged myself away from Sebastian. Rose was holding up a threaded needle, Emily staring at it in concentration.

"Mr. Kent, go to him slowly, but if you think it's too much, come back. We don't know what his power is like right now." Rose was wringing her hands, betraying her calm voice. "But we must find a way to stop that bleeding."

Mr. Kent took a cautious step to Sebastian, testing each one, gritting his teeth as he got closer. "I think I can manage for a few minutes."

Sebastian was not moving, and I could not control my panicked gasps.

"Rose, Rose, we have to—"

"I am. I am." She caught my arm, but her eyes were on Mr. Kent as he used his metal hand to lift the layers of fabric so Rose could see what needed to be done. She and Emily moved closer, blocking my view of Sebastian.

"Emily, you need to go slowly and neatly; think of it like embroidery—" Rose explained what she would have to do, while Emily took control of the needle, testing it. Mr. Kent was getting paler and blinking his eyes to stay conscious when Rose told him he had to pull out the dagger.

"As swiftly as possible, then press hard on the wound."

Sebastian's eyes did open then, and the sound he made was something I never wanted to hear again.

But he was alive.

Emily worked the airborne needle seamlessly, Rose guiding her every stitch. They found their rhythm and finished as Mr. Kent fell into a coughing fit.

"So, so tired." There was no jest in his voice, and Rose cut the thread and sent him away urgently. He made it back to me, leaning entirely against the stone wall, gasping for breath.

"Will he be all right now?" I called to Rose, begging her to tell me the worst was over.

"I don't . . . I don't know." Rose handed Emily a bandage lined with tape, which she telekinetically pressed down. "Miss Kane, can you get him downstairs?"

Mr. Kent tried to help me up, but we were both too unsteady after our long exposure, pulling each other down. Rose had to get between us, her small frame stronger than I had thought, as she helped us slowly to the stairs.

Emily concentrated on Sebastian, untying his restraints and gently floating him up. She slowly descended the narrow spiral stairs backward, maneuvering him down after her. His limbs and head dangled like a rag doll's, and I begged him to stay alive.

Outside the White Tower, our friends were waiting. Woozy, exhausted, and heartsick, I nearly collapsed into Arthur's arms, while Miss Chen and Laura hurried to help Mr. Kent and Catherine held Rose.

"Arthur, is he still . . . ?" I asked. "Can you hear a heartbeat?"

Arthur brought me a few steps closer to Sebastian's floating body, and tilted his head for an agonizing moment before nodding. "I can 'ear it, but it's weak."

Alive then, for now. Thank heavens. Just a little while longer.

We made a sad but terrifying parade as we slowly trudged back through the tower, over the rubble, and around the smoldering flames. All around us, on the tower green, the outer ward, and along the battlements, bodies lay sleeping and vines slowly moved them outside the walls. Miss Tolman sat tied up in one corner, her mouth stuffed with a rag and her baleful glare saying enough.

We made it over the moat and to the last tower, where William, Mr. Adeoti, and two carriages waited for us. Emily lay Sebastian down gently in the first one, then stumbled back in exhaustion into Rose's and Catherine's arms.

"Army's on their way," William said, peering off into the darkness to the north. "Preparing to storm the place, looksit."

"We should disappear quickly. For Mr. Braddock's safety and theirs," Catherine said. "I don't know if they are coming because of Captain Goode's illegal takeover of the tower, or because of the battle."

From not far off, I could hear the calls and stomps preceding the arrival of the army. What the soldiers would do once they arrived and found this scene, I did not know. But we couldn't leave everyone else here.

"What about all the Society members?" I rasped. At some point I had either cried myself raw or lost the energy required for speaking. "We need to keep the dangerous ones bound. But most of the others don't deserve to be punished. Not with Captain Goode forcing them."

"George is moving them to a raft," Miss Fahlstrom said, emerging from the Thames side of the tower.

My body stiffened instinctively at the sight of her, but Mr. Kent was quick to put in his reassurances.

"She stopped helping . . . Captain Goode after the trial," he said, his breath heavy.

"I'm sorry I helped him," she said, coughing and grasping the stone tower next to her, weak from Sebastian's power, too. "I only wanted to protect everyone with my warnings."

Mr. Adeoti hastened over to give her support. "I can sort out who should be left for the police to arrest."

"I'll take the others to our secret rooms," Arthur said. "Let them decide what to do from there."

"Thank you," I said.

"You best be goin' now," Arthur said, giving William a wave. "Braddock's country home is in Barking. Long ride but the safest place for 'em."

I nodded, barely understanding, and tried to climb into Sebastian's carriage. About ten arms pulled me back and many insistent points were made about me dying if I stayed with him for the ride. But I refused to let him travel alone, imagining we would find him dead when we arrived. Miss Rao grumpily agreed to get in with him but would knock at the roof once she could take no more.

With Arthur staying behind, Miss Chen volunteered to drive the other carriage. The rest of us piled inside, Laura in Mr. Kent's arms, clinging to his neck with tears sliding down her pale cheeks. I rested on Rose's lap, she and Catherine stroking my hair and murmuring sounds of reassurance. Emily dozed off immediately on Catherine's shoulder. Miss Fahlstrom left me with a short message before the door was shut and we set off.

Every ten minutes or so, the carriages stopped, and someone new volunteered to go with Sebastian. Each time I received a full report of him still being alive, still breathing. Rose tried to convince me that it was good that he was still unconscious and therefore unbothered by the jerks and buckles of the carriage.

The journey must have been about three hours, but it could have been days. All I knew was that the sun was rising when we finally arrived at Sebastian's estate. No one would let me see him as he was removed from the carriage. And Miss Fahlstrom's three words were all that repeated in my head, words I hoped were true.

"He will live."

Chapter Twenty-Five

DEATH. All that was left was the book labeled *Death*.

My footsteps echoed through the empty Society of Aberrations library. The leather cover felt soft under my fingertips as I traced over the golden lettering. The last entry would need to be rewritten—Sebastian Braddock's biography was hideously distorted. But there would be time for that.

Time for him to change what having his powers meant.

"Is this everything?" Miss Chen asked, picking up the last stack of books.

I cleared my throat. "I think so."

"You do know that half these historical records are probably nonsense?" she asked, looking through them dubiously.

I did know. But for the past three days, I had been driving everyone mad worrying over Sebastian, despite Rose's constant assurances that he would be well. I found it impossible to be easy until his power was lowered and I could see him with my own eyes. Helping him this way was the next best thing.

"Even the smallest bit of information might be important," I said, clutching the volume to my chest. "Besides, Catherine would kill me if we left anything behind. Or let any of these get damaged."

Miss Chen's gaze snapped up and away from them. "That is a very good point," she said, leading the way out.

The wooden library doors closed behind us with a great ache.

The building sat silent—none of the usual muffled sounds of training sessions or mission meetings. It had been three days since the Tower of London attack, and not a single member had returned. With Parliament still locked in discussions over what to do with the Society, we thought it best to make the decision for them. Starting with the removal of all the records, so powered people couldn't be tracked and turned into tools for the government.

We circled the first floor one last time, checking for anything we might have missed. We passed familiar rooms and sights, the place barely changed under Captain Goode's command. His office was eerie, and it felt like he had left only moments before. It still smelled like him—a thick, overwhelming scent of burnt lavender that filled the small room, finding its way into the pores of the wood paneling. It was neat, free of dust, and the only thing left was a thin notebook lying in a desk drawer. We took that, too, and continued down the quiet corridors, striding away from his ghost.

But there were ghosts everywhere, my stomach turning at the memories provoked by the morbid tour. The parlor where Miss Grey had accepted Captain Goode's offer, eager to help the world. The garden where Oliver had trained and played. The foyer where Mr. Redburn had dropped us all after our trip to retrieve Sebastian. I hated that the Society hadn't been what Miss Grey wanted. I hated that it hadn't given her and Oliver the safety and guidance they needed. I hated that they had died for it. All I could do for them now was ensure their successors had better lives, the lives Miss Grey and Oliver had deserved. That still didn't feel like enough, but I didn't know if anything ever would.

A loud crack and a bang wrenched my attention back to the

present. A large portrait came crashing down, the image of the Society's founder shattering into several pieces, strewn across the foyer's marble floor.

Miss Chen cocked her head, admiring her handiwork. "Wanted to do that every time I walked in here. Smug bastard."

The rest of the group came running, alarmed by the noise, then amused by the sight. Mr. Adeoti clutched a satchel full of items he'd collected for research, his face shining. Emily was followed by a few floating sculptures, and Laura wobbled in, dwarfed by the heavy paintings she was attempting to carry in her skinny arms. The girls had great ambitions to help Mrs. Tuffins decorate her next boarding house.

"This is the last of it from the downstairs offices," Mr. Kent said, emerging from a corridor behind them. He pushed a small handcart loaded with piles of papers and ledgers, pausing at the broken painting on the ground. "Oh, well done. I found a portrait of Captain Goode and added some rather untamed nose hairs, so if anyone ever finds it, that's how he will be remembered."

"And this is why we entrust you with the most important jobs," I said.

"London does need a new hero. I can already tell the newspapers are getting desperate for stories," Mr. Kent said, tapping his metal finger to his chest. "I am willing to step forward and make that sacrifice."

Even though he was being his usual facetious self, I found there was a part of me taking that seriously. I could somehow see him that way. Not just in his square jaw and blazing eyes. He'd done the brave thing countless times for me, for all of us, and without hesitation.

"I really think you could," I told him.

"And maybe my brothelgänger will finally get more customers," he added, ruining it.

Miss Chen snorted, and I pushed Mr. Kent and his cart toward the exit.

Outside, the night was dark and cool, the moon covered with clouds, and the streets filled with fog. Mr. Kent's cart rattled across the cobblestones, toward the carriages, Tuffins waiting with one, William the other. Tuffins turned to us from his perched seat up top, a flustered smile crossing his face, which must have been a trick of the light, because Tuffins never got flustered. Next to him, Miss Rao calmly stepped down from the carriage and opened the door. With her telekinetic power, Emily easily loaded the rest of the records and the collected artwork into the back of the carriage.

And we were done. Almost. Just one last matter.

We all turned back to the Society of Aberrations.

"Does anyone have any last words? A change of heart? An insatiable desire to take it over?" Miss Chen asked.

The last one was tempting. And it was what Miss Grey would have wanted. I couldn't help but imagine everything I might do if I were in charge. Gather every power as soon as it emerges anew, research them to learn every benefit and quirk, teach the children to use them responsibly, capture the people who didn't, send our powers to other countries in an instant to peacefully solve any crisis. We'd protect the world. We'd bring peace all over. We'd save everyone.

But that's what Captain Goode had claimed the Society of Aberrations had wanted to do. And somewhere along the way, their purpose got twisted and rationalized into protecting England first at the cost of the rest of the world. Someone had risen to power, using the Society for selfish gains, keeping people against their will, forcing them to maintain an empire. And it would happen again. I was not the right person to save the world. There really *was* no person who could do that. Even if we had the best intentions, it was dangerous to gather the powers together to be wielded like weapons. They needed to be spread out, shared, and balanced—shields to prevent anything like this from happening again.

"Good riddance," I said.

Miss Chen took that as her cue. Cracks snaked their way up and down the brick facade of the Society. Windows shattered, walls exploded, the street rumbled, and the building groaned. The center crumbled away first, floor by floor, and the rest of the building collapsed inward with a massive boom and a rush of dust and debris that Miss Rao's winds blew away from us. As everything settled and silence fell upon the street again, we found a pathetic pile of crushed brick and splintered wood where this epicenter of power had stood.

Now we were done.

Mr. Adeoti stared at the ruins, his face solemn. "There are probably going to be many more secret societies out there soon," he said. "Hopefully one will be good." I took his arm and gave it a quick squeeze as we turned back to the carriages.

"That's everything, Tuffins," I said, closing the door on the records and books. "Thank you. Please tell your mother we will call soon with plans for her new boarding house."

"I will," he said, giving me a nod, then a second to Miss Rao. "And, Miss Rao, I will consider your offer."

She bowed her head regally, and Tuffins set the horses off. His carriage disappeared into the fog toward Catherine's house to drop off the last of the Society's property.

"And what offer is that?" Mr. Kent asked, unable to resist.

"I invited him to India to help me rid it of all the Englishmen," Miss Rao answered with a frown. "If I keep doing this alone, I'll only be deemed a villain like your deadly friend, so I need many others. The rest of you may come if you must. Except you, truthseeker."

An angry growl of thunder shook the sky.

"Well, all this noise must have woken a person or two. We should probably leave," Mr. Kent said, hurrying to William's carriage.

We settled ourselves in, sharing smiles at a job well done. A pleasant silence reigned for a moment, before Mr. Kent found the courage to speak again and clapped his hands. "So, Miss Rao has her very good plan that I will not ask anything more about. What about you, Miss Chen?" he asked.

She shrugged, of course, but looked out the window thoughtfully. "Find my family in New York, I think. I'd like to see my brother. Want to come visit?"

"Ah, I've heard horrible stories of deceit and debauchery from there. It sounds lovely," Mr. Kent said. His eyes slid toward Laura and Emily. "But I don't believe I can quite destroy my family's name yet."

"Laura and I have decided to never marry," Emily announced. "Maybe that will help."

Mr. Kent nodded at her gratefully.

"We are going to be *spinsters*!" Laura agreed, like it was the naughtiest word she knew. "And grow old together as the best of friends. We shall have five puppies."

Mr. Kent was looking rather skeptical but admitted grudgingly, "I should like to see my stepmother's house overrun with muddy dogs."

"Oh! Can you give the house to Mrs. Tuffins?" Laura asked, bright eyed and overflowing. "She would take such good care of it. And we can all live together!"

Mr. Kent fixed her with a thoughtful look. "Now that's an idea, Kit. . . ."

The rest of the drive passed merrily, with everyone batting around ideas for the future—places to travel, ways to make Mr. Kent even more disreputable. But I found myself growing anxious the closer we got, the lighter the sky grew. It was almost time, finally.

My thoughtful sister seemed to be well aware of that. When our carriage rolled to a stop at Sebastian's country estate, dawn breaking lightly over the trees, Rose came out to meet us, bleary eyed and wrapped in a blanket.

"How did it go?" she asked.

"Well, I think everything is settled," I said, "given what our most pressing concerns are now. . . ."

Behind me, Mr. Kent and Miss Chen were loudly arguing about whether blackmail or the destruction of buildings was more satisfying and Mr. Adeoti was offering to settle the matter by experiencing both with his power.

"Perfect," she said, a true smile settling peacefully on her face. She reached one arm out of her blanket and pulled mine in under it. "His powers should be low enough now. Shall we go visit him?"

"Yes," I said, holding tightly.

"Miss Wyndham!" Mr. Kent called after me. "Don't forget to tell Mr. Braddock that he is back to owing me his life!"

"I'm sure he'll be thrilled to hear that," I replied.

"Who wouldn't want an excuse to keep me in their life?" Mr. Kent asked.

There were a couple replies from the group that made Mr. Kent frown regretfully over asking the rhetorical question, but my honest response—"I couldn't possibly imagine."—seemed to help.

He looked at me speculatively for a few heartbeats, his warm eyes sparkling with the sunrise, lips smirking. Then he turned smartly back to the house, catching Laura around the waist and hoisting her off her feet, sending into her a fit of giggles and shrieks as they went inside.

Rose's hand was warm on my arm, and she was quiet as we slipped away, heading out to the parson's cottage. The morning dew dampened our skirts as we climbed the rolling hills. The air was warm, and flowers were beginning to open their buds as the sun called to them. The thought of spring sent a reflexive shudder through me. A new London Season would be starting soon.

"I wonder what Mother would say about the coming Season," I said. "After all this."

Rose gave me a sad smile. "I believe she'd be rejoicing over arranging the match between you and Mr. Braddock."

"Oh yes, she'd take full credit for it," I said, feeling a pang of sadness that I'd never get to argue with her over that. "And she'd be making big plans for your debut."

"I don't think she'd have planned for my choice of suitor," Rose said. "Or what I want to do."

"Medical school?" I asked.

Rose shook her head. "No, maybe one day, but . . . well, Catherine and I have been thinking about setting up a . . . a sanctuary, of sorts, with Mr. Adeoti. We thought it could even be . . . something of a place powered people can visit for some peace. A second home in London. We want to speak to Mrs. Tuffins and see if she would like to live there with us. We owe her a house, after all."

"Mr. Kent may be in the middle of offering her his home, but it's a wonderful idea," I said. "But what about . . . your worries about . . . Catherine?"

Rose gave me one burning look, then lowered her eyes. "Well, I talked to Mr. Adeoti about Mr. Jarsdel's lost love for me. He suspects my powers' effects could have properties like Mr. Braddock's. They likely wear off when I'm away from someone longer than I'm with them."

I stopped walking. "So . . . if you're with someone for a day and then you leave for a day, they return to normal?"

Rose nodded hesitantly. "At least I hope so. Catherine is going to go stay with her parents for a while. And when she returns . . . if I could know, could really know if someone . . . felt something for me, not as a part of my powers, well. Then maybe . . ." She trailed off, but the light didn't leave her yet.

I hugged her to my side, hoping it was true. God, I hoped it was true. Rose deserved it. She deserved to have the life and home she wanted.

I finally let go of her, letting her breathe again. "I think it good that one of us will stay here." Only as I said it did I realize that I would not remain in London, in England.

She did not protest as I expected. Just sighed and gave me a sidelong look. "I always thought London was too small for you."

"Yes, tiny city, pathetic, really," I said.

We resumed our walking, and after a few minutes we finally made it to a small cottage nestled by a stream. It looked abandoned, tall grass and ivy half covering it. I felt suddenly shy, and Rose gave me an amused look before stepping forward and knocking solidly on the front door.

"Mr. Braddock?"

No response. She knocked again, louder. My heart beating, I pushed the door open and found the reason for the silence. The room was empty, the bed in disarray, and the window open, curtains swaying in the breeze. Sebastian had run away again.

"I am going to kill him," I growled. "And then I'm going to somehow heal him and kill him again."

"Ev, don't be hasty—" Rose said.

"Where's my dagger fan?" I asked.

"It's . . . right here," Sebastian's voice called from behind us.

He was coming from the stream, soaking wet, the dagger in one hand, a shirt in the other. He was naked to the waist and very suddenly aware of that fact upon seeing our expressions. My mouth was open, but I was entirely unable to shut it. A sunlit, bare-chested, and wounded Sebastian was too much for me, and he seemed to realize it. He muttered an apology and gently eased his shirt on, which got rather wet and clingy in the process, doing little to help his indecent appearance once it was on.

The entire sight made it difficult to figure out what to do with my words, hands, life, and even anger, but it had to go somewhere. "You! You-you shouldn't be out of bed . . . cleaning things!" I threw my hands up wildly, aware that I needed to find some control over myself.

He frowned. "I needed to wash up. I was careful with my woun—"

"I thought you ran away!" I said.

"I'm sorry I didn't wait attentively at the door for you for three full days," he countered, crossing his arms.

"Well, I'm sorry I didn't visit sooner," I retorted. "But I was recovering, and you would have killed me."

"Oh look! Foliage!" Rose declared. "How fascinating. I will leave you two."

She hurried off back toward the main house. In silence, we watched her disappear over the hill. I felt vaguely ridiculous.

"I'm glad you're all right," he said, almost stubbornly.

"I'm glad you are, too," I replied. We stared out along the green of the estate, the beauty of the day creating a hazy, dreamy shimmer.

"I didn't think I'd ever see this place again," he murmured, staring at the stream and the edge of the woods.

"It's beautiful here," I begrudgingly admitted.

"When the Lodges visited, Henry, Mae, and I used to come

here to play games," Sebastian said. "We had one where we each wrote a secret of ours on a piece of paper and picked a hiding place in this area. Then the other two would ask five questions each about the hiding spot and try to find it."

It was physically impossible to stay angry imagining a young Sebastian running about the trees with Mae and her brother. A happy, unencumbered Sebastian. A Sebastian before his power emerged.

"What were your secrets?" I asked.

"Back then, they were all the little things I felt guilty about. Like losing a toy I had received as a gift or breaking a glass. Henry's were usually things he wanted to do. Places he wanted to visit. And Mae's . . . I don't really know."

"What do you mean?" I asked.

"We usually weren't able to solve hers," Sebastian said. "Either her clues were too difficult, or we were abysmal at guessing. The one time I do remember solving hers, the secret was a very straightforward tract explaining why she liked ants."

"Ants?" I asked.

He smiled. "She was always a mystery."

"Then you never found the rest of her secrets?" I asked.

"I imagine they are all still hidden here somewhere," Sebastian said, his voice a little thick. "Maybe I will find them someday. I like thinking I might."

"Me too," I said, watching the water trickle by. I was glad there was still more to be learned about Mae—that kind, guileless, but somehow inscrutable girl.

"Thank you for not killing me," Sebastian said after a moment.

"Thank you for not letting me," I said, feeling another wave of relief run through me. "You could have given up. I was terrified you did when you fell unconscious."

"I think I dreamed of you yelling at me," he said.

"I have to admit, that wasn't a dream."

"I thought about what you said to me that night I turned myself in," he said, lowering himself to the ground with a little wince of pain. "About the next person who would receive my power. Maybe it would be different fourteen years from now, with the powers being public knowledge. But I still couldn't help imagining the power first emerging. How my inheritor would more likely than not hurt the people they loved first. If I could keep that from happening . . . or delay it until we had a system to protect them and help them control it . . ."

"We will. I promise," I assured him. "We have a lot to do."

Sebastian took my hand, gently tugging me to sit, his power meeting mine in the middle. For a long while, we sat in the grass on his estate, the brilliant sun shining on us, drying the dew even as it collected on my skirts. We might be the only ones out there with these specific powers, these wonderful and terrifying abilities, but we were not alone. We had each other. We had friends who risked their lives for us. We had the power and the past lives of our predecessors somewhere deep within our souls.

And though there was a part of me that wanted to stop thinking about the future and lie here forever, all those connections made it impossible. I had been so selfish for so long, my only real goal in life to find amusements beyond England. But I was coming to realize, there were things we had to do because we weren't alone. There were people who needed to return home. And there were homes that needed to be returned to their people. And now that I knew that, could truly see it, I could not shrink from it.

"Before any of this happened, I wanted so badly to travel the world." My voice was quiet, but the air was still and he was so close. "I had no thought of leaving it a better place. Of truly helping others."

His calm gaze caught my nervous one and held tight. "I think you would have come around to that."

"But you have always helped people," I said, my heart suddenly beating a little faster. "I don't know what you wish to do now; you deserve rest. I know many of our friends deserve that, too. But I . . . I don't think I can right now. I think I should try and do some good with this power."

I couldn't look at him as I continued to voice my doubts and hopes. "I had thought, that is, I do not know where exactly to start. But I do owe Miss Rao for her help. She's returning to India to free her country, and I know I would likely be in the way, but I could at least be there to heal her if she needed, could keep her healthy. I could be with her as she fights and, well, it just seems like a good place to start." The words rushed out of me, and I realized I had possibly never been so nervous. I knew that Sebastian cared for me, very deeply, but I still did not know what he would say to my sudden suggestion.

"Are you certain?" he finally asked.

"I am."

"Are you absolutely certain?" His expression was deathly serious.

"I—What do you mean?" I asked, sitting up to keep my heart from sinking. A shiver ran through me, and it almost felt like my healing was gone and I could be hurt again. He didn't want to come. I shouldn't have been surprised—he couldn't be expected to drop everything and follow me across the world. But I'd assured him that I'd always stay by his side. I couldn't break that promise.

He took my hand in both of his, in that gentle way one delivers the worst of news. "I feel I have an obligation to tell you that your suggestion reminds me of someone."

"Who?"

"Someone who spent the last years of his life fighting for Greece's independence."

I blinked. "Oh lord."

"Yes, oh *lord*, indeed." A wide grin broke out on Sebastian's face, and my lips could not resist smiling—no, no, crying, definitely crying—for he was so close and so dear and, finally, so full of light. It softened the sharp angles and his eyes were a brilliant, gold-threaded green when they caught mine. I could not think of how to respond to a Sebastian like this for a long moment.

"Fine," I said with a deep, elegiac sigh. "There's no avoiding it any longer. I admit it. I'm not only Byronic, I'm a Byromaniac. It's a tragic curse."

"It is," he said, pulling me down next to him, cradling me gently against his shoulder. I felt his lips on my forehead as he brushed a tingling kiss there. "But I'll help you fight it. I'll help you control it. I'll go with you to India, I'll go with you anywhere. You'll never be in danger of taking a solitary walk on the moors or writing moody poetry, because I'll always be with you. By your side until you're absolutely sick of me."

"Good," I said, my hand curling over his, our powers joining. "Then I think that gives us all the time in the world."

Epilogue

My friend,

If you are reading this, I am long dead. I have been informed that this is a melodramatic and terrible way to begin a letter. My apologies, but it is also true. I pray that you are reading this far into the new century and that I was able to delay anyone receiving this power for as long as possible. But receive it you have.

I'd like to believe that you understand more than I ever did about what this power is and what it will do, but there are a few things I wish to say, as someone who understands what you are experiencing. The first is: You are not evil. You are not in any way at fault. You have a power that might terrify you, but it does not define who you are and what actions you might take. It took me a long time and one quite insistent person to understand this. It took making many mistakes and some very evil men using me for their own ends. But that is not your fate. Your heart is your own, and you can make what choices you wish, for good or for bad.

The second is this: You can control this power. It will take time and effort, but I promise you, it can be done. As I write this, I have been attempting to lessen my effects on others this past year and a half. It is not gone, and I don't think it ever will be. But there is improvement. And if some days I still want to run away and hide from the world, want to flee my own skin, I try to remember that I am better now than when I started. And that is what gives me hope.

Perhaps you will take this all very differently than I did. But if you feel, as I have at times, that you do not deserve to be counted among the good or the living, you are wrong. You deserve a life, a full one. You may just have to work a little harder than most to find that.

Finally, I do not know what your world looks like, but if you can, look for the powerless. Look for those who are fighting for something better for everyone. Look for those who are sharing their power to create a brighter, bolder world. I can only suggest that you join them, fight alongside them, and listen to them. I can tell you that it has given my life meaning I was missing.

And if you ever find yourself in need of help, make your way to 57, Golden Square in London, look for the sign that says "Tuffins's Boarding

House," and ask for Miss Rosamund Wyndham, Miss Catherine Harding, or Mr. Joseph Adeoti.

There will always be a home there. You aren't alone.

Sincerely,
Sebastian Braddock

PS: If you meet someone who can compel you to speak the truth, avoid them at all costs. You will constantly say the wrong thing and wish you could use your power on them. It is easier to avoid them entirely.

Acknowledgments

————

THERE WERE TIMES—and more than a few—when we thought this book would never be finished. We wondered to ourselves, would it really be *so* terrible if the series ended at *These Ruthless Deeds*? Leave 'em wanting more, right?

Well, if you're reading these words, we can only assume the book *is* finished, and if that's the case, there are a lot of people we need to thank. First, last, and always, is Holly West. Holly, you have been a lot more than just an editor to us over the past three years. (My God. Three years.) Ranging from mentor, cheerleader, therapist, head fangirl, life coach, confidante, biggest supporter, and kick-in-the-butt, you've suffered our hours-long phone calls, desperate last-minute changes, and pleading for extensions. And yet, against all reason, you still answer our e-mails. All the best parts of these books are because of you. Thank you, from the bottom of our hearts. You made our dreams come true three times over, and that's not something we can easily repay, but we promise to try.

Laura Zats, our dear agent, you are relatively new to our lives but became instantly irreplaceable. Thank you for all the support and advice you have given us so far. Having you on our team, with your fight and your verve, is the best present we could have asked for in 2017. We are so very excited to see what the future brings with you.

The Swoon production team: To Hayley Jozwiak et al., we have not made your lives easy. You have rushed and worked late and been endlessly patient as we toss things in at the deadline. Thank you for all your work making a beautiful book with significantly fewer typos.

Lauren Scobell, we are still suspicious you might be a figment of our imaginations. Can anyone possibly be so insightful, so cheerful, and so easygoing? All at once? It seems impossible. Thank you for all that you have done for us over the past years—the books you have piled into our arms, the squealing over great authors and OTPs, the lunches, and the brilliant input. We are so lucky you found Swoon and that you brought us into the Swoon family.

Emily Settle: We are pretty sure you are our guardian angel. Thank you for clicking "read" on our manuscript. Thank you for telling Holly to read it. Thank you for being our advocate and friend in the years since—your e-mails have brightened our days and, on a memorably bad one, been the reason we kept writing. You are our favorite Emily, even if you don't have telekinetic powers. Please know that in our head-canon, Emily goes on to have a life full of adventures and joy and weirdness.

To our designers: Kathleen Breitenfeld, Rich Deas, Liz Dresner—thank you for a trilogy of stunning covers and gorgeous interiors. It is your fault that we can't walk by masks, fans, and brooches without buying them. Our apartments are becoming a little bit weird with all our books displayed, and we wouldn't have it any other way.

To the people in the publishing world who have become so dear to us, we are lucky to count you as peers and friends: Allison Senecal, Gaby Salpeter, Heidi Heilig, Kerri Maniscalco, Lily Anderson, Destiny Soria, Jessica Cluess, Tara Sim, Stephanie Garber, Tracey Neithercott, Kyra Nelson, Tricia Levenseller—we are a little in awe of your talents and immensely excited to read all

your future endeavors. Thank you for all your support of us—we probably wouldn't have made it here without you. Go forth and write more books for us to devour, okay?

To our incredible and growing Swoon Squad: Sandy Hall, Danika Stone, Jen Wilde, Lydia Albano, Shani Petroff, and all those we have not met, this journey would not be the same without you.

Thank you to Judith Flanders for writing a fascinating, inspiring, and indispensable book about the history and culture of murder in Victorian England. And thank you to Dr. Elliot Handler and Dr. Mariam Amin for answering our creepy questions about stabbing people.

Thank you to all our friends, you know who you are because we are going to hug you and beg you for vitamin D the second we emerge from our writing caves. We love you all so much; thank you for being patient with us.

As we have said before, we are both lucky to have stunning parents. They supported us when we told them we wanted to be a screenwriter and actress, they supported us as we began writing a book, and at every turn since. We are sorry you will always have to worry we are about to be broke, but thank you for rooting for us as we pursue these long-shot goals. We know the success we have now and in the future is because of your love.

And to you, the person reading this: Thank you for sticking with us and Evelyn through everything. One thousand pages later and you're still here, which is pretty incredible and a little terrifying. Thank you so much for reading. We are so thrilled this story resonated with you. Most of all, we hope you know how extraordinary you are, whether your powers are superhuman or not.

Love,
Kelly and Tarun

Check out more books chosen for publication by readers like you.

Mild-mannered assistant by day, milder-mannered writer by night, **TARUN SHANKER** is a New York University graduate currently living in Los Angeles. His idea of paradise is a place where kung fu movies are projected on clouds, David Bowie's music fills the air, and chai tea flows freely from fountains.

tarunshanker.com

Tim Goodwin Photography

KELLY ZEKAS, a New York University graduate, writes, acts, and reads in New York City. YA is her absolute favorite thing on earth (other than cupcakes), and she has spent many hours crying over fictional deaths. She also started reading Harlequin romances at a possibly too-early age (twelve?) and still loves a good historical romance.

kellyzekas.com

These Vengeful Souls is their third novel.